Copyright © 2017 J.C. Paulson
All rights reserved.
ISBN 978-0995975606

Adam's Witness

One

Dread weighed on the bishop's soul as he emerged, shoulders hunched, from the confessional at the back of the church. He walked slowly past the pews, aware that a small light was the only illumination in the vast, domed cathedral. The stained glass windows were only a faint glimmer of blue, gold and red in the darkness.

He had just finished the final confession, and tried to shake off the uneasy feeling it produced. He wondered why no lights were on. Did no one know he was still in the church?

As bishop, Howard Halkitt heard few confessions; the priests managed most of them, but someone had to plumb their sins. When the bishop was in the cathedral, he would often take on one or two parishioners. It was always good to know what was going on in the hearts and souls of the congregation, he thought.

This last one, though, was disturbing. The man in the confessional was confused, the bishop thought, and so angry. Even crazy. The parishioner, if that was what he was, seemed to be less interested in confessing and more interested in confrontation. Rarely did a confession cause the bishop enough concern that he wished he could disobey his vows and call the police, or at least a psychiatrist.

But there had been no truly overt threat. He could only call on God.

As he approached the altar, Halkitt looked up and began to pray for guidance. As far as the bishop could gather, the man hated nearly everyone who was not white, heterosexual, and Christian. He particularly hated gay people.

One of those.

God knew there were a few of them out there, although they were reasonably rare in Saskatoon. Immigrants were starting to come into the community in larger numbers, and Halkitt could sense the city becoming more open-minded, more welcoming, due to the cosmopolitan influence.

But then there was this man. He expressed himself in strange, clipped sentences, sprinkled with profanity. He constantly asked the bishop to agree with his point of view. A confessional was not supposed to be about agreement.

"So the guy. Faggot. Came on to me at the bar," said the confessor. "Had to give him a piece of my mind. Right? What would you do? Slapped him upside the head."

That kind of thing.

"You don't feel that you did anything wrong, though?" Halkitt had asked him, wondering why the man was confessing.

"Need to know if I'm okay. Last time this happened, I got popped by the cops."

The bishop suggested several Hail Marys, and pointed out to the confessor that he was really asking for

4

secular, not sacred, forgiveness. With a humph and a few more epithets, the man finally left.

Halkitt was almost before the altar, turning over the confession in his mind. Was the man's admission that he slapped someone reason enough to call the police? But how would that help, since he didn't know the man's identity?

Then he heard steps . . . soft steps, creeping toward him down the carpeted aisle.

"Ed? Is that you?" asked Halkitt, expecting the janitor.

"No," said a voice Halkitt thought he recognized. The steps came more quickly; hard breathing filled the air. Halkitt started to turn, then looked up — surprised to see a flash of gold over his head. There was a shriek of fury, then no more words. The heavy object, encrusted with gilt and precious stones, caught the bishop on the side of the head with a sickening thud.

He fell to the floor. There was no time to call for his God.

The phone rang for the twentieth time in three hours. How, Grace asked herself, was it possible for the phone to ring that often on a Sunday night in Saskatoon? Full moon? She was already scrambling to write four stories for the Monday newspaper, and still had police checks to do.

"StarPhoenix newsroom, Grace Rampling speaking."

"Hi, Grace," said a resonant tenor voice. "My name is Bruce. I'm a member of the Pride Chorus. Do you have a minute?"

Did she have a minute? It was an unusually busy news day, already six o'clock and the copy editor was putting on the pressure. She could hear the bustle on the news desk as the front section was put together. Her four stories were destined for that section. The last deadline was ten o'clock. Grace sighed. How much longer would she be the weekend reporter at the newspaper? Damn it, she was almost thirty. It was time for Monday to Friday, and maybe a social life.

"What can I do for you?" she asked, resigning herself to an even busier night.

"Something has happened, and I'm wondering if you'd be interested in doing a story."

Everyone started their story pitches this way. It was always a little frustrating. How can you tell someone if you're interested in a story when you know nothing about it?

"Give me the short version? Then I'll tell you whether it's newsworthy."

"Well, our chorus — are you familiar with it?"

"I am."

"We were supposed to sing tomorrow night at St. Eligius. Our director just got a call from the church office — I think it was from the secretary — to say they aren't going to let us sing in the sanctuary. It was a concert, you know, not part of a church service or anything, and now they're backing out on our contract. I mean, we pay for the use of it."

The four stories she was working on — well, at least three of them — would have to wait. A gay men's choir being booted out of a Catholic church venue these days was not only a good story, it was also a human rights issue.

"Bruce, do you feel comfortable giving me your last name?"

"I . . . I guess so. Are you going to quote me?"

"Probably, yes — I'd like to speak to your choir director, too."

There was silence on the other end of the line.

"Okay," said Bruce at last. "My last name is Stephens."

"And the director's name?"

"Alan Haight."

"Tell me about the concert, Bruce. What were you going to sing? Was it religious music, show tunes, or was it something — well, something the church would consider sacrilegious?"

"It was supposed to be our usual spring concert," said the singer. "We do Broadway tunes, both solos and full choir, light operetta numbers — Gilbert and Sullivan, that sort of thing — and a few pop songs. Nothing salacious. Or sexy. Honest," he added.

"Why were you going to sing at St. Eligius?"

"Third Avenue United was already booked. It's our usual venue. We decided to try St. Eligius; it has fantastic acoustics. Ever been?"

She had, actually. While covering arts, she had seen many acts there — mostly instrumental trios and quartets, but also a few singers. The effect was transporting. It was a beautiful church.

"I have. I take your point. What reason did the secretary give your director?"

"He just said they changed their minds; that hosting our chorus was not appropriate for the cathedral. Wow."

Bruce halted.

"It's okay, Bruce," said Grace, who could hear him choking up. "I know it's upsetting. Can you tell me what the fee was?"

"I think it was five hundred dollars, but you'd have to ask Alan."

"How many singers are there in the Pride Chorus?"

"Fifty, more or less. All men, of various ages. We're thinking of inviting women, but the choir started as a gay men's thing . . . art mixed with support, you know?"

"Sure. Could you please give me Alan's number? I'd better get going, or I won't reach anyone at the church. And your number, too, please."

Bruce Stephens provided the requested numbers, then asked, tentatively, "How will the story be received?"

"Most people who read the story will understand the problem. I'd bet that will be about eighty percent of them. Try not to worry about that, Bruce."

"I'll try not to. I had to call, you know?"

"Absolutely. Thanks, Bruce. I'll be in touch."

Grace hung up, amazed at what she had heard. What was the matter with the church management? No church administrator in his right mind would do such a thing, if only from a public relations standpoint.

A quick call to Alan Haight confirmed Bruce's information, but calls to three numbers at the church office brought no answer. Balance, in news, was everything; it was crucial to get the cathedral's side of the issue. Grace leapt to her feet — it was already after six-thirty. Pulling on her parka and scarf, she approached the madly-typing news editor, looking pale and harried under the bright fluorescent lights.

"I have a story for you."

"You have, I hope, four stories for me," said John Powers, looking at her list, then expectantly at her.

"I don't think so," said Grace. "We have a gay choir getting kicked out of a Catholic church."

"What? Which church?"

"The cathedral. St. Eligius."

"When?"

"The concert was supposed to be tomorrow. Pretty shitty for them to pull the plug at this late hour."

"No kidding," agreed John, looking at his watch, and then at the four holes on his dummy pages, waiting for copy.

He grunted. John was nothing if not a true newsman, and Grace knew he smelled a story with legs. Unfortunately, she knew he also saw vast tracts of white space in tomorrow's paper.

"I'll make you a deal. If you finish the fire story, you're off the hook for the other three stories if and only if you deliver the gay choir. I'll find some more copy from Canadian Press or the Leader-Post, or something. I hope."

"Thanks, John." Grace was already dashing for the back door.

"Where the hell are you going?" he called after her.

"To the church. Can't reach anyone by phone. Be back soon."

"Okay," John yelled at her back.

St. Eligius and its offices were located directly behind the StarPhoenix; it was an easy dash from the back door. Grace pulled a scarf around her thick auburn curls, slipped her gloves on and checked again for her notepad and cellphone.

Door pass card? Check. It would be nice to get back into the newspaper building once the interviews were done. The security guard could not be trusted to answer the bell, and if he did, couldn't be trusted to actually let you in without giving you the third degree. Grace didn't always win those battles.

It was cold, not that twenty-five below zero in March was that unusual in Saskatoon. It was also getting dark as she walked across the parking lot and down the alley toward the church office, skin already tingling and brown eyes watering in the icy breeze. She shivered from exhaustion and cold. Her empty stomach growled.

As she hurried down the alley, she thought how ridiculous it was that this kind of thing still happened to gay people. At least, that appeared to be the issue. She thought the local churches were rather enlightened, but this showed otherwise.

She arrived a bit breathlessly at the office door and knocked loudly. No lights were visible, so it was unlikely anyone was still there. Still, she tried the door. It was locked.

There was another door at the east end, so she walked over to it and knocked again. Nothing. Damn it. She'd have to go back to the newsroom and start looking up the names of the priest, bishop and secretary, and try to find their home numbers.

Shifting her heavy bag from one shoulder to another, she turned back toward the alley, and started to hurry back. Wait, Grace asked herself: what if someone is in the church? It was mostly dark, but she thought she could see one small light at the back.

Mist swirling up from the half-frozen river cloaked the beautiful brick cathedral with gothic mystery, and for a second or two, Grace admired the eerie majesty of it. A few steps more took her to the beautifully carved, heavy wooden door, with its arched top and wrought iron trim.

When she went up to knock, she discovered it was open, just a crack. Grace felt a bit of a thrill; it wasn't a fool's errand after all. Someone was about.

Knocking again, she pushed the door open and walked directly into the cathedral's sanctuary. Stained glass windows ringed the long room, and the wooden pews, oiled to a soft shine, glowed in the dim light. Church sanctuaries, at least the lovely ones, always awed her a little, despite her secular views.

"Hello?" called Grace. "Hello! Is anyone here? I'm from the newspaper."

There was no answer — in fact, no sound at all. Grace walked toward the altar, away from the dim light — a little reading light, perched over a music stand — and into the gloom.

Calling "hello?" rather more softly, Grace peered along the pews and peeked at the confessionals, wondering if a priest was cloistered inside one of them.

Then her foot hit something — something soft, but not yielding. She almost tripped, but held her balance as she realized it was not something, but someone lying across the aisle.

Shocked, Grace let out a strangled yell and looked down at a man in clerical clothing right at her feet.

Backing up with speed and suddenly breathing hard, Grace pulled out her cellphone, clicked a button to turn on the screen light, and pointed the phone at the person. A priest lay in front of her, bleeding copiously from the head. Gore was congealing on the floor.

Grace sank to the floor, hand on her stomach, and tried not to throw up. Maybe he had fallen and hit his head, but more likely someone had done this to him. If it was the latter, was that someone still in the church?

Panicking, as the possibility of someone watching her sunk in, she crawled into the closest space between two pews and punched 911 on her cellphone. An operator answered immediately.

"911. What is your emergency? Do you need police, ambulance or fire?"

"Police. I've found a man lying on the floor in St. Eligius Cathedral," Grace said in a stage whisper. "I think he's a priest, and he may be dead."

"What?" Even the operator sounded flummoxed. "One moment please." Grace could hear her dispatching the police. Then she came back on the line. "Why do you think he might be dead?"

"He's been struck in the head and there's blood everywhere. He's not moving."

"What is your name, please?"

"Grace Rampling. I'm a reporter at the StarPhoenix. I was here to cover a story."

"Are you safe?" asked the operator.

"I don't know," said Grace, still in a stage whisper. Thank God the operator could hear her. "I don't know if anyone is here."

"Police are on their way. Please stay on the line."

"I can't. I have to call someone else. Thank you," said Grace, hanging up. Then she hit a speed dial button. John answered in one ring.

"John," she hissed. "I think there's a dead guy in the sanctuary. He's bleeding all over the place — can you hear me?"

"Grace? What the hell? I can just barely hear you. Are you all right?"

"I don't know. I can't see or hear anyone, but I'm crouched between two pews."

"Do you know if he's dead? Or are you guessing?"

"I'm guessing. I haven't felt for a pulse or anything. There's an incredible amount of blood, though."

"I'll call 911. And I'll be right there."

"I already called 911. But if you could come, that would be great. Thanks, John."

Grace hung up, then threw up. Wiping her mouth, she looked over at the body again, and took as deep a breath as her pounding heart would allow.

She crawled toward the man lying before the altar, stretched out an arm, and found his wrist.

He was definitely dead.

Two

Grace couldn't look at the man on the floor again: the gore, the staring eyes, and the gaping hole in his head were too revolting. She couldn't see much by the light of her phone, but what she could see was stomach-twisting. There was, in her view, no doubt that he hadn't fallen. He had been struck, and hard.

It occurred to Grace that she was not just the primary reporter, but the primary witness in this likely murder case. She had seen dead people before, especially on the weekend news beat, but this was the first one she had discovered.

"I'll be damned," she said to herself, then became aware she had said it out loud, in a normal tone of voice. Brilliant, she thought sarcastically. Was there someone lurking in a confessional? Behind the font? Did he hear her?

Stuck until help arrived, she started scribbling notes, describing what she had done, what she had seen, and how she had nearly tripped over the bloody, lifeless body.

Huddled between the pews, with half an eye on the body, she felt she could die herself of thirst and disgust.

14

Sirens. The cops were fast, especially considering what a busy day of crime they had faced — as, therefore, had she: there was the fire, which was almost certainly arson, considering who owned the property; several domestic disputes, two of them violent, according to the police scanner; a few downtown drunks, one of them with frostbite; and myriad other scuffles and intoxications.

This was, though, the first murder. Saskatoon did not normally have more than six or eight murders a year, so it was unlikely another violent death had marred the city's peace that day. And here she was babysitting the corpse.

She was reasonably sure it was the priest, judging by his clerical garments, but she had never seen him before and knew little about Catholic garb. If she was right, this was going to be one hell of a mess. High-profile murders were extremely rare in the city.

"Police!" said a booming voice. "Do not move!"

Grace froze. She doubted that the directive was intended for her, but the authority in that voice was visceral.

"Grace Rampling! Where are you? Police!" The 911 operator had done her job thoroughly. The officer knew she was there, and by name. His huge voice clanged and echoed around the acoustically-lively sanctuary; anyone hiding inside couldn't possibly miss its reach.

"Here," croaked Grace, her voice thick from fear and vomit. She tried to clear her throat.

"Grace?" asked a more familiar and less terrifying voice. "Grace, it's John. Come out. It's safe. Come on out, now."

Into the bright beam of a flashlight, she gingerly stood up, emerging from between the pews with her tangle of loose curls showing first, followed by her pale face and chocolate eyes, and finally the rest of her. She stood slowly, testing the strength in her cramping legs as she clung to the back of the pew.

"Hi," she said a bit weakly, thinking some stronger greeting would have been more impressive.

Grace squared her shoulders, an unconscious action she often used to raise her confidence. Get it together, she scolded herself. "I'm Grace Rampling," she announced to the police, with a little more self-assurance. "As you can see, there is a body here."

Four police officers approached her, three in uniform. It was quite the sight, like a scene from a movie.

"Are you all right?" asked the tall plainclothes officer with the booming voice, looking down at her with concern on his face.

"Yes. Apart from . . . well, the obvious."

"You smell wonderful," said John, who had come up behind the officers, sniffing.

"Thank you so much," said Grace, finding her sarcasm. "You try finding a dead body covered in blood."

John gave her a quick hug, just around the shoulders, and handed her his water bottle. Grace, determined not to cry, accepted the water gratefully, impressed by John's presence of mind in grabbing it on his way to the church.

"Thanks," she said, after taking several large gulps. "I'm fine."

Sergeant Boom then took over.

"Ms. Rampling. I'm Detective Sergeant Adam Davis. What brought you to the church at this hour? What were you doing here?"

Grace started to explain, as the other three officers strode to the body. Other officers appeared and began to search the church.

"I've taken some notes. Would you like me to email them to you?"

"That would be great, thank you. However, I need you to tell me the whole story, now."

Grace quickly described the phone call from Bruce Stephens, and explained the issue faced by the Pride Chorus.

"I couldn't reach anyone by phone at the church office, but St. Eligius is so close to the newspaper, I decided to run over and try to find a spokesperson. No one was at the office, so I came over to the church," she told the sergeant. "I wasn't exactly expecting . . . him," she said, pointing toward the body.

"What happened when you got to the cathedral?"

"I knocked, and then noticed the door was open, just a crack. I came inside calling 'hello.' There was no answer, but I kept walking down the centre aisle and almost stepped on the . . . the man. It was pretty dark; I could barely see."

By now, police officers had found the switches to turn on more lights in the sanctuary, and were looking into the confessionals, along the pews, and around the altar.

"Did you see anyone, or hear anything else?"

"No. In fact, it was incredibly quiet."

Grace turned in reaction to a sound behind her, and now saw the dead man in full light.

"Who is he?" she asked unsteadily. "Was he killed, do you think?"

"We don't know yet," said the sergeant. "We just got here. What happened next?" he asked, which helped Grace keep her focus.

"I was a little scared. I didn't know if he was dead, for sure, or if someone had done this to him. I crawled into that pew, and called 911. Then I called John. I pulled it together and checked for his pulse. There wasn't one."

"Thanks, Ms. Rampling. Hang around for a few minutes, will you?"

"Yes, Sergeant," said Grace, by now wanting to get back to the familiarity of the newsroom. There was also the issue of writing and filing the story.

She walked a bit further back toward the door, John in tow, and sat down. What the hell, time is wasting, thought Grace; she pulled out her notebook again and starting to write.

"What are you doing?" asked John.

"We still have a paper to put out, in case you've forgotten. I'm writing this story."

"You're going to have to change the lede later, you know," John said.

"No kidding. Now shut up. Let me write."

They would likely have to wait — perhaps until late — for the dead man's identity, and for a confirmation of whether he had been murdered or not. That would indeed be the lede, the term news people use for the first paragraph in the story; but meanwhile Grace could start on the other details.

Photographs were taken of the body where it lay, while other officers looked around for evidence. Then one of the police officers made a strange noise — a combination between indrawn breath, whoop and strangled yell.

He had turned the body over.

"Sarge," he called. "Adam! Damn, it's the bishop."

Three

A dead bishop. Soaked in his own blood.

Well, there's the lede, thought Grace.

The victim's identity had an electrifying effect on the police officers, for whom this would likely be the highest-profile killing they had ever worked on. The sergeant strode over to the body, and from his considerable height bent and peered into the man's face.

"James, how do you know this is the bishop?" he asked the younger officer. "His face is pretty bashed up and covered in blood."

"I recognize him," the officer said simply. "I've met him a couple of times. It's definitely him."

"Hell," Adam said, under his breath. "Okay, everyone, we have a murdered bishop here. Jeff, call communications and tell them what's going on. I'll call the chief. Is the crime scene unit here yet? And someone find the priest and the church administrator, or secretary, or whoever the hell."

From her spot at the back of the church, Grace had to admit she was impressed by the efficiency of the police officers, under the direction of the tall sergeant. They were rapidly covering every angle of this homicide, from investigation to public relations.

She was madly writing everything down.
It was going to be great colour for future long pieces about the murder, the community and hopefully, the perpetrator, too.

Adam Davis walked back to the pew she and John were occupying.

"I guess you know who the victim is."

"Does that mean he has been murdered, for sure?" asked Grace.

The sergeant looked like he could kick himself. Grace knew it was because he had used the word victim, instead of a less obvious term like dead man or corpse. She tried not to smile at him, but failed. A crooked grin also passed over the sergeant's face, and a small nod of the head said he accepted his mistake gracefully.

"Yes. There's no possibility he could have fallen and done that kind of extensive damage to his face and head. The bishop has been murdered, no doubt."

"Any idea as to the murder weapon, or how he was killed?"

"Not yet. And if I did know, I wouldn't tell you this early on in the investigation."

"If I may butt in," said John, "we have a newspaper that has to get out tomorrow morning. Is there any chance we could go back to the office, and get at it? We're at least two, maybe three hours behind. And we have to find a picture of the bishop. Fast," he added, to Grace.

Adam thought for a minute. "Go ahead. Make sure your phones are on, and write your numbers on this notepad," he said, handing it over. "And don't leave town."

"Very funny," said John, scribbling down his office and cell numbers, as well as Grace's.

Grace was not as amused. "What do you mean by that?"

"You're our star witness, Ms. Rampling. Please do not leave town without letting us know. I mean it."

"Yes, Sergeant," she said, rather more meekly than she would have liked.

There was something exceptionally authoritative about this policeman. There was no doubt that this was his show, and even she was going to have to play her part in it. It wasn't up for debate.

"I also have to ask you not to reveal the time of death — or, more specifically, the time of discovery," said Adam. "The fewer details we provide to the public right now, the better; but particularly not the time. We would really appreciate it."

"Okay, Sergeant," agreed John, who made the calls on what details made it into news coverage. "It won't make that much difference to the story. We'll avoid that nugget."

"Thank you, Mr. Powers. Ms. Rampling. Good night."

John and Grace put their coats back on, collected their cellphones, cameras and notebooks, and headed back down the alley toward the welcoming warmth of the office. It was even colder than before.

"You know how I always suggest, on Sundays, that someone find me a story? Make it up, if necessary? Create one, if desperate?" asked John.

"I do," Grace said. "And I always think it's funny, too," she added kindly, in deference to the old news editor's joke.

"You've gone too far this time."

21

They entered the newsroom, where the staff had little knowledge of the events of the last hour, and John quickly pulled them together around the night desk.

"I know this is going to be a little hard to digest, but Grace has just literally stumbled on the deceased body of the bishop of Saskatoon," he said, maybe a bit grandly, to a general round of gasps and exclamations of "you are kidding" and "shut up" and "holy shit."

"We have some eye witness information from her — how he was found, how he looked, and so on. Now we have to cobble this story together. It won't be a scoop, obviously, by tomorrow — the cops will have to get this out right away — but we sure have details no one else will have.

"Lacey, I need you to help Grace write the main story, and get a few paragraphs up online. It's getting really late. Call the mayor and try to find the priest. Grace, just start cranking out what you know, and figure out how you're going to get that gay choir into the piece. And get in touch with the chief of police.

"We're going to be late. Jim, call the pressroom. Tonight, we really are going to stop the big white spools. And Kathy, start looking for a photo of the bishop. What the hell is his name? Does anybody know?"

Grace felt overwhelmed; her brain wasn't clicking. What the hell was his name? She couldn't remember. She was shaking with hunger, thirst, and the uncontrollable physical reaction that comes after a shock. Lacey McPhail, who luckily was in the newsroom writing a theatre review that might not see newsprint tomorrow, looked appraisingly at Grace and solicitously dragged her over to her desk.

"What do you need?" asked Lacey, soft green eyes peering into Grace's black-rimmed brown ones. "Honey, you look done in. And," she sniffed, "you smell awful."

"I barfed," said Grace piteously, letting down her guard now that she was with a friend.

"I knew that," said Lacey. "Can you eat something? I have some hummus and veg, a granola bar, maybe a banana? Might be over-ripe. Anyway, I think some ginger ale might help."

Grace was incredibly hungry; the desire to vomit had left her. Besides, there was absolutely nothing in her stomach. Even Lacey's Mother Earth food would work for her. Mostly, she just wanted to write the story, and maybe get some sleep soon. But first, food. She was collapsing from a lack of blood sugar in her system; she was pretty sure she couldn't stand up, on her own.

"Thanks, Lace. I'd really appreciate that."

"Okay. Let me set you up with sustenance, and we'll rock and roll."

Grace wolfed down Lacey's food, and started to hammer out the story on her computer. Lacey picked up the phone and started making calls. The desk was remaking the front section of the paper. Even for the StarPhoenix, it was a wild Sunday night.

Four

Saskatoon StarPhoenix, Monday, March __

BISHOP MURDERED

Howard Halkitt found dead
in St. Eligius sanctuary

By Grace Rampling
and Lacey McPhail
of The StarPhoenix

Saskatoon's Catholic bishop, Howard Halkitt, was found murdered on Sunday, lying in a pool of his own blood before the altar of St. Eligius Cathedral.

Saskatoon police confirmed his death after responding to the scene after a call from this newspaper.

"We are devastated. How could this happen to our bishop?" said St. Eligius's priest, Father Paul Campbell, on Sunday night. "It is beyond understanding."

The bishop was a devout and sympathetic spiritual leader, said Campbell.

"It is impossible to overstate his importance to the Saskatoon Catholic community — indeed, the entire community," said Campbell. "It is a terrible loss."

Police said they had no suspects in the early hours of the investigation, and would not say how the bishop was killed. However, from eye witness observation, he appeared to have been attacked at the head, and lost a lot of blood.

Born in Ontario, Bishop Halkitt came to Saskatoon ten years ago as a priest, and was named bishop two years later.

He began his spiritual career in the town of Westmoreland, Sask., as teacher and headmaster at the boys' school and priest for the congregations at the Catholic churches in Westmoreland and nearby Pierce.

He then was transferred briefly to Brandon, Man., and later to Thunder Bay, Ont., before coming to Saskatoon.

Halkitt has two brothers and a sister, all of whom live in Canada, and several nieces and nephews. None of them could be reached for comment Sunday.

Saskatoon Mayor David Wolfe expressed horror and sympathy upon learning of the bishop's death.

"It's unbelievable," said Wolfe. "I extend my profound sympathy and support to the bishop's family and the Catholic community."

Police chief Dan McIvor said the police service would work around the clock to solve the crime. McIvor also expressed his sympathy and concern, but said no further details would be available until after an autopsy could be performed.

Earlier on Sunday, St. Eligius Cathedral revoked a contract with the Pride Chorus for the use of the sanctuary, which forced the men's choir to cancel its performance at the church for tonight.

The performance, under the circumstances of the bishop's death, would not have gone ahead anyway, since the cathedral has been closed as police investigate.

However, Bruce Stephens, a member of the choir, said he was shocked and hurt that St. Eligius would take away their venue due to the group's gay membership. He said the cathedral's secretary had contacted the choir's director, and told him the Pride Chorus performance was not appropriate for the cathedral.

Reached after learning of the bishop's death, Stephens said he was horrified.

The church secretary, Ellice Fairbrother, could not be reached for comment.

Police said there is no obvious connection between the bishop's murder and the cancellation of the concert.

The Pride Chorus was to perform Broadway tunes and operetta favourites at their annual spring concert, which was booked at St. Eligius when their usual venue, Third Avenue United Church, proved unavailable. The chorus has about 50 male members.

Choir director Alan Haight said he was "devastated" to hear of the bishop's death.

Five

G race poked her key into the lock after three stabs, stumbled across the threshold, dropped her purse and work bag, and collapsed into the nearest corner of her faded couch.

She was quite sure she had never been this exhausted, not even when she had serious jet lag after flying back to the middle of the Canadian Prairies from Australia two years ago.

"Take tomorrow morning off," suggested John, just before she left the newsroom.

"I already have the day off, mister; I've worked all weekend."

"Well, I hate to mention this, but you might want to show up. After you get some sleep. Steve is going to want to debrief and figure out how we're going to handle this as the story develops. If you want to keep covering it, you'd better be there."

"I know," said Grace. "I'd thought of that. At the moment, I think I could sleep for a week straight."

"It's been quite the night. Go home, Grace. Call me when you get up."

"Okay. John, thanks for everything."

"No, Grace. Thank you." He looked exhausted.

She gave him a shaky smile, and headed out the south door.

In the parking lot, she had a moment's discomfort. It was late, and there was a murderer out there, somewhere. He had killed the person he was looking for, but just the same, she walked rather quickly to her car, hoping it would start in the cold. Start it did — bless the little beast — and after waiting a moment for it to warm up, she left for home.

But she couldn't resist driving past the cathedral. As long a day as it had been, the police were pulling even tougher hours. There were still four squad cars there, and uniformed officers were swarming the area. Well, there was little point in stopping; they wouldn't let her back in, and the paper had finally gone to press, hours after deadline.

Grace capitulated to exhaustion and went home — not too far a drive from the paper, over the steaming river to the tree-lined neighbourhood of Buena Vista, where she could just barely afford a little bungalow on her unspectacular reporter's salary.

After a few minutes of sitting in the dark, Grace made her way into the kitchen; she was hungry again, despite having scarfed down McPhail's hummus, vegetables and granola bar. Peanut butter on toast with bananas: That sounded good, and quick.

She barely made it through her little meal. She fell onto her bed, removing her clothing from a prone position. Teeth unbrushed, sticky with peanut butter, she fell asleep.

_____

The phone was ringing. Damn it. What time was it? Why was her mouth full of fuzzy cotton?

Ah yes, peanut butter. Grace came up through layers of sleep, and tried to focus her crusty eyes on her alarm clock. It was noon, or so it said.

You've got to be kidding, she thought. Noon! Nine hours had passed, as if they were a moment. She reached for the bedside phone, and realized it wasn't ringing. It was her cellphone. Where the hell was it?

Still half-dressed, she stumbled into the living room and started searching for the phone. It had stopped ringing, which didn't help in finding it, but then started again. It seemed to be coming from the crumpled bag lying in the corner.

There you are, you blasted implement, thought Grace.

"Hello!" she said, sinking onto the couch. "It's Grace."

"Ms. Rampling. It's Adam Davis," said a powerful baritone voice.

Okay, I know that name, said Grace's barely-awake brain.

"Sergeant Adam Davis," the voice added, its owner obviously perceiving the pause.

"Oh! Hello, Sergeant. How are things going? Have you found the murder weapon? Do you have a suspect? Is . . ."

Adam cut her off, laughing.

"Ms. Rampling, I can't answer those questions just yet. How are you doing? You had quite the night. I'll bet that even in a reporter's life, yesterday was a bit unusual."

"You could say that, yes. I'm fine. I managed to get nine hours of sleep."

29

"Yikes," said the police officer, actually sounding contrite. "Did I wake you up?"

"No, I was up. I had to answer the phone."

"Very funny. I thought that joke went out with Don Rickles."

"I have an extremely sophisticated sense of humour," said Grace, having to laugh. It was a bit strange, talking to this policeman she had just met as if he were an old acquaintance.

"Sorry to wake you, really. I was wondering if you could make it down to the police station this afternoon. There are a few details I'd like to firm up."

"I could, but I don't know when. I have to meet with the editor sometime this afternoon, and the news editor, whom you met last night — John. Four o'clock might work, but could I call you back, after I check in with the bosses?"

"No problem. Here are my numbers," he said, reeling off three phone numbers in quick succession. She hoped she wrote them down correctly.

"I'll call you back as soon as I can, Sergeant."

"Thank you, Ms. Rampling."

"It would be okay with me if you called me Grace. Ms. Rampling makes me sound like a suspect. Or my mother."

"Thank you, but I'm not sure that's appropriate just now. Talk to you soon."

"Yes. Okay. Thanks, Sergeant."

Grace hung up, wondering if she should be worried about the formal way he addressed her. She also wondered if Detective Sergeant Davis had had any sleep at all. Then she wondered why that thought had even occurred to her.

Six

Well, Grace. You had quite the night," said the editor, Steven Delaney, when she appeared for the editorial meeting at two. "In thirty years in this business, I can definitely say this has never happened before – at least, not on my watch."

"Hi, Steve," said Grace, dropping into one of the square, stained easy chairs in his office. "I guess it's a rare thing for a reporter to find the body."

"Extremely rare, I'd say. So, here we are, to discuss what comes next. Has anyone else had a similar experience, here or in any other newsroom?" asked Steve.

Everyone shook their heads. John was in his usual place in the corner by the window; Steve, as always, drew up his office chair in the middle; city editor Claire Davidson took up the chair on one side of Steve, with managing editor Mark Williams taking up the last spot.

"The closest thing I can come up with is the time Robert, by luck or coincidence, was on the scene when that woman drove off the bridge," said Mark. "Great pictures at the scene, but then he felt he had to go and help the lady out of the river, instead of getting a picture of her."

31

He shook his head with mock severity at Robert's putting the woman's life before a photograph.

"It's not the same, though. He was a witness, but obviously there was no crime. It was an accident."

"I hate to ask this question, but will Grace be just a witness? Or will she be, theoretically at least, a suspect?" asked Steve. "She was first on the scene."

That cast a pall over the room. Grace went white. Despite the joke she had made while talking to the sergeant, about not calling her Ms. Rampling because it made her feel like a suspect, she hadn't seriously considered it.

"Hell. Can they really think I'm a suspect?" she asked.

"Well, the sergeant told you not to leave town," John said.

"That's because I'm their star witness, he said!"

Another pause in the conversation, as the editorial group grappled with the implications. They were all so familiar with the legal aspects of journalism — libel, publication bans, conflict of interest — but this was new territory. Grace could be in conflict as a reporter on the story, if the police did indeed consider her a suspect.

"I suppose we don't know she's a suspect until they tell us so, right?" Steve said. "And again, it would be a procedural, a theoretical thing. They can't possibly think that she might, indeed, be the killer.

"So let's just carry on as usual, until and unless they tell us otherwise. She is indeed a witness, but that doesn't bother me a lot; journalists are witnesses. That's one of the things we do in society. It's no different because she actually found the body. That's my view. Anyone else?"

"The police may see it differently," Mark said slowly. "They may not entirely trust Grace if she is both a witness and the reporter covering the story. For example, if they question her, can she report on that?"

"That's a good question. We better find out. Grace, have you been in touch with the police today?"

"Yes. The sergeant called and invited me down to the police station. I meant to tell you when I came in. He would like to ask me more questions. I said I'd be there about four; is that okay with you, Steve?"

"Of course, that's fine. But I'm going to get on the horn with our lawyer. I hope Bill's in today. I want to know exactly where you stand, Grace, on what you can report. "

"Who's following the story today?" asked Claire. "I assume, Grace, that you want to stay on it? But you're going to need some help; and, if we find out you can't continue, we need a second reporter up to speed on this.

"I don't need to say this out loud, but it's going to be one of the biggest stories of the year, and possibly the next two or three years, depending on when they find the killer and when he goes to court."

"Lacey was helping Grace last night," said John. "Thank God she was here. And she was really good, too — caught up to the mayor and found the priest within about an hour, while Grace was putting together her story and talking to the Pride Chorus guys. No luck finding the secretary, though."

"Let's find out what other stuff Lacey is working on. She's been helping in arts while Brenda is away; can they spare her? Otherwise, I have no problem with that," said Steve.

"Can I just say," broke in Grace, who was feeling a bit emotional, "how absolutely fantastic John and Lacey were last night? Not to mention Jim and Kathy. Thanks, John," she added, trying not to get maudlin.

"You were pretty amazing, too, Gracie," said John.

What a lovefest, she thought. But really, the team was incredible when it was on its game, and it was, very much so, the night before.

"Well, now that I know I have the best damned news team in the city, verified by themselves, can we get rolling?" said Steve, in his slightly snarky but kind way. He smiled at Grace and John. "I'll call the lawyer. Grace, put off heading to the station as long as you can; I'll try to reach Bill before you go. It's a whole two minute walk, so you can wait until just before four."

"I'll go and get the news releases from the police, and see what the other outlets have published by now," said Claire to John and Grace. "Meet me at my desk in about ten."

Grace went to her desk and poked her computer's on-button, threw her purse in a drawer, and sat down. She called the police station to confirm her four o'clock interview. Immediately after she hung up, the phone rang.

Naturally, thought Grace. Why would today be any different? She could see the red light flashing, indicating waiting messages. Someday, she mused, I will take my revenge on the damn phone and beat it with a stick.

"StarPhoenix newsroom, Grace Rampling speaking."

"Hello, Grace, my name is Frank Stephens."

"Hi, Frank."

"I'm Bruce Stephens' father."

"Oh, hello. How is Bruce today?" she asked. She was actually quite concerned about him. It was brave of him to stand up for his choir, to call her and to provide attributed quotes. She quite liked him. He was, as far as she could tell yesterday, pretty forthright.

"Bruce is doing quite well, although he is shocked about the death of the bishop. Quite a bizarre turn of events," said Frank Stephens.

"But the reason I'm calling is to thank you for the story on the choir. It's not always easy to have a gay child. I appreciate your support in this regard, if you understand me. I think that kicking Bruce's choir out of the church was a . . . a terrible thing to do."

"I appreciate that, Frank, thank you. But it is my job. We try to cover stories that are human rights issues, and hopefully make the city a better place. So no thanks are necessary."

"Well, still, I'll bet reporters don't always get a lot of positive feedback. And that must have been a very late night for you. So, I thought I'd call and let you know someone appreciates your efforts."

"Thank you. That's very nice of you. Tell Bruce if they reschedule the concert to let me know. I'd like to come."

"I'll do that, Grace. Thanks. And thanks again for your story, even if it ended up being overshadowed by the bishop."

"I guess it did. Thanks for calling, Frank."

Well, that was nice, thought Grace, on her way to the city editor's desk.

"Anything new from the police?" she asked Claire.

"Not much. No killer, no murder weapon, no witnesses besides you, and no motive. Perfect. What the hell are we going to do for a folo?"

"Offhand, I can't think of anything brilliant. Maybe something will come to me after I see the police. John?"

"We can get some reaction. Try to get more of a bio going on the bishop, what's happening with the church — how long will it be closed, how the parishioners feel, that kind of thing — until we get more facts. We can get going on that, and then see what Grace brings back."

"Good plan," Claire agreed. "I'll assign the bio and the church update. We'll re-evaluate when Grace gets back from the cop shop."

Grace was not entirely looking forward to her meeting — or would that be interrogation? — at the police station. She was usually the one asking the police questions. It was going to be strange sitting on the other side of the tape recorder.

She was somewhat armed with the lawyer's advice, which as usual erred on the side of the journalist. The reporters loved Bill Cooke. He was always on their side, as much as he possibly could be within the law. Basically, she was free to report anything, unless the police actively made a strong argument as to why she couldn't.

"Don't ask for permission, Grace," said Bill. "Just do your job. If they bring it up, we'll discuss. And if you become something other than a witness, we'll regroup."

Grace headed out the south door just before four, getting a few supportive thumbs up from her colleagues as she went.

"Tell that cop to keep his voice down," John called after her. "You know. Sergeant Boom."

Grace laughed. "I'll see if that makes any difference."

The police station was exactly a block and a half away from the StarPhoenix, if you used the newspaper's front door. She walked quickly, past the brownstone apartments and along the dirty melting windrows created by snow cleared from the winter streets. It wasn't Saskatoon's most beautiful time of year.

She presented herself to the desk sergeant at two minutes to four, and explained that she was there to see Sergeant Davis.

"Have a chair, Ms. Rampling. I'll call the sergeant."

Grace spent her short wait checking her notebook. She really wanted to be helpful and clear, and did not want to dither.

"Ms. Rampling," said a big, now-familiar voice.

Grace looked up at the sergeant and in that moment felt her heart stop. He stood towering over her, with his head slightly cocked to the side, considering her.

Oh my God, thought Grace, he's . . . beautiful. Why didn't I notice that last night? Right. Because I was terrified and throwing up all over the place.

Damn, Grace's brain added. That's just great, having unprofessional thoughts about the sergeant. Please, don't let me show that on my face.

"Hello, Sergeant," she managed to say, standing up and offering her hand.

"Thanks for coming down," said Adam, his big hand taking hers. "We'll go into one of the rooms down the hall. James will join us."

"James?

"James Weatherall. He's the police officer who identified the bishop last night."

A sharp and sudden memory of the noise James made when he turned the body over came to her, as if it had been taped and replayed.

"Right. I remember him."

They reached the little room. Grace found it daunting. It was grey and airless, without windows, and furnished with a small table, a recording system and four very uncomfortable-looking chairs. A bright light was suspended from the ceiling. It really is like those awful interrogation rooms in TV police shows, Grace thought.

She thought about making a joke. "I confess!" was almost out of her mouth, in an effort to make the room seem less intimidating. But she bit it back. It didn't seem professional, under the circumstances. And who knew if they would take it seriously?

"Please take a chair, Ms. Rampling."

The door opened to reveal James Weatherall, who came over to Grace and introduced himself by name and rank, shaking her hand.

"How are you, Ms. Rampling? That must have been quite the night for you," he said.

"I'm fine, thank you, Constable Weatherall," she said.

"Would you like coffee? Water?" he asked.

"No, I'm fine, thanks."

"Ms. Rampling," started Adam, managing not to break the light with his voice. "We will be recording this conversation, as I'm sure you know. Can you please start by stating your name and occupation."

Grace complied.

"Ms. Rampling, you were in St. Eligius Cathedral last night. Can you please tell us again how you came to be there."

Grace almost asked him why she had to go over that again, since she had explained her reason for being there last night, but then understood with a small, unpleasant thrill that they could be testing her response. They would compare it to what she said last night.

"We just want it on tape," said Adam, seeing the shadow cross her face. "It's all right, Ms. Rampling."

Grace went over the evening's events again, hoping what she was saying matched exactly with what she said last night, starting with the phone call from Bruce Stephens and ending with nearly tripping over the body.

"Did you at any time hear anyone or anything in the cathedral, or see anyone?" asked Adam.

"I did not. It was very quiet. After I found the body, I looked around as much as I could. I was a little, well, worried."

"What were you worried about?"

"That there was someone in the church, and he or she had killed this person."

"Did you know the bishop was dead?"

"Not until later, but he looked awful. There was a lot of blood, he was very pale and that sort of thing, so I thought he might be."

"When did you realize he was dead?"

"After I called 911 and my editor, I got up the courage to crawl over to him — I was hunched between two pews — and check his pulse. There was no pulse, and his hand was cold. I was then quite sure that he was dead."

"Those would be good indications," said the sergeant, with a little smile. "Did you notice the quality of the blood? I mean, was it . . . sorry," he stopped, as she paled a little. "Was it, well, runny or congealing? Sorry," he said again.

Why was she being so squeamish? She had seen lots of pretty awful things. But somehow, this was very different. And there was so much blood.

"I . . . I'm not sure. It wasn't still flowing, anyway," she said. "For what it's worth, I had the feeling he had been dead for a while. Not a long while, but not just a few minutes, either."

"And what time was this?"

"It was about seven-ten. I think I got to the church just after seven. I started by looking for a source at the office, and left the newspaper about six forty-five," said Grace, checking her notes.

The sergeant and constable couldn't conceal how impressed they were with Grace's steady and specific testimony, and looked at each other with eyebrows cocked. It would be great if all witnesses were reporters, their expressions said, not for the first time. Fat chance.

But Grace didn't notice. She was too focused on her notes.

"Did you know, or had you ever met the bishop?" asked James.

"No, I had never met him, and I didn't recognize him."

"Do you know anyone in the congregation?"

"I don't know for sure. I don't think so. I mean, I'm not aware that anyone I know is a member of that church. I'm not Catholic," she added in explanation.

"Do you have any idea who may have killed him?" asked Adam.

"No. Why would I? Oh . . . " she trailed off, thinking of the Pride Chorus. Grace realized they might think she suspected Alan Haight or Bruce Stephens. But she didn't, not really — at least, not Bruce. She had only spoken to Haight for a few minutes, and had neither a good nor a bad feeling about him.

She shook her head again. "No."

"Thank you, Ms. Rampling. We appreciate you taking the time to come down."

"It's no problem, really. I don't know if I've been helpful?" She wasn't sure what to say.

"It's early days. Everything helps right now. I'll see you out. James, I'll meet you in a few minutes."

"Okay, Sarge."

Adam Davis opened the door and gestured rather chivalrously for Grace to precede him into the hallway. He walked her to the front door, and thanked her again.

"My pleasure," said Grace, looking up at the tall officer with the big baritone voice, and then blushed, thinking her response was ridiculous. But it was true. "Feel free to call if you need anything else."

"Oh, I will, Ms. Rampling," said Adam, eyes dancing just a bit. Obviously, he would call, for God's sake, thought Grace. He was in charge of the case.

For a second, they stood there, just looking at each other, Grace oddly unsure about how to end the conversation. Somehow, it didn't feel like it was over. Then she pulled herself together and walked out the door, with a simple, "goodbye, Sergeant."

"Goodbye, Ms. Rampling."

And that was that. He didn't suggest that she was a suspect, and didn't tell her what she could and couldn't report, so it seemed all good . . . apart from the fact that Grace was very worried she wouldn't be able to get his face, or his voice, out of her mind.

41

Seven

Who killed the bishop? Grace wondered as she walked slowly back to the newspaper office.

How old is Sergeant Davis? The thought intruded. Grace shook her head again, her usual tactic to clear unwanted thoughts. Stop it. He could be married, or gay, or messed up, or psychotic, or any number of things . . . but he seemed so kind, quite empathetic, for a police officer.

Don't go there, she told herself. It's just too much work, and much too strange, since I'm a damned witness and he's the sergeant on the case. That relationship would be a world of hurt.

So, who did kill the bishop? She tried to focus on that thought. She was, of course, positive that the police were going to interview every single member of the Pride Chorus, and ask them all where they were between, say, four and seven on Sunday night.

It was possible that one of the choir members lost his temper, she supposed, over being kicked out of the church. Was that really a motive for murder, though? It seemed ridiculous, but it could be. People did terrible things with very little provocation.

The Pride Chorus was definitely made up of prime suspects one through fifty.

It couldn't be Bruce Stephens, though, could it? He seemed so thoughtful, if upset. It would be interesting to meet him in person, thought Grace. She could get a better feeling about what sort of a person he was; and maybe she could also get a longer interview on the issues facing the chorus, which might make a good read.

Maybe I'll call him when I get back to the office, thought Grace. How tall is Sergeant Davis? asked another cell in her brain. Damn.

"Hello, Bruce Stephens? It's Grace Rampling calling, from the paper."

"Hello, Grace. It's me. How are you?"

"I'm fine. I am, however, a witness in a murder investigation, which isn't something I've ever aspired to, but otherwise fine. How about you?

"I'm fine, too — although I am a suspect in a murder investigation, and I haven't aspired to that, either. Isn't this bizarre?"

"It is. And I'm afraid you're right, that you and the rest of the choir are going to fall under suspicion, but try to remember it's just that you're obvious suspects; it's not personal."

"Well, I'll try to remember that, but it's still damned uncomfortable. Do I need to say, for the record, that I didn't kill him and was nowhere near the place on Sunday?"

"You don't need to, but thanks for that. Remember that line when the police call. Listen, I'm wondering if you would be willing to get together and chat about all this. I'm thinking about a story on the chorus; it may balance the coverage, and we could talk about the issues a choir like yours faces. What do you think?"

Bruce paused. "I'm not sure. I feel a little exposed as it is. But I see what you mean. Maybe we could have a coffee or a drink or something, and just talk about it a bit more, face to face?"

"That'd be great. When could we do that?"

"Why don't you meet me at Divas? Say, Wednesday night?" asked Bruce.

"That would work. What time?"

"Eight? Before things get rolling at the club?"

"Better make it nine. I might not have my story finished by eight. Would that be okay?"

"It might start getting a bit loud, but we'll make it work. I'll see you there."

"And what do you look like, exactly?"

"I will wear a rose in my lapel. I'm just over six feet, dark brown hair, blue eyes, hundred and eighty pounds. But I will find you. Remember, your picture is sometimes in the paper."

Ah, yes. The byline photo.

"And if you don't find me, I can always phone. See you in a couple of days, Bruce. And thanks."

"See you later, Grace. Don't thank me yet."

Tuesday dawned as cold as the day before, ice crystals brittle in the air, the river generating so much steam that visibility on the Broadway Bridge was reduced to nearly zero. Saskatoon's river never froze in the winter; the Queen Elizabeth power plant discharged so much hot water, the South Saskatchewan didn't turn to solid ice until well upstream. That fact was a regular traffic hazard when the temperature dropped below minus twenty.

Grace drove to work carefully, quite aware that she was distracted by the events of the last two days swirling through her brain and the image of Sergeant Davis's face securely lodged in her mind's eye. The road conditions were awful. Thank God she lived close to work, and didn't have to take the freeway.

Something else was nagging at her. Her mind searched all the files of her memory banks: what was it?

Grace had an interview booked for nine-thirty, a date made before the bishop's death for a very different story on the pending construction of an enormous new commercial building. Usually, she loved that stuff, but now she was obsessed with the murder. She tried to set it aside, as she collected her gear from her desk and prepared for the morning's work.

"I think I'll walk," she said to Lacey. "It's only four blocks, and God knows if I'll find a parking spot."

"It's cold," warned Lacey.

"I realize that," said Grace, smiling at her friend, and putting her rather enormous and very warm parka back on. "But it's less frustrating than driving around the block twenty times. See you later."

Adam and James were in Adam's office, planning their next moves.

"We need to interview Bruce Stephens, James. And the choir director, the priest, and the church secretary. Can you get that lined up? I have to go to provincial court on the Lassiter case. I should be back in an hour or so."

"I'm on it, Sarge. See you later."

Adam always walked to court, if he had time. It gave him ten or fifteen minutes to clear his head, focus on the case ahead of him and — in the summertime, at least — enjoy the freedom of wandering the streets and people-watching. It was much nicer to walk to the Court of Queen's Bench, which was perched rather elegantly overlooking the riverbank park, but provincial court was his destination today.

It was a fairly routine case, and Adam was indeed finished in forty-five minutes. It was bloody awful out — the wind had kicked up considerably — and Adam was starting to regret not driving to court. Instead of heading straight back to work, he turned onto Second Avenue and ducked into the Starbucks, craving good, hot coffee. It was never so at the police station.

Every head turned when Adam strode in. Sometimes he caught people staring at him, and he wondered why. Because of his size? He did look like a cop, he knew, even in plain clothes. But sometimes they were looking at his face. He'd been told he was handsome, and the number of women who had thrown themselves at him seemed to suggest it, but he never quite saw it. He just saw himself.

He got in line and was waiting as patiently as possible when the door opened. An icy gust ushered in Grace Rampling, face pink from the cold, swaddled in her parka, her hair partly covered in a soft black scarf. As she joined the lineup, she drew the scarf down, shook out her curly mane, pulled off her gloves and opened her handbag.

Adam contemplated her for a couple of minutes, aware of how much he was enjoying watching her without her knowing. As the line moved along, they were eventually standing directly across the fabric barrier from each other.

"Ms. Rampling," said Adam, looking down at her. Adam almost never said hello. He got right to the name, or to the point.

Grace, who was absorbed in reading her notes from the interview, looked up with a little start.

"Hello, Sergeant. How funny to meet you here."

Adam smiled. "It is, kind of. We work a block away from each other, never met until two days ago, and now you can't get rid of me."

"Not at all," said Grace, politely. "How are you? How is the case going?"

"Slowly but surely. May I buy you coffee?" asked Adam, stretching the barrier fabric up as far as possible for Grace to duck under.

"That's very nice of you . . . please, don't feel you have to, I'm fine . . ."

"I'd like to, Ms. Rampling. Please. You've done a lot for us. Never allow anyone to offer you coffee at the station again, though. It's vile."

The touch of humour seemed to break through Grace's confusion; she laughed and slipped over to Adam's side of the lineup. No one objected. No one ever objected to anything Adam did.

"What would you like?" asked Adam, as they neared the till.

"Mmm," said Grace, perusing the options. "I'd love a latté, please."

Adam ordered the latté for Grace and an Americano for himself; they chatted about coffee preferences, and the relative merits of Starbucks over Tim Hortons, as they prepared to leave.

"It's awfully cold for March, even in Saskatoon," said Grace, juggling her coffee, handbag and reporters' gear as she tightened her scarf around her head. "I can't wait for this to break."

"Amen," agreed Adam. "Are you from Saskatoon?"

"Yes. Born here, and I've lived here most of my life, except for Regina while I was in journalism school. And I'm still not used to winter. How about you?"

"No. I was born on a farm, near a very small town close to the Alberta border. My parents still farm there. I came here to attend the University of Saskatchewan."

"Did you? Why the U of S?"

"I didn't want to be too far from home — I like to help with seeding and harvest when I can — so I wanted a university in Western Canada. I came to check out the campus and I liked it best."

"And you stayed," prompted Grace.

"I applied for the police force right after graduating, made it in, and I've just stayed, yes. I really like Saskatoon. It's beautiful — at least in the summer. How long have you been at the StarPhoenix?"

"About seven years. I started right after J-school, and I'm happy there. Actually, I love it there. It's a great place; and, my family is all here in Saskatoon. I'd really miss them if I moved away."

Grace's face clouded, just for a second, and she quickly looked down when she mentioned her family. Adam wondered if he should ask why, but thought it might be a bit personal. He had only met Grace two days ago. But obviously, something caused that look.

By now, they were almost at the police station. As if cued by the sight of the building, Grace changed the topic of conversation.

"You know, there's been something bothering me all morning. About the case. It just clicked. I'm not sure if this means anything or not," she said, then paused.

Adam, a little surprised, chuckled and raised an eyebrow. Obviously, she was just as interested in this case as he was.

"That was a quick segue. But tell me. What are you thinking?"

"Yesterday, just before I came to the station, Frank Stephens called me," she said, a little reluctantly. "Frank is Bruce Stephens' father. You know, Bruce from the Pride Chorus?" she asked, and Adam nodded.

"I feel really uncomfortable about this," Grace said, with a little sigh. "He seems like a nice man. But it was a bit strange. He called to thank me for the story on the choir getting kicked out of the cathedral; said it was hard to have a gay child, sometimes. That's a bit unusual — he was also right that reporters don't get a lot of positive feedback — but then he said to me, something like, 'you must have had a late night.'

"It may just have been something he said, to sound supportive. Or he may have said it because he knew I called Bruce for a comment mid-evening. But I thought it was odd. We kept the time of discovery out of the paper, at your request."

"So he was either making polite conversation, or he knows something and didn't realize he was revealing that," said Adam, mulling this piece of information over. "Thanks for telling me. That's interesting."

They were both shivering at the door of the station.

"I better get going," said Adam, reluctantly. "I have an interview with the choir director. If you think of anything else, please call me," he added.

Then he realized he didn't want her to leave; didn't want to stop talking with her. Suddenly he was thinking, please call me if you notice the sun going down. Or the traffic light turning green.

"I will. And I better get back to work before I freeze to death out here. Sergeant, thank you so much for the coffee. That was lovely."

You're lovely, thought Adam.

"You're very welcome," was what he said. "Least I could do."

"Goodbye, Sergeant," said Grace, turning to head to the StarPhoenix.

Adam didn't go inside, just yet. He watched her walk down the street, head up and shoulders straight despite the hunching cold, her slim figure obscured by the voluminous parka, silky auburn curls escaping from her scarf.

He had watched her eyes for ten minutes as they talked, intrigued by how dark brown the irises were, how enigmatic that deep colour made her gaze. Now he was watching her back, her graceful walk, the shape of her — as much as possible, considering the parka.

Something stirred in Adam. Something he had never been sure he would ever feel; that he was even incapable of feeling. It was very disconcerting. He pushed the feeling down, and went inside.

The interview with Alan Haight didn't take very long. Haight had booked a rehearsal with the chorus soloists from three until six in the afternoon on Sunday. Then he had driven one of them home, stayed for a drink, sworn up a blue storm and gone home. He had also made a lot of phone calls.

If he was telling the truth, he had alibis for the time of the murder.

"What did the church secretary say, when he called you?" asked Adam.

The call had come to Haight's cellphone right after rehearsal had begun. "He simply said the church had decided to cancel our concert; that it was unseemly. I argued, but he wouldn't say any more, just repeated that. I asked whose decision it was, and he just said the church's."

"How quickly did you inform the choir?

"The four of us split up the list and called everyone we could reach right away. I think maybe we couldn't get in touch with ten, or so. There was little point, at that moment, in continuing with the rehearsal."

"I'll need a list of the ones you reached," Adam said.

Haight paled, as the significance of this sunk in, but nodded.

"Thank you for coming, Mr. Haight. Please let us know if you have to leave town."

"Right. Goodbye Sergeant, Constable."

Well, they learned a few things. Hopefully, Adam thought, they would learn more tomorrow, from the priest and the secretary.

He returned to his office, and replayed the tape of Grace Rampling's testimony.

He told himself that he wanted to review it. But that wasn't really true. He had pretty much memorized everything she had said.

He wanted to hear her voice.

Eight

It was after eight on Wednesday night by the time Grace finished a follow-up story on the bishop's death, known in short as a folo in newsrooms. It really wasn't much of a story, but at least it kept the murder in the paper.

Grace headed to the women's bathroom to freshen up. She didn't usually wear a lot of makeup, but she did want to look like she was going out, not going to bed.

Handbag tucked under her arm, she approached the mirror with trepidation. Tired eyes looked back at her, with black half-circles underneath. She looked pale, too, but that wasn't really unusual for an overworked redhead. Blessed with beautiful if untamed curls, Grace's hair was holding up, but she patted a little concealer under her eyes, added a bit of lipstick, swept on some mascara and felt a bit better.

Walking out of the newsroom and waving to John, Grace felt quite vindicated to be leaving in the middle of the evening instead of at two in the morning, as she had three nights before. That being said, she was going to talk to a potential suspect and certainly a good contact, so the workday wasn't really over yet.

Grace drove the few blocks to Divas and lucked into a spot on the street not far from the club's entrance, which was located down a fairly dark and forbidding alley. At this time of night, not a lot of people were headed for the club — it was much too early for the serious clubbers — but a few were walking down the alley, laughing, chatting and teasing, coming down for an early drink.

Grace had been in plenty of forbidding places in her reporting life and experienced little fear, but heading into the dark was a little different so soon after finding a body. She was glad for the other club-goers.

She was a little earlier than she expected to be, so the music was not yet deafening and the conversation was still a thrum instead of a full-out bellow. Coloured lights were swirling and flashing, and it took a few moments for her eyes to adjust. She looked around for Bruce, wondering if he had arrived yet.

"Good evening, Grace," said a voice on her left. She turned to see a tall man with his thumb and forefinger extending his lapel, which indeed bore a lush, red rose. His entire face smiled at her, eyes twinkling, as he executed a slight bow.

"Hello, Bruce," said Grace, extending her hand and feeling a wide grin spread across her face. "Beautiful rose."

"Thank you. I did have to dress up a little, in order to actually wear the rose. A little upscale, perhaps, for this scene."

"I appreciate the effort," said Grace, taking in the man's appearance.

"It wern't nothin', ma'am," said Bruce, in his best John Wayne accent. "Let's grab one of those tables at the back. It should be quieter there."

He was wearing a blue silk jacket, complete with a rose hole, over a white shirt and dark blue jeans. Gentlemen with dark brown hair and navy eyes look very nice in blue, thought Grace, who had noticed that several times over the last few days. Much like Adam, she realized, Bruce was very attractive, very at home in his body, and she could see the humour in his face. Meeting him, she understood why she liked him so much on the phone.

Divas was a gay club, but no one looked twice at Bruce leading Grace to a table. The crowd at Divas was accepting of any and all combinations of couples or groups.

Bruce carried an imported beer, and after asking her what she wanted, ordered a dry white wine. Grace felt a twang of guilt over having a drink while working, but thought, what the hell. She could use a little lubrication after the last twenty-four hours. And she wanted to fit into this environment as much as possible.

They made small talk as they settled into a booth. Then Grace started to turn the conversation to the topic at hand.

"Have you rescheduled your concert?" she asked.

"Not yet. It seems — well, unseemly," said Bruce. "The bishop dies in the church where our concert was supposed to be, but we got kicked out. Then we rebook in another venue down the street. I don't know; it feels insensitive, somehow.

"The other thing is, I wonder how we'd be received right now. We could get lots of support, but maybe not. I'm just not sure. Alan thinks we should wait a bit, and I agree."

"Point taken. I hadn't thought of it that way," said Grace. "Have you talked to any chorus members? How are they feeling about the bishop's death? I mean, it's likely you're all suspects, as we said on the phone."

"A couple of them are a bit scared," said Bruce. "There are always the more-sensitive types, and those who are more relaxed about things. The sensitive ones are a bit jumpy. I don't think anyone likes police interviews. That being said, as far as I know, the police haven't contacted any of us yet aside from Alan and the soloists."

"Tell me a bit more about the chorus. How long has it been around? Have you had any other issues?"

"Oh yes, plenty of problems. The chorus has been together about fifteen years, I think; I joined a few years ago. We've had heckling, and in the early days, we had to really hunt for venues. But the last three or four years have been great, with no venue problems until we got booted from St. Eligius. That's not to say some of our members don't get harassed; but as a choir, we are doing really well, generally speaking."

"Do your concerts make money?"

"Not much. Enough to keep us in black pants, white shirts and sheet music. We're strictly a community choir; there is no profit motive."

"Profit motive," repeated Grace. "What exactly do you do for a living?"

"I'm an investment banker," said Bruce, laughing.

"Ah," said Grace. "I hate to ask this, but do you think there is any serious animosity among the choir members toward the church?"

"Of course. They are . . . " Bruce hesitated. "They're angry. It's so offensive. The chorus is a professional group — I mean, most of us are professionals. We don't show up for concerts dressed in drag, for Christ's sake. Although if we did, that should still be our prerogative. And the Pride Chorus is not an activist organization, either. We do it for the fun, the art, and the social connection." He stopped, and swallowed. "Sorry. I think I'm preaching."

"No, no. I asked, remember." Grace realized she was raising her voice. The music was getting louder. "What would you think of a story about a few of the members? Who they are, what they do for a living, a few personal details? We could add some information about the chorus itself, its history and so on. I think, especially considering recent events, that people would find it very interesting."

Bruce thought for a moment, contemplating Grace across the table.

"Can I give it some thought? I'm not entirely against the idea. It might be good for us; it might have some nasty side effects. This is not yet the most open-minded community on Earth. We just got kicked out of a church, after all, bizarre as it is. It is getting better, though."

"Of course you can think about it. I realize it's a big question." Grace handed over her card. "You can always reach me at these numbers."

"Thanks, Grace. I do appreciate the opportunity, you know. I just have to make sure I think it's the right thing to do."

Bruce glanced to his right, and Grace, following his eyes, landed her own on a familiar figure.

Approaching them was the police constable, James Weatherall, looking very much unlike a policeman apart from his official haircut. Grace tried to hide her astonishment, but when James hugged Bruce and gave him a light kiss, she gave up.

"Hi, Ms. Rampling," said James. "You look surprised to see me."

"Hi, Constable Weatherall," said Grace. "I suppose I am. I'm sorry. I'm very sorry about my uncontrollable face. I think I'm more surprised that you know each other."

"Grace, James. James, Grace. Can we do first names at the club, or is that a breach of protocol?" asked Bruce, who knew from James that Grace had been at the police station giving a statement.

"I don't know," said Grace. "I was definitely Ms. Rampling at the police station."

"I think it's okay," said the constable. "Grace."

"James," said Grace, inclining her head in a nod along with the new greeting.

Now what? she asked herself. Should she determine if Bruce and James were a couple, or just dating, or what? Was it her business anyway? Should she just leave?

"I know what you're thinking," said Bruce, clearly reading her mind. "And yes. We're a couple. It was going to become apparent sooner or later, and besides, what is there to hide, really? Except that my spouse is a cop investigating a murder in which I am probably the prime suspect.

"No problem," he added, bitterly. "What could go wrong?"

"I'm sorry," said Grace. "That must be tough."

"It is," said James. "It has only been — what, about three days since you found the bishop? And we've really had to be extra nice to each other. It's pretty weird. We'll get through it. I'm going to have to figure out a way not to be there when they call Bruce in for an interview, for sure. I may have to remove myself from the investigation. That would suck."

"I think we should dance," Bruce shouted. "It's really getting too loud to talk much."

"When you say, 'we?'" Grace asked, at the top of her voice.

"All three of us. Let's dance."

Grace loved to dance, and couldn't resist. It was really a riot, dancing at a club with two of the handsomest men in the room.

The hotter elements of the Divas experience would come later. Some nights, hetero men who found a gay male audience erotic and exhilarating would hit the stage to strip. Men in flamboyant drag would do the same. Sometimes, confused and lost members of the public would wander in, experience shock, and either stay for the fun or leave appalled. And sometimes, a lunatic homophobe would appear. The security guards were therefore very, very large — even bigger than Adam Davis.

It wasn't Grace's first time at the club, but it was her first time as a patron. Soon, it dawned on her that the fun should really be over; she should be keeping some personal distance from Constable Questioner and Prime Suspect.

A bit breathlessly, Grace yelled in Bruce's ear, "I really should get going. Have to work tomorrow."

"Too bad, Grace. Are you sure?" he yelled back.

She nodded. "But thank you. It was great meeting you, and don't forget about my request."

"I won't. I do appreciate the offer, as I said," Bruce said in her ear. "I'll walk you to the door, so we don't have to yell."

Grace waved goodbye to James, gathered her stuff, and headed for the door. She shook Bruce's hand.

"Thanks again."

"Should I walk you to your car? It's dark and can be a bit intense out there. How far are you?"

"I'm just half a block up on Third Avenue."

Grace thought about his offer. Who was safer out there? A female reporter or a gay man just leaving Divas? But there were always people coming and going in the alley.

"I'll be fine," she said, finally. "We'll talk in a couple of days?"

"Absolutely. Cheers, Grace. Take care."

Grace ventured into the alley, looking both ways first. She started walking quickly down the cobblestoned, garbage-strewn, stinking corridor.

The shadows surrounding the massive garbage cans were great places to lurk, thought Grace. She was only a few feet from the main street, and started to relax.

"You fucking fag-loving bitch," came a growl from the shadows. "You fucking fag lover."

Grace didn't have to think about it. She ran. The voice's owner was in hot pursuit. With a sickening mental lurch, she realized instantly that this person was unbalanced. How did he know she was at Divas? Why did he care?

Grace had been trained not to confront and attempt to reason with crazed people in solitary situations — she was a journalist, not a cop — so she said nothing and ran, tripping and sliding on the greasy stones. He was gaining on her and spewing filth as he came.

Then he was right behind her. Grace screamed as she felt his presence, smelled his stink over the reeking alley, not a foot away. A whoosh of air behind her told her he had a weapon.

"Grace!" someone shouted, just before a blow landed on the side of her head, and glanced down on her shoulder.

She felt consuming, intense pain, as the cobblestones seemed to rise up, meeting her hip and knee and face. All she could see was her own blood as it ran into her eyes. Then nothing.

Bruce Stephens lingered at the doorway. It was quieter and cool, and he kept an eye on the reporter, who perhaps didn't really need to walk down the alley alone.

He watched Grace as she became enveloped by darkness near the end of the alley. She was almost at her car. Just as he turned to rejoin James inside, he heard a voice. Then he heard her scream.

"Grace!" he yelled. "Grace!" No response came. "Answer me!"

But there was silence, apart from a brief scuffling sound. Bruce started running, calling over his shoulder for the security guard to get James and then get his ass down the alley.

It was slippery and dark, but Bruce was moving fast. He found Grace less than a minute later. He crouched over her, saw the blood flowing from her wound, then cradled her head against himself, away from the hard cobblestones. In seconds, his blue jacket was as red as his rose.

———————————

Adam was sort of enjoying the reasonably quiet, relatively crime-free evening. It made for a long shift, but if he had to be in the office, it was a good time to read over the details of the Halkitt murder.

"Hey, Charlotte," he said to one of the constables, who was reading the same information. Charlotte Warkentin had a fantastic mind for details, and for crime scene visualization. Adam was always glad to have her working on his cases, especially for testing theories. He was very, very fond of the older constable.

"Says here that Halkitt was five foot nine. Not a tall guy. That means pretty much half the adult population, or more, could have bashed him on the head.

"Plus it looks like he, or she, I suppose, was right-handed. If the killer was left-handed, he would have landed the weapon on the back of the head, not on the side of the head. Right?"

By the way the body was lying in the aisle of the cathedral, it appeared that Halkitt had turned slightly before the attack.

"Exactly right," said Charlotte, who cared about exactitude. "That doesn't exactly narrow down the possible murderers, does it? Anyone five-six or taller could have done it — although probably not someone very tall — and someone right-handed. I bet he or she had mousy brown hair and blue eyes, too," she added, sighing.

"How strong would someone have to be to raise the murder weapon, whatever the hell it is, and then bash this guy to death, do you think?"

"Depends on the weapon, of course — how heavy it is, which we know is pretty heavy by the look of the wound, and how long. It wouldn't likely be someone slight or weak, but it wouldn't have to be someone incredibly powerful, either. Again, it's the universal suspect."

A quick knock at the door was immediately followed by a head poking in.

"Sarge, got a 911 call. Weatherall says you need to be there," said the police officer.

"What the hell is he doing responding to a 911 call?" asked Adam. "He has the night off."

"He called it in, Sarge."

Adam was momentarily stunned into silence. That was really bizarre.

"What the hell is going on?" he asked the constable.

"Beats me, Sarge," the constable answered, retreating.

Adam's cellphone started to ring, and James's name appeared on the screen. He snatched the phone off the desk and answered it quickly.

"James. What the hell is going on?" asked Adam, repetitively.

"Adam, the reporter, you know, Grace — um, Ms. Rampling — has been attacked. The ambulance is just arriving," he added, although that was obvious to Adam, who could hear the sirens approaching over the phone.

"She's bleeding like crazy and unconscious."

"What the — where the hell are you?"

"In the alley behind Divas. They're putting her in the bus now . . . she's headed for . . . just a sec," said James.

Turning to a paramedic, he asked, "Where's she going?"

A mumble in the background. "She's going to RUH, right now," James said, returning to Adam.

Royal University Hospital was the closest open emergency room, and possibly less likely to be backed up than St. Paul's at that hour.

"I'll meet you there," said Adam. "You can tell me what the hell is going on at the hospital."

"Right, Sarge," said James, reverting to protocol as he heard Adam's loud and very cranky voice. "See you there in five to ten."

Hanging up, Adam grabbed his jacket, turned to Charlotte Warkentin and said, "I'm going to the Royal's ER. The reporter, our only witness, was just attacked."

"Oh, no. How is she?"

"Don't know yet," said Davis, snagging his mobile phone as he headed out the door.

"Want me to come, Sarge?"

"Yes. Okay. Good idea. Let's go."

James was pacing around the dirty and much-too-small triage area at RUH, waiting for Adam. He wouldn't be more than a minute or two behind.

When the Divas security guard came flying into the bar and got right into James's face, hollering at him to get out into the alley, James sprung to his feet.

Someone had been bashed on the head – for the second time in just over a day?

He pushed his way through the crowd and hit the alley at a dead run. James was spectacularly fit and could go from zero to twenty-five in less time than it took most people to get out of bed.

He reached the scene in seconds and found Bruce with Grace, saw the blood flowing out of her head and all over Bruce. Instantly he grabbed his phone and called

911, not sure if the security guard had had the presence of mind to do so.

Then he called the boss. A very, very cranky boss.

James saw Adam coming rapidly through the emergency room door, Charlotte Warkentin a step behind. At least a full head shorter than the big sergeant, and several years older, she was doing well to keep up with his long stride.

"What the hell is going on?" Adam boomed at James, turning the heads of all the medical staff and the patients in triage. "And where the hell is Grace?"

So much for 'Ms. Rampling.' And how many times had he said "hell" in the last ten minutes?

Taking a deep breath, James responded, as quickly as he could, "Grace, er, Ms. Rampling was at Divas meeting Bruce Stephens of the Pride Chorus. I guess she wants to do a story about the choir. She left, and just a few moments later someone attacked her. Hit her on the head. Pretty hard, too, Sarge."

"Is she okay?"

"She's alive, if that's what you mean. I wouldn't say she's okay. Big wound on the head and a lot of blood loss."

"Where is she?" asked Adam, his voice rising again.

"She's in one of the ER rooms getting checked out. But Sarge. Adam," said James, stepping in front of his boss and looking him directly in the face.

"I'm sorry if this is out of line, but you have to calm down a bit. I think you have everyone a little freaked out."

Adam looked around, and finally noticed that every eye was trained on him and his constable.

He cleared his throat, and in a slightly quieter tone said, "Sorry, James. She's so — she's our main witness in this case. And she didn't deserve this."

"I know, Adam. Do you want me to find out how she's doing? We'll need to talk to her about the attack . . . if she's going to be okay, I guess . . . "

"Yeah, let's find out. Let's go. She better be okay."

Nine

Adam and James strode down the corridor, in perfect step as if they were on a military training ground. Charlotte headed for the cafeteria. The constable's den-mother instincts said three high-calorie drinks were in order, to keep everyone going on this long night.

"Excuse me," said Adam to the nurse at the desk. "Sergeant Davis from the Saskatoon Police. I need to know how Grace Rampling is doing. She was brought in a few minutes ago with a head wound. Can you help me."

It wasn't a question. It was a command.

"Just let me check, sergeant," said the nurse behind the admitting desk, staring for a few seconds at the big, handsome sergeant. "I believe they've taken her straight in for an MRI."

Oh, man, that didn't sound too good, thought Adam. The worst emergencies always took first place in the triage line.

"How is she doing?" he asked, anxiety spilling into his voice.

"I'm sorry, sir. I really don't know, and I don't think anyone will until after the MRI."

"We need to know if we can talk to her, and the sooner the better. She was attacked and we have to find the assho . . . person who did it," said Adam.

"I understand, sergeant. Just give me a few minutes to track down her doctor."

The nurse bustled off toward radiology, asking another nearby nurse to take her place. Adam and James, unaccustomed to not being in charge, stood shifting from foot to foot and trying not to look at each other as they waited. Adam knew by now that for some reason, he was not quite as detached from this case as he usually was. He was trying to keep the expression on his face from revealing that.

Several minutes later the nurse reappeared. "She is in MRI, gentlemen. I'm afraid she is not conscious. As soon as she knows something, the doctor will come and talk to you."

"Has anyone called her family?"

"Not yet. It's only been a few minutes and we've been racing to get her stabilized."

"How bad is this injury?" asked Adam, alarmed.

"It's pretty bad," the nurse admitted. "At the very least she will have a serious concussion."

"And at the worst?"

"Let's just see how she does, and what the MRI shows. It's too early to speculate," the nurse said kindly, observing the sergeant's face. "You know this patient?"

"Yes, we know Grace Rampling. She's an important witness in a murder case, and now she has also been attacked, so you can see why we are very concerned."

"Oh dear," said the nurse, her brow furrowing. "Well, we are doing our very best, and we will keep you informed. I promise," said the nurse, peering up at Adam to emphasize her words.

He cleared his throat. "Thank you," he said. "Much appreciated."

Adam and James were forced to retreat to the waiting room, as patients and nurses and gurneys flowed around them in the admitting area. There was no excuse for holding up the emergency room's business.

After several minutes of silence, Adam finally spoke.

"You called this in," he said to James.

"I did. I was there."

"At Divas?"

"Yes."

"May I ask why?"

"I was there with Bruce Stephens, and with Grace. They were meeting to talk about possibly doing a story on members of the Pride Chorus," said James. He took a breath. "Sarge. Bruce is my spouse."

"The chorus guy? Isn't he a banker or something?"

"That's right. Investment banker. We've been together for a couple of years. I thought I'd better tell you; it could be a problem if you call him in for an interview. I couldn't be there."

"Damn right you couldn't. Talk about a conflict. Why didn't you tell me sooner?"

"It's only been a few days since the murder," James pointed out, sounding a little defensive.

"That's not what I meant. I didn't know you had a spouse. Of course your personal life is not really my business, officially. I just thought . . . maybe you would have told me."

James looked appalled.

"I'm sorry, Adam," said James, sincerely. "I don't know what to say."

Adam turned to James, with the slight incline of the head that always showed he was considering or accepting someone else's point of view.

"It's okay, James. I understand. I really do. But I'm glad to know, and always want you to feel you can tell me anything you want to tell me. You know you're the best cop on the force, right? And I'm proud to work with you."

"Thank you, Adam," James choked out. "That means a lot to me . . . "

The nurse was suddenly in front of them. "Gentlemen. It's time to visit Grace."

"Here," said Charlotte, emerging from behind the nurse's shoulder with chocolate milk containers in both hands. "Drink this first."

Grace looked like hell. Adam was shocked when he saw her white face, auburn hair stained darker red with blood, and a big gash on her temple. She didn't look at all like the smart, brave reporter he had met in the cathedral, rising from between the pews like some wild-haired Venus, nor the professional woman he'd bumped into at the coffee shop. She looked tiny, vulnerable and beaten up.

His heart contracted. Damn it, he thought: what is it about this woman? Why do I feel like this? And how is that going to help me solve this murder case?

Well, it's even more than that now, he realized. She's a witness, but now also the victim of an attack, and, thank God, not dead. Did he have a serial killer on his hands — who just missed killing Grace as well as murdering the bishop?

When I catch that asshole, he is so going to be charged with attempted murder for this, thought Adam viciously, his blood rising. Then Grace stirred.

"Hi, Sharge," said a tiny, slurred voice from the bed. Grace's eyes opened, just a bit. "How are you?"

"She's very groggy, and she does have a concussion," said the nurse, sotto voce. "Keep it short, please."

Adam forced a watery grin over his face, feeling it stretch unconvincingly over his teeth. He nodded at the nurse, acknowledging her request.

"Hi, Grace," he said quietly, for him, abandoning the Ms. Rampling farce. "How do you feel?"

"Gross," said Grace, honestly. "My head hurts awf'ly."

"I'm so sorry this happened to you. Can you tell me who, or how, at least?" he said as gently as possible.

"Don't know who. Stinky."

"Stinky?" repeated Adam, trying to swallow a laugh burbling in his chest. The word sounded funny, even adorable, coming from a normally-erudite but now-befuddled Grace. "Did he smell awful? Was it a he?"

Grace tried to nod her head, but groaned when it hurt and made the room spin.

"Ugh. Feeling barfy again," she managed.

"It's okay, Grace. I'll come back later, when you're feeling better."

"No, no, Sharge. It's okay."

The nurse dove in and put a cool cloth on Grace's forehead, then gave her some Gravol. "She won't be awake long," she warned the police officers.

"He smelled awful. He," added Grace for emphasis. "Low voice. Strong."

"Did you see him at all? Tall, short, skin colour, clothing?"

"Uh uh. Dark," said Grace. "Tallish. Could tell from by where voice was coming."

Great English for a reporter, thought Adam. But that helped.

"Can you remember anything else?"

"Called me a fucking fag-loving bitch. Noticed that."

All three police officers stood stunned, staring at Grace, shocked by the epithet. This was definitely no random act. The attacker knew Grace, or at least knew she was a patron at Divas.

But that second possibility didn't make sense, thought Adam. Why didn't he attack her on the basis of being lesbian, then, as opposed to a "fag-lover?" No, this was personal. Someone knew she, Grace Rampling, was at Divas, and perhaps followed her there from work.

Adam and James looked at each other, both with alarm in their eyes. Did Grace need protection?

For a second or two, Grace's revelation had turned the room into a frozen tableau. Then Charlotte, who had been taking notes, broke up the scene by looking up at her colleagues, wide-eyed. "I've got it all, Sarge," she assured Adam.

On the heels of her words, there was a flutter of the privacy drape, and a considerably smaller, slightly younger version of Grace pulled it aside.

"Oh, Grace," breathed the tiny interloper. "Oh no. Oh no. Oh no."

Grace's sister beelined for the bed, completely ignoring the medical and law enforcement people in the room. She dropped her purse and pulled off her coat in one smooth movement and crawled right into Grace's bed, half on top of her.

Crooning and smoothing Grace's sheets, blankets and hospital gown, Hope Rampling hugged her sister, murmuring, "Oh, honey, you look awful. I love you, are you okay? Oh, sister."

Everyone stared at the loving little scene, unwilling to move and break it up, but also a little amazed by its audacity. No one had ever seen that kind of single-minded, focused drive to comfort someone before. Hope didn't seem to even notice the other six people crowded into the little draped-off ER room.

"Hopey," mumbled Grace. "So glad you're here."

Hope's face was screwed into an attempt not to cry or scream. She just held her sister and crooned, "just shhh, sister. You're going to be fine. I'll make sure of it."

Adam cleared his throat, partly to get the sisters' attention, and partly to clear the lump that had formed in it.

No sign of hearing him came from Hope, so he continued.

"Miss? Who are you? Grace's sister, I assume?"

Then Hope finally looked around, and up — way up — at the tall sergeant's face.

"I'm Hope Rampling. Who are you?" she demanded.

"Detective Sergeant Adam Davis. I'm the lead police officer on your sister's case."

"You're going to find the bastard who did this, correct?" Hope instructed him.

"There is no doubt, Ms. Rampling. I will find him," said Adam confidently, drawing himself up to his full height. Not unlike Napoleon, Grace's sister was clearly one little person you didn't want to mess with. Even Adam felt her intensity.

The nurse finally intervened. "The patient could use a little peace and quiet, and she's going to be asleep soon anyway because of the medication. Sergeant, could you come back in the morning? Preferably very late morning? If you leave your card, I'll let you know if anything changes."

"Yes, nurse," said Adam, more meekly and quietly than one might expect from him, handing over his card. "Grace, I'll see you tomorrow. Please get some sleep, and take care." He took a step toward the bed, his hand reaching for hers. Hope bristled, but Grace raised her hand slightly.

"Tanks, Sharge," she said, touching his hand. "Tanks, conshtables," she added, trying to look at James and Charlotte around her bandages.

"Nothing to thank us for, Grace," said Adam. "See you tomorrow."

As the police officers slipped through the gap in the curtains, they heard Hope telling the nurse, "I'm not leaving. Don't even try me."

They didn't get very far after leaving Grace's ER room. Standing in the triage area again, Adam started handing out orders.

"Someone's obviously out to get Grace. We need an officer here at all times, and when she goes home," he said, then paused. He wasn't willing to entertain the thought that she might not go home — and she did seem to be doing reasonably well, considering.

"When she goes home," he repeated, a little more loudly, "we'll have to be there as well. Charlotte, see what you can arrange.

"And get Bruce Stephens into the station, pronto, first thing in the morning. Sooner, if possible. I will interview him.

"James, see if you can round up all the stories Grace has ever written on human rights cases, especially relating to the LGBTQ community, or find someone else who can do it. And move those other two interviews; we have to deal with this first.

"We have a hater out there."

Ten

Grace and Hope Rampling had agreed many years before: they were very glad the last child in the family was a boy.

David. The giant killer, and their baby brother. It had biblical connotations, but it beat the hell out of Peace, or Constance, or Charity, or worst of all Chastity. God knew what excellent quality a third daughter would have been named for.

Now the youngest, but by far the biggest, member of the family poked his head through the curtain.

"Grace? Hope? Can I come in?" asked David.

"Shurr you can, brother," said Grace, opening one groggy eye. "But I'm not mush for conversashion."

David was at her bedside in two long strides. "Grace, honey, you just rest," he said, kissing her forehead, then swallowing hard. "I'll be here when you wake up."

He turned to Hope and gestured at the curtain. "Jesus, Hope. What happened?" he asked as they briefly went into the hallway.

"I don't know exactly. She was apparently at Divas — some work-related reason — and was attacked as she left. That's all I know. The police sergeant was here just before you came. Maybe he can tell us more tomorrow."

"Have you called the parents?"

"No. Was hoping you would? How much longer are they going to be in Florida?"

"Couple weeks, I think. I'll call them, Hope. In the morning. It's one a.m. in Florida. Let's not freak them out tonight unless absolutely necessary."

"I can't go through this again, David," said Hope, her voice cracking and tears coursing down her cheeks. "I can't. I can't."

David wrapped his big arms around his tiny sister. "Me neither, Hopey. We just have to hang together, like we always have. We'll be okay. She'll be okay. I promise."

There had been another Rampling. Saint Paul.

The eldest brother, a few years older than Grace, had decided to go into engineering, despite gentle entreaties from his lawyer parents to follow them into their profession. He wanted to build things. He spent hours as a child with his blocks, then his Lego, then the cushions from every couch and chair in the house.

Paul eventually started using scrap pieces of wood to create pet shelters, tiny sheds, miniature doll houses for his little sisters. Yet his empathy, and the caring way he treated his younger siblings, spoke to another calling. His sweetness earned him the nickname, Saint Paul.

He did well in his first two years of structural engineering at the university, where he met Melissa — an arts student he often saw in the cafeteria. They soon connected at a campus dance and became an item. Then, in the middle of his second year, Paul proposed. He was madly in love with Melissa's pretty face, the adoring way she looked at him. He wanted to marry her.

Strangely, as it would turn out, it was falling in love that gave Paul pause about his chosen career. Love had become the most important thing in his own life; he wanted the world to feel it, the way he did for his fiancée. The only member of the family who was deeply serious about spirituality, Paul felt himself increasingly led by his faith.

He decided. He was going to be a minister. He couldn't wait to tell Melissa, and his parents and sisters and little brother. His family was not surprised. But Melissa looked at him strangely, out of big eyes with long, mascara-coated lashes.

Why, she asked, would you want to do such a stupid thing?

Paul blanched. He tried to explain how his love for her had inspired him to seek a more meaningful career, helping people. But Melissa tossed her head. Think about it, she said.

Paul was confused by her reaction, but he had also made up his mind.

He talked to his family about his decision, and they all said it was up to him; whatever made him happy would make them happy. His mother kissed him tenderly on the cheek. You are an amazing child, she said. We love you.

Two weeks later, he told Melissa he would leave engineering and enter the Lutheran seminary. Melissa broke their engagement. She didn't want to be a minister's wife. Goodbye.

Paul whirled out of her apartment. He called his mother, told her the news, and said he was upset, but okay. He was going for a drive to calm down before he came home.

He climbed into his car and started driving, tears blurring his vision, anger and rejection and sorrow tearing his heart. He went north on the Prince Albert highway, wiping at his eyes. Distracted as he was, he didn't see a patch of ice and hit it at highway speed. The car spun around and flew off the highway, missing the first power pole on the southbound side. But it hit the second, smashing the car flat and ripping Paul's body apart.

His death was like a bomb, blowing the family to pieces. Unable to face each other's grief, the Ramplings scattered into private spaces, emotionally and physically. They could not comfort each other. The funeral was sheer hell, and things got worse when Grace saw Melissa at the little reception afterwards.

"How dare you," Grace hissed at her. "How dare you come here. You killed Paul. You killed him, as if you were in that car with him. Get out!" she screamed. "Get out!"

Everyone heard Grace. Melissa left the funeral. Grace ran out of the church basement; Hope followed, but Grace was well ahead. She couldn't catch her. Grace wandered the streets until after nightfall, and then crept home.

Weeks went by. Grace was pale and silent. Hope was anxious and frightened. David, still so young, was baffled, quiet and vague. Their parents were destroyed, and as desperately worried as they were about their remaining children, they couldn't help them.

One night, Hope was unable to sleep, as usual. Just fifteen, she was profoundly the stereotypical middle child, the one who mediates, who manages the family emotions; but she didn't know how to do that now. She slipped into the dark kitchen to get a drink, and as she passed Grace's bedroom, heard her sister weeping, gasping with grief. Hope's heart broke, wide open.

Hope didn't knock, as she usually did. She walked into Grace's room, crawled into her bed, and half-covered her body with her own, hugging her sister closely. There was nothing she could think of to say, so she just shared her physical comfort. They wept together until they couldn't weep any more, then fell asleep.

The next morning, Hope and Grace looked at each other with swollen red eyes, and found a glimmer of courage together. They found David on the back step, looking forlornly into space, and both put their arms around him, letting him cry. They went to find their parents, and put their arms around them, too.

And so they began to come together, slowly and painfully; they could finally comfort each other. But a small seed of distrust was planted in the hearts of the Rampling children, and particularly Grace, now the oldest. She could not understand, and never would, how Melissa could have agreed to marry Paul for his occupation, maybe his arresting looks, but not for himself — his sweet, caring, somewhat innocent self. Did love, for some people, really work like that? And how could you tell who they were?

And Hope and David couldn't fathom losing another sibling. Although it seemed that she would survive, Grace's attack still scared the hell out of them.

Eleven

It was eight o'clock in the bloody morning. Bruce Stephens was normally an early riser, but eight came much too early on this particular Thursday.

After the grim events of the night before, Bruce had a lot of trouble sleeping. Once Grace had been whisked away by ambulance with James right behind her, Bruce was left standing, shaking, in the alley. Daril, the bouncer, finally came over. He was, if a bit rough around the edges, a very nice guy with a very big body who gave a powerful damn about the safety of gay and lesbian people. He put an arm around Bruce's shoulders and led him back inside.

"No point freezing out here, man," said Daril, who was not much taller than Bruce but perhaps twice as wide. "Let's go in. Gotta warn folks about what happened, too."

They returned to the warmth and noise of the club, and the bouncer left Bruce in the care of a friend. He told the DJ to turn off the music. Now.

"Folks," Daril's voice boomed over the microphone. "One of our guests has been attacked in the alley. I know, this is not totally unusual, but she was hurt bad, and there's a bad dude out there. Nobody leaves alone. Am I clear? No one."

As the club buzzed with the news, Bruce prepared to slip away. As he reached the lobby, Daril caught up to him. "Oh no, you don't, Stephens. You are going nowhere by yourself."

"I'm sure he's gone. I'm just going to get in my car and drive home," said Bruce, still vibrating from the shock of finding Grace.

"Good try, Stephens. Let's go."

Daril followed Bruce to his car and watched him drive away before heading back to the club.

Once at home, Bruce locked the doors. Sleep was sporadic, so by the time he presented himself at the police station at eight sharp, he was more than a bit worse for wear.

"Bruce Stephens," he heard a big baritone voice saying. "Sergeant Adam Davis. Thank you for coming."

"Sergeant. Nice to finally meet you," said Bruce, who could have been looking in a mirror, or at least at a brother, so similar was Adam in colouring and physique.

"Call me Adam. We have a good friend in common. As you know. If you'll just follow me. Coffee?"

"Oh, yeah. Could use some right now. Thanks."

"Thank God you were there, Bruce. What happened?" Adam asked, once they were settled in an interview room with bad, bitter black coffee.

Bruce described the entire evening, starting with why Grace came to Divas to meet him, and ending with watching her walk out the door, then hearing her scream.

"I just had a feeling. I mean, it's really never a good idea for a woman to walk down a dark alley late at night, but somehow, with the bishop's death and everything, it seemed — well, it was top of mind. She turned down my offer to walk out with her, but I walked her to the door and then just stood there for a while, watching her for as long as I could see her. I was right there. Then I heard some scuffling, and her scream. I didn't really expect anything to happen. It was so bizarre."

"Did you scare him off, do you think? Would he have hit her again?"

"I'm not sure. I'd like to think so — that I scared him off, I mean. I yelled her name right after she screamed, so it's possible."

"Sorry for the strong language in this question, but Grace said he called her a fucking fag-loving bitch," said Adam. "Did you happen to hear that?"

"No, I didn't," said Bruce, stammering. "That's . . . awful."

There was a pause. Both men stared into their coffees, absorbing the meaning of the man's profane and disgusting comment. Then Bruce asked, "is it stupid to ask if you think this is the same person who killed the bishop?"

"Not stupid, no. I'm not sure I can answer that, and I certainly shouldn't. It looks that way, though, doesn't it? We'll know more after the bishop's autopsy, I hope."

It seemed obvious that Bruce had not attacked Grace, or at least, he had very little time to do so. Mental note, thought Adam; ask the bouncer if he saw Bruce at the door. But if that were true, then he also had not attacked the bishop — if, of course, the two attacks were done by the same man. At least, thought Adam, he knew

Grace's attacker was male. That was a start, anyway, if not much of one.

And furthermore, James loved this man. James was an intelligent, intuitive, ethical and sometimes brilliant cop. Adam assumed he was the same in his private life. He felt sure that Bruce Stephens was not the killer. Still, he had to be careful. On the face of things, Bruce was perhaps the prime suspect in the bishop's death. Adam just found it hard to believe.

"I don't suppose you caught a glimpse of this asshole."

"No. He took off, I'm sure, right after he heard me yell, and I was much too focused on finding Grace."

Adam sighed heavily. "That's what I thought. Obviously, you did the right thing. Is there anything else you can tell me? Anything else you noticed?"

Bruce shook his head. "It's a blur. It was pretty awful, and I didn't sleep much last night, so my head's not clear. Maybe something will come to me later."

"OK. Thank you, Bruce. Let me warn you though; there's a bad guy out there. I'm going to catch him, but in the meantime, you're not safe. No one in the LGBTQ community is, and no one connected with the community, however distantly, is either. Am I clear?"

"Yes, sir," said Bruce, not sarcastically. The honorific was an automatic response to the authority in Adam's voice.

He laughed, a bit ruefully. "Yes, Adam. I heard that story from the bouncer, too. Thank you."

"Just watch yourself, go nowhere alone. I'll stay in touch. Thanks."

Bruce unsteadily left the police station, and went straight home. He locked all the doors and set the burglar alarm.

———————————

"Boss," said John Powers, knocking at the editor's door, with Mark Williams right behind him. "Got a minute? It's about Grace."

"Come in," said Steve. "What's up?"

"Grace is in the hospital, Steve. She was attacked last night. Bad concussion, not sure what else."

Steve was speechless. He stood up from his chair and looked at John, unblinking, for many seconds.

"What happened? Are you sure?"

"She was at Divas, the nightclub, last night. She was talking to a member, or maybe members, of the Pride Chorus. She left about ten, I think, and someone was in the alley with a weapon. He tried to bash in her skull, apparently, but didn't quite manage it. She has a gash and a bump and a concussion, and possibly a cracked collarbone. Worse than a glancing blow, but not a full force bang on the head. I gather we're lucky she's more or less okay."

"Dear God," said Steve, closing his eyes for a few seconds. "Have you seen her?"

"No. Visiting hours were over by the time she got to the hospital — all this was only about twelve hours ago. I thought I'd try to go just after lunch."

"I'm coming with you. We're going to have to have a very serious talk about whether we should cover this."

"I know," sighed John. "I've never come across this situation either. First, she's a witness. Then, a suspect, if theoretically. Now, she's a victim. What the hell?"

"Yes. What the hell."

Twelve

The forensic pathologist was measuring something on the smashed-in skull of the Bishop of Saskatoon when Adam Davis walked into the reeking but antiseptic room.

Jack McDougall was seventy years old, and had made it clear to his superiors that he had no intention of retiring from his position. Death fascinated him, and killers horrified him. There was no better job in the world for McDougall, and a little arthritis in his hands, to match the grey in his thinning hair, wasn't going to stop him.

The police, the health region and pretty much everyone who knew him agreed. McDougall was, if a bit stubborn, among the best pathologists in the country. Maybe the world. If he told you how someone died, you could take it to the bank.

"Doc," said Adam.

"Adam," said McDougall severely. "You're early. I'm not yet finished with the bishop."

"I see that. I was just hoping you could give me a preliminary verdict. Someone else was attacked last night, a woman. A reporter from the paper, no less. She found him," he added, indicating the bishop's body.

"I need to know if it was the same guy, and I don't even know what killed the bishop yet. I don't have a murder weapon. So, I have nothing, and I have at least one murderous bastard freak on the loose," Adam said, with feeling.

McDougall looked at Adam sharply.

"It is not, Sergeant Davis, my practice to provide preliminary verdicts. Could send you down the wrong damn rabbit hole," he said, peering intently over his glasses.

"Come on, Doc," said Adam. "Give me something, anything, to go on. More people could get killed. I'm not exaggerating. I am seriously not kidding."

McDougall rolled his eyes toward heaven. "Fine," he said, gruffly, which told Adam he was moved by his plea. "Come here and look at this wound, then. It's really quite unusual."

"Did the bash on the head kill the bishop?"

"Yes. I'm positive. But look at the shape of this. It's a blunt instrument, certainly, but what kind? Very heavy, quite large. I've just been measuring it. About six to eight inches long, and at least an inch and a half wide, your weapon."

"Shovel? Crow bar? Brick?"

"No. None of those. Shovel would be too big, crow bar would not be heavy enough, plus the wound would be a different shape. Brick is closer, but that's not quite right either. I don't know what it is, but like I said, six inches at least, by one and a half. Plus, the wound is deeper in the middle — see here? — than it is at the ends. So there's a point on the weapon, as well, of some kind."

Adam looked closely at the messy wound. With McDougall's explanation, he could clearly see what he meant. What the hell had killed the bishop? Adam knew if he found the weapon, or at least knew what it was, he would be a lot closer to finding the killer.

That wasn't always the case; a knife was a knife, and a handgun was a handgun, even if the length of the blade or the ballistics helped narrow it down. But blunt instruments were remarkably varied, and often said something specific about their wielders.

"Thanks, Doc," said Adam. "I really appreciate this. And I won't hold you to your opinion. But obviously, someone hit him on the head, hard, with something unusual, and that killed him. I can work with that."

"You're welcome, Adam. Don't bloody well make it a habit to show up here before I'm done," said McDougall, but there was a gleam in his eye, and warmth in his voice.

"You got it, Doc," Adam said over his shoulder, automatically. He was already halfway out the door, and heading for the cathedral.

"What's missing from this church?" Adam asked Ed, the janitor.

Minutes earlier, Adam had marched into the cathedral and started looking in every nook, confessional, side room and office. He didn't care who he found — a priest, staff member, choir director, even a congregation member.

He was damn well going to start getting some answers.

He finally encountered Ed, sweeping the floors in the basement's social area. Identifying himself, Adam dragged the janitor up to the sanctuary, and told him to look around.

"What's missing?" he asked again, for emphasis.

Ed, looking around a bit wild-eyed, was not the most confident of men and more than a little intimidated by this authoritative police officer. Adam, seeing his eyes, relented a bit. Ed, he thought, was not a likely killer. Even if he was, being aggressive wouldn't help Adam get the information he needed. Back off, he told himself.

"Take your time, Ed," said Adam, more kindly and more quietly, which helped calm the janitor. "You're not in any kind of trouble. But I really, really need your help in solving this crime. Did you know that the reporter who found the bishop was also attacked? There's a scary person out there, and I'm going to find him. And you can help me."

Ed nodded. "Yes, sir. I haven't noticed anything yet, but I'll take a look around, if that's okay."

"Absolutely. Go ahead," said Adam, encouragingly. "I can wait."

Adam reasoned that since the attack occurred in the church, and the murder weapon was a strange size, shape and weight, there was likely something actually in the church that would make a good weapon, different from the usual crowbars and hammers. Candlesticks? Statues? What?

Since no bloody weapon was found — and the police had been very thorough — Adam also assumed that the killer had taken the weapon with him. Ergo, here he was, asking Ed what was missing. Thank you, Jack McDougall.

Ed was spending a lot of time in the apse, looking under the choir's pews, poking through cupboards behind the altar. Suddenly he straightened up, with one of those Eureka looks on his face.

He practically ran down the steps from the altar to the pew where Adam was trying to sit patiently, but was actually fidgeting.

"Sergeant!"

"What?!" said Adam upon seeing Ed's face, and jumping to his feet. "What did you find?"

"It's the monstrance, sir. It's usually kept in that locked cupboard over there," he said, pointing behind him. "The monstrance is missing."

Thirteen

W hat the hell is a monstrous?" asked
Adam, who was not Catholic and had
misheard.

"Monst*rance*, sir," said Ed. It was hard to correct someone as confident and authoritative as the sergeant. "A monstrance is that big sort of holder — a vessel, they call it — that contains the host. It's used on high holy days, for the communion, you know."

"What does it look like, exactly? More importantly," he added, "how big is it?"

"It's a big round thing with a cross, sort of. It's pretty. It's all golden with gems and things in it. It's about . . . " Ed considered. "About so high, I guess," he said, demonstrating about two and a half feet with his hands, "and maybe a foot wide at the top?"

Adam shook his head. He couldn't picture it.

"So there's a round cross at the top, it's about two and a half feet tall and a foot wide . . . Is it all one big round thing?"

"No, no, the cross part is held up by a shaft, and the shaft is supported by a base at the bottom. It has a case and a pedestal, too."

"How big is the base?"

"I don't know for sure. Maybe eight, nine inches? It's square."

"Holy shit," said Adam, rather too loudly and profanely, forgetting himself and his present location. "How heavy is this thing?"

"It's pretty heavy. I'm not sure what it's made out of underneath, but it's entirely plated in gold, and like I said, there are some gems set into the top part. Maybe eight, ten pounds? The bishop or the priest has to be able to carry it high up," said Ed, demonstrating with an imaginary monstrance, "so it can't be too heavy. But it's pretty heavy. I've had to lift it a few times, mostly to clean it, polish it and put it away."

Adam forgot himself again. "Holy shit," he said, advancing on Ed. "Sir, you are officially my favourite person of the day," he declared, clapping Ed on the shoulder. He really wanted to hug him.

"Thank you, Sergeant," said Ed, stammering. "I'm glad I've been helpful."

"You have no idea. I'll be in touch. And thank you."

Back at the station, Adam looked it up. "A symbol of the Blessed Sacrament, the *monstrance* is the sacred vessel which contains the consecrated Host when carried in procession." There were several pictures of monstrances alongside the description, and while they were varied, there were also similarities.

He phoned Charlotte. "Hi, Adam," she answered, seeing his name come up on her phone.

"Charlotte. I've found the murder weapon."

91

"What?" she said excitedly. "Holy cow. What is it? Where is it? Do you have it in your office? Is it in the evidence room?"

"Sorry, Char, I overstated that. I haven't found the actual thing; but I know what it is. It's a monstrance. And I actually have no idea where it is. That's why I'm sure it's the murder weapon. It's the right shape, the right size, probably the right weight, and it's missing from the cathedral."

Charlotte groaned. "The search continues."

"Can you pop into my office? We have to do some research on this thing, and find out if anyone in the congregation has a photo of it. The priest, maybe, or the secretary. Someone will. Then let's find out what these things are made of. Would it be heavy enough to kill the bishop? Would it be easy to swing? That kind of thing. Drop by and we'll make a list of what we have to do next."

"Be there in two secs. Had anything to eat lately?" said the motherly constable, always equating food with well-being and crime-solving capability.

"Umm . . . " Adam couldn't actually remember the last time he ate.

"I'll bring some snacks. See you in a jiff."

A little research, conducted over crackers, cheese, pickles and orange juice, confirmed that a monstrance could indeed easily weigh eight to twelve pounds, and even more for the really big ones.

But something was nagging at Adam. While an eight or ten pound piece of brass covered in gold could indeed have made a wound like the bishop's, he was none too sure the wound on Grace's temple had the same authorship. He would have to go and see her again, check out her head more closely and talk to the doctor. It would

92

have to be the next morning; it was getting late, and he couldn't justify waking someone as banged up as poor Grace Rampling.

He realized he was looking forward to the next day. And Adam Davis hated hospitals.

It was widely understood throughout the police service, and particularly among the female members, that Adam Davis was a very good catch. He was tall, had thick, wavy dark hair and deep-blue eyes, a well-cut jaw, a beautifully and unusually-curved mouth; in short, he was ridiculously handsome, and even rather sensitive. He was known as a straight-shooter and a hell of a good cop, maybe even brilliant at police work; and that big, resonant voice was rich as chocolate and sexy as hell.

So, why was he so very single? Asexual? Some hidden deformity?

It was, partly, the same reason he hated hospitals.

Born on a farm near the Alberta-Saskatchewan border, Adam grew up fast and by age eighteen was already powerfully built, athletic, remarkably serious and very ambitious for a young man. In his municipality, there was no local police force; the RCMP enforced the law. From a young age, he found himself admiring the officers, who had a tough job riding herd on cattle rustlers, teenage joy-riders and various other rural annoyances over a wide area. And there was also the day they probably saved his mother's life. That day, and most of the days following, he thought policing was the best profession in the world.

The city eventually beckoned. Adam was a smart kid. He wanted to attend university, and his parents were more than supportive. Considerably closer to Saskatoon than to Calgary, he visited the campus of the University of Saskatchewan and found it pleasing: beautiful architecture, lovely green spaces, a good reputation, and located in a city of a decent size with an affordable standard of living. Also, he'd be closer to home, convenient for helping out on the farm. He was accepted to the U of S, earned a science degree and promptly applied to the police force.

His superiors detected a natural. Adam flew up through the ranks: he landed, and solved, some of the toughest cases and made sergeant in just a few years.

But the early years were hard, and shaped Adam in ways he could not have foreseen. While still a beat cop, Adam did a stint on the wrong side of town, in the days before guns were common on the streets of small prairie cities. One dark night, he was called for the dozenth time to a particularly nasty skid bar. It was not an unusual scene; drunken, stoned men were brawling inside the bar and out, yelling and punching, and Adam and his partner dove into the melee to break it up.

Things calmed down somewhat, at first, when the police officers arrived. A few of the brawling men, tired, chastened and breathing heavily, sat down on the cold pavement, snot and blood flowing from their noses. The less co-operative were still half-heartedly swearing at and shoving each other.

Then there was a loud crack, from inside the bar. Adam and his partner doubted it was a firecracker. Drawing their guns, they made for the door and pulling it open, yelled "Police! Freeze!" Adam heard another shot, and instantly felt a searing, savage pain in his shoulder, as his body swung involuntarily and violently to the left. Seconds later, a similar pain exploded in his leg.

Shock had its way. The next thing Adam understood was that he was in the hospital, with an oxygen mask over his face and people shouting orders over his body. He couldn't speak; he wanted to ask what the hell was going on.

Then everything faded away, until after surgery.

He awakened to the usual antiseptic room, the grogginess and nausea from a long bout under anaesthetic, and incredible pain emanating from his shoulder and leg. The bar scene came back into focus, and Adam knew he had changed forever. He no longer felt invincible.

The city was growing, changing, becoming more violent. He had taken for granted that people would indeed freeze when he told them to; after all, he was big, loud, fierce and a cop. So much for law and order.

Stuck in the hospital for two long weeks as his shoulder and leg began to heal, he learned to loathe the lack of freedom enforced by the health care system. Adam was determined to get back to work, more than ever wanting to save the world from violent criminals. Even if it killed him.

But spending several weeks recovering at home, crazed with boredom, and then sidelined to a desk job sent Adam into a spiralling darkness. He began to drink at night, hitting the bars to assuage the profound loneliness and frustration he couldn't beat back. Women threw themselves at him, and, uncharacteristically, he let them. He plunged into a whirl of sex and drunken nights on the town. Out of his mind with anger, and having something to prove, he started a bar fight or two, and was lucky to be held back by friends from the force.

Post-traumatic nightmares followed Adam into sleep. The drinking made them worse. He woke up sweating, shaking, screaming in the night, reliving the gun shots and the medicated blur that followed. The nightmares terrified a couple of young women he had taken home; he reacted badly, and yelled at them to get out of his house.

Haggard, hungover and furious, Adam dragged himself into the office late one morning. He threw up on the way to his desk, a place he didn't want to be. Minutes later, noticing his lateness and pale, sweating face, Charlotte marched over and placed her hands widely on the surface before him.

"What the hell are you doing, Adam?" she asked him. "This has to stop. It must stop. You have a great career ahead of you; a great life ahead of you. For God's sake, don't ruin it. Can I help you? Please, let me help you."

Shocked, Adam almost responded with rage: Get the hell out of my life. Then he realized, with horrified amazement, that people had been cutting him slack but they knew what he was doing. Charlotte certainly did. He was fucking up.

The realization snapped something in his brain, and Adam collapsed. Charlotte half-dragged him into a quiet room, held him and told him it would be okay. With her behind him, Adam started to pull himself together. He stopped the heavy drinking and meaningless sex, finally decided to talk to a psychologist and slowly started to come back to himself. Forever afterward, he credited Charlotte with saving his life and his career.

He swore to himself that he would never subject a woman to that kind of behaviour again. No one should put up with that kind of shit. He had behaved like an asshole. It was also incredibly embarrassing that such a big, fierce guy was awakened by the terror of nightmares, which also terrified his bedmates.

He would rise above it all. He would not be a victim. He would also never drag a woman into his uncertain life, as long as he was on the front lines. He could die at any moment; that had become clear. He wasn't even sure if he deserved a partner, considering how he was capable of behaving. He had learned that he was not in control, not even of himself.

It had been a few years ago, and Adam had healed, somewhat; he had returned to his true disposition. He had had a few flings, a few one-night stands since then; he was, after all, a beautiful and healthy man. He began to trust himself again, but he couldn't entirely shake the lonely superhero façade, visible only to himself. It helped him get through the bad time, and it still felt like protection.

But he had never fallen in love, and whether the right person had not appeared in his life, or whether he simply couldn't allow it, it was hard to say.

That night, the nightmares — which had abated somewhat over the last couple of years — returned. Adam was walking down a sticky, wet alley, past piles of filthy clothing and garbage that often moved as he stepped over them. It was raining, dark, and the atmosphere reeked humidly of misery and excrement.

At the other end of the alley, he could see a streetlight, and in its beam, Grace Rampling. Dressed in diaphanous white, she was walking toward him, calling his name.

Then, the inevitable shot that came in all his nightmares rang out. But this time, the bullet wasn't aimed at him. Grace crumpled, fell to her knees, and cried out, as the bullet flew through her body and came straight at him.

He deked to his left, and watched the bullet fly by him, with the strange slow-motion sight often bestowed in dreams. But he was sure Grace was dead. He ran toward her, and lifting her up, saw the huge hole in her torso, ripped apart by the bullet. He yelled and began to tear her clothing away to see the wound, to stanch it . . . but it was no use . . .

He woke up, streaming sweat and tears, his muscular body stretched taut in reaction to the agonizing realism of the dream. It was the first time, in his dreams, that the bullet didn't hit him, wasn't aimed at him. Why?

He heard his subconscious reminding him that Grace, lying at RUH in her white hospital gown, was still in a lot of danger. And that he apparently cared, a great deal, whether she lived or died.

He wiped his eyes. Damn.

Fourteen

Adam Davis had learned two things about himself the night before; they were both good and terrifying, and they were both related to Grace. It didn't matter right now, though. He couldn't do anything about those things, and he had a job to do. He was going to pull himself together and get down to the hospital.

First, he pulled on sweats and sneakers and ran a few miles down the Meewasin Trail, near his condo, trying to burn off the nightmare and the realizations that it brought. Then breakfast, shower, teeth brushing: the routine calmed him a bit.

It also occurred to him that he had probably eaten seven or eight hundred calories the day before, not exactly enough to support the energy requirements of a two-hundred pound, six-foot-two, thirty-two-year-old police officer. He boiled two eggs, fried some ham and made four pieces of whole wheat toast, plus an orange. Hopefully that would hold him until lunchtime.

He met James at the station, and the two hopped into the unmarked car Adam had at his disposal when on duty.

"It's a monstrance," Adam informed James, with whom he hadn't spoken since the interview with Ed. "The murder weapon. It's a monstrance — a very fancy vessel for carrying the host on special holy days."

Adam explained what had happened at the forensic pathologist's lab and at the cathedral the day before.

"It's got to be the monstrance," he ended. "It's missing, it's the right weight and it has a heavy base with a sort of sculpted edge."

"It's got to be," agreed James who, being Catholic, knew exactly what a monstrance was but didn't say so. "Now all we have to do is find it."

"Yeah, that would be the problem," said Adam. "So today, we're catching up to the priest, right? What's his name. Paul Campbell?"

James nodded.

"And the church secretary. I want to see if one of them has a picture of the monstrance. But first, we see Grace. I want to try to determine if she was bashed by the same weapon. We'll see if she and the doc let us see her temple. It was all bandaged up yesterday."

"And her shoulder," added James. "Whatever she was hit with also landed on her shoulder."

Adam stared at James. "Did I know that?"

"Maybe not, Sarge. It looked as though it hit her head at a funny angle, then sort of slipped and banged down to her collarbone or shoulder. It's pretty bruised too, the paramedic said."

"Maybe I forgot, or maybe it didn't come up at the hospital. You said the paramedic told you this?"

James nodded again.

"Yep, he took a quick look while they were getting her on the gurney and into the ambulance, and he told me."

"That's good to know, actually. We'll see if we can take a look at the shoulder, too."

Adam, considering this information, thought that if the attacker had used the monstrance, Grace would be dead. Just like the bishop.

Hope Rampling never left her sister's side, apart from slipping out to get some food. She was still in bed with Grace, curled up sleepily on her side, one leg over Grace's leg, and one arm over Grace's abdomen. A large, bewhiskered blond man was in an armchair in the corner, sleeping. It was ten in the morning.

The two police officers, having checked in with the nurse at the desk, stopped at the curtain surrounding Grace's bed, and hearing nothing, hesitated. Was she asleep? They waited for a moment, and then saw a doctor heading toward them.

"Good morning. I'm Dr. Bergen," said the doctor, holding out her hand. "You are the police officers dealing with this attack?"

"Good morning, Doctor. I'm Detective Sergeant Adam Davis; this is my colleague James Weatherall, and yes, we're on this case. We were hoping to talk to Grace this morning. How is she?"

"Hanging in there. She has a nasty concussion, cracked clavicle, significant shock and loss of blood. Let me see if she's awake."

The doctor slipped through the curtain, and Grace opened her eyes. The doctor smiled at her.

"Good morning, Grace. How are you feeling?"

"Ugh," said Grace, speaking through a mouth that felt like it was stuffed full of rotting cotton. "Okay, I think. Foggy. Can I have some water? Juice would be better."

"Of course," said the doctor, pouring her some water. Hope moved just enough so Grace could sip it through a straw. "I'll see if breakfast is in your future. Do you think you could talk to the police? They're just outside the curtain."

"I think I can. Sure."

The doctor opened the curtain and motioned the police officers to come in. "Not too long," she warned. "She's going to be really tired for a few days, and she needs to heal."

Adam and James nodded, and slipped inside the curtain. They noticed the big man sleepily rubbing his eyes in the corner, and then Hope, still hugging her sister.

Seeing Hope draped over Grace hit Adam in the stomach. More than anything, he suddenly wanted to remove Hope from the bed, ask the man in the corner and James to leave, and crawl under the blanket with Grace, assuring himself that she was fine and warm and alive and that the bastard in his dream didn't really leave a gaping hole in her chest. That dream was just too real.

He tried to clear his head, swallowing the erotic effect of the thought of touching Grace, and remembered that the reality of her injuries was bad enough, a dream encounter with a gun notwithstanding. There was that big bandage over her head, and probably something protecting the clavicle under the hospital gown.

"Grace," said Adam gently, in nothing like his usual big voice. "How are you feeling? Is it all right to ask you some questions? I brought James, too."

"Hi, Grace," said James, moving into her field of vision. "How are you doing?"

Hope roused herself, rolled partly onto her back, took Grace's hand, and said, "she sucks. Right? Someone tried to kill her. Just pointing out the obvious."

"Hopey," said Grace, chastising her sister, but with adoration in her voice.

"I'm okay. Well, more or less. How are you two?" she asked the policemen, peering at them through one eye, since the other was partly covered by the bandage.

Adam and James had to laugh.

"We're fine," said Adam. "We're not in a hospital bed, though. I'll try to make this short and easy, Grace. Can you remember anything else about this man who attacked you? His height, for example, or, well, anything? I know it was really dark."

Grace's face, or at least what could be seen of it, suddenly changed. She was obviously dragging her thoughts back to the attack, and the horror of it came flooding back.

"Oh God," she breathed. Her lip quivered for a moment, and then she pressed both lips together, swallowing hard.

"He . . . he had a fairly low voice," she began.

"Take your time honey," said Hope, while David, who had awakened, came over to take Grace's free hand and introduced himself to the police officers.

"Nice to meet you, Mr. Rampling," said Adam, while James nodded. Then they returned their attention to Grace. "Do you remember telling us what he said, Grace?"

"I do. He called me a fucking fag-loving bitch. You don't forget that sort of shit," said Grace, bitterly, and then remembered that James was gay. "Oh, no — I'm so sorry James," she added, but James shook his head.

"It is what it is, Grace. Just tell us what happened, and for God's sake don't worry about my feelings."

"Still, James, I'm sorry. About all of it," said Grace, taking her hand out of Hope's and reaching for James's hand. He took it briefly and squeezed it, smiling down at her before giving her hand back to Hope.

"I think he was pretty tall," Grace resumed. "Not as tall as you, Sarge, or as David — but not short or average height. It felt like he was talking down to me by a considerable margin, and his stink — God, he reeked — seemed to come from above me."

"I have to ask you something else," said Adam, as James took notes. "Is there a way we could see your wound? If the doctor allows it, are you okay with that?"

"Why?" asked Grace.

"We are trying to establish the kind of weapon he used."

"And you're trying to establish if it's the same weapon used on the bishop."

Even with a concussion, she didn't miss much. "Yes," he said. "That's right."

"Well, it's okay with me as long as it doesn't hurt too much. You'll have to find the doctor or a nurse to help."

James left the room to find Dr. Bergen again, and found her along with a nurse talking in the hallway.

"Doctor, Sergeant Davis has asked Grace if we may look at her wounds. I know, I know, a bit weird," James added quickly, seeing the doctor's face.

"Fact is, we really need to establish what kind of a weapon the attacker used. It's really important," he added.

"Did she say yes?" asked Dr. Bergen.

"Yes, she did. As long as it doesn't hurt too much," he added.

"I guess we can manage that. Nurse? Can we gently uncover that gash? And what about the clavicle?

"That too, I gather," James said. "The sergeant is wondering how the attack happened, hitting her head and then the shoulder area. It's part of the puzzle."

The three headed back into Grace's room. Dr. Bergen asked for Grace's permission to uncover the wounds, while Hope flinched and David turned slightly gray.

"Is this really necessary?" asked Hope. "It's going to hurt and it's going to be ugly."

"It's not necessary, Ms. Rampling, and we could manage, but it will be very helpful in finding the attacker, and figuring out whether the assailant also attacked the bishop," said Adam, feeling like a jerk. "But we don't want to upset you or Grace, or Mr. Rampling, either."

"It's fine, really," Grace said. "I'd rather you found this guy before he hurts someone else, like Bruce."

Good point, thought Adam, wondering how James was taking that comment.

The doctor and nurse came to Grace's bed, and carefully drew back the bandages. The head wound was a gory sight, and the area around it so bruised it was hard to tell what had caused it, but Adam was quite sure it was very different from the bishop's wound. Pulling out a small camera, he took a quick photo of the wound. This was something Jack McDougall had to see.

Grace was breathing heavily, and gasping. The air swirling around her gash was not making matters better.

"Do you have what you need?" asked the doctor. "This is obviously causing some distress."

"No. I'm okay," said Grace firmly, if a bit weakly.

"No. You're not, and I'm finished. Thank you for this, Grace, we are really grateful," said Adam. "We'll let you know more, when we do. Take care."

Adam and James walked out. A few metres down the hallway, Adam stopped, and propped himself up against the wall, breathing deeply for a minute or two. Causing Grace pain was not his favourite thing. James watched him silently.

"Let's go," Adam finally said, pushing off from the wall.

"Where to, Sarge?"

"Back to McDougall. I need his call on what caused this wound."

Fifteen

I f I had to guess, and you're not the world's greatest photographer, Sergeant Davis," said McDougall with mock severity, "this looks like a pipe wound. Heavy pipe, but maybe an inch in diameter. Then you say her clavicle is badly bruised?"

"Yes. On the same side . . . although that might seem like a natural assumption, but to be clear."

"Well, it is remotely possible that a pipe of some kind could have given a powerful but still glancing blow that landed on her clavicle, or there was a second attempted blow. Either way, I don't think it's the same weapon."

"That's what I thought," said Adam. "And I think I know what killed the bishop. It was a monstrance."

McDougall's eyebrows flew up. "No kidding? That's fascinating. You could come up with plenty of disturbing religious motivations behind the choice of *that* murder weapon.

"Yes, that could be it," he added thoughtfully, remembering the autopsy.

Coming back into the present, McDougall asked, "how did you figure that out?"

"The monstrance at St. Eligius is missing. It weighs perhaps eight to ten pounds, is about two and a half feet tall, all told, and has a heavy base. Inch and a half around the edge. Sound about right?"

"Bingo, Sergeant. It sounds like you have your weapon. Now about this one. It doesn't necessarily mean it can't be the same attacker, does it? Who lurks in alleys carrying monstrances? Maybe a pipe was just more convenient."

"Hell. You're right," said Adam. "I thought for a minute that, at the very least, we had determined there were two attackers. But it still might be one. It would simply be hard to sneak down an alley with that big a weapon."

"What about motive?" asked James. "Could both attacks be related to homosexuality somehow? Grace's certainly was, based on what she told us. 'Fag-loving bitch'. Remember?

"But we don't know why the bishop was killed. Not really. It could have been someone connected to the Pride Chorus, but that's circumstantial so far. And that would be the opposite motivation of Grace's attack — someone, admittedly derangedly, supportive of the gay community."

"Well, for what it's worth," said McDougall, "it looks like two different killers, or potential killers, despite what I said. But you're right. Hard to tell."

"Let's get back to the station," Adam said to James. "We need to talk to the priest and the secretary. Thanks, Jack. As always."

"You're welcome, Adam. As usual."

"Who's first on our must-interview list?" asked Adam.

"The secretary. Are you ready for him?"

"Yeah. Let's get this over with. With Grace's attack, I feel like we're running behind on these interviews. Is he here?"

"Yep; I'll go get him."

James went out to the waiting room and saw the secretary waiting, a medium-height man with thinning brown hair and imperfect skin. Ellice Fairbrother appeared to be in his mid-forties, and perhaps not brimming with self-confidence.

"Mr. Fairbrother? Hello, I'm James Weatherall, one of the constables working on this case. We're ready for you. Please follow me. Would you like some coffee?"

"No, thank you," said Fairbrother. "I've had enough caffeine today."

Arriving at the interview room, James introduced the church secretary to the detective sergeant.

"Thank you for coming, Mr. Fairbrother. Please take a seat," said Adam, preparing the recording device.

"First, if you could, please tell me where you were on Sunday between about four-thirty and six-forty-five p.m."

"I was at the office from after the morning service until about five, five-thirty, and then I went home," said Fairbrother.

"Can anyone verify that?"

"No, I'm afraid I was alone in the office most of the afternoon, and no one was home."

"Did you know the bishop well?"

"Fairly well," said Fairbrother. "I've been at the cathedral for about four years, and I see the bishop quite often."

"Did you see or hear anything unusual the afternoon, or early evening, of that day?"

"No, nothing. It seemed to be a very normal day. I was terribly shocked when I found out about the bishop."

"Have you noticed whether anything had been disturbed, or taken, at the church since?"

"I don't think so. What sort of thing?"

James was about to mention the monstrance, but caught Adam's warning look. Adam was considering telling Father Campbell, who would find out soon enough that his vessel was missing, but he didn't want anyone else to know — unless, well, they already knew.

"Anything that could be used as a weapon."

"No, no, I haven't noticed anything like that. Oh, dear, oh, dear," said Fairbrother, sounding rather like the White Rabbit in Alice in Wonderland and rubbing his hands together. "A weapon. Oh, dear."

"And about the Pride Chorus. I understand from the choir director that you called to inform him the cathedral would not allow their concert to go ahead. Is that true?"

"Yes, I did."

"On whose authority?"

"The bishop's," said Fairbrother. "He made all those decisions. Unless, of course, it was a directive from the Catholic Church of Canada. The bishop didn't say."

Adam toyed with asking Fairbrother what he knew about Grace's attack, as well. But it was not yet public information that the person attacked at Divas was, in fact, Grace.

He settled for asking, "could you also tell us where you were on Wednesday night?"

"At home."

This wasn't going anywhere, thought Adam. The man either didn't have any information, or Adam wasn't asking the right questions. He seemed an unlikely suspect, worried and pensive.

"All right, Mr. Fairbrother. Thank you for coming down. We may need to interview you again, so please let us know if you have to leave town for any reason. James, can you show Mr. Fairbrother out?"

James did, then met Adam back in his office. "Interesting that he said the bishop cancelled the concert," said James.

"Yeah, that's about all we learned. We can't ask the bishop about it, unfortunately. What did you think of him?"

"He seemed quite upset, to me. He's not overflowing with personality. I didn't get much of a read on him."

"Me neither."

"Father Campbell is here, sir," said the receptionist.

"Thanks, Amanda. I'll be right out."

Adam closed the file he was reading and went down the hall to stick his head over James' carrel wall. "He's here," said Adam.

"On my way," said James, who had returned to his desk between interviews.

Adam went to the front to gather up the priest, who was standing in the entry looking ashen, tired, but determinedly upright. In full clerical garb, Paul Campbell looked particularly pale against the black cloth, and Adam felt a bit sorry for the priest. He was undoubtedly having the worst week of his life, at least professionally.

"Hello, Father Campbell. Adam Davis, detective sergeant in charge of the investigation into the bishop's death."

He put out his hand and enclosed Campbell's icy fingers in his grip.

"Nice to meet you, Sergeant," said Campbell, with a small nod, looking straight into Adam's eyes. His voice and gaze were strong and unwavering, contradicting his complexion.

They headed down the hall, making small talk about the nasty March weather, toward the interview room. James was waiting for them.

"Can we offer you some delicious police station coffee, Father?" asked James, sarcasm dripping from his voice.

"You make it sound so enticing," said Campbell. "But thank you. That would be nice."

James went out on the coffee mission, having determined that Campbell took no sugar but cream — well, whitener — and Adam set up the recorder for the interview.

"This is an interview with Paul Campbell, priest at St. Eligius Cathedral," said Adam, also identifying himself.

"Father, can you tell me where you were and what you were doing the day the bishop was killed."

Campbell cleared his throat.

"It was like many other Sundays, or at least it started that way. The bishop was coming to the cathedral that morning to deliver the sacrament and a sermon, so I was in a secondary role that day.

"He arrived about nine o'clock; we had a good talk and prepared for the service."

"Did you use the monstrance that morning?" asked Adam.

"Yes, we did," said Campbell, brow furrowing. "Why do you ask?"

"I'll explain later. Please continue."

Looking a bit disconcerted, Campbell started to ask another question, but the expression on Adam's face stopped him.

"Well, the service was not unusual in any way. Afterward, we had some lunch and the bishop later heard confession. He was determined to hear as many confessions as possible; it always made him feel more connected to what the people were thinking. I heard confessions as well, then left for the manse about four-thirty."

"What happens to the monstrance after the service?" Adam asked, just as James returned with coffee.

"It's cleaned and then stored in its cabinet," answered Campbell, thanking James for the hot drink with a nod.

"Which is locked?"

"Yes. Monstrances are expensive and hard to replace, and congregations are quite attached to them — they are unique and people feel connected to their monstrances. One would not want it stolen. Again, sergeant, may I ask why you are so concerned with the monstrance?"

Adam was glad he had told Ed, the janitor, not to reveal that the monstrance was missing. Obviously, Ed had taken it to heart. And there would not have been a reason for Campbell to check on the monstrance just a few days after the service. The priest seemed truly puzzled by the questions, which was telling Adam a great deal.

He would find out very soon that the vessel was missing. Adam would have to tell him, or wait until the priest discovered it himself. He mentally weighed the benefits of both approaches.

"Sergeant?" Campbell said. Apparently Adam had taken a long pause.

"Father Campbell, your monstrance is missing," said Adam, making a decision.

"Missing! Why have I not been told? How do you know?"

"Only two people know, besides the police. Your janitor, and the killer. Unless they are one and the same."

As this information sunk in, Campbell went paler yet, and sat back in his chair looking profoundly shocked.

"I'm telling you now," added Adam.

"You are saying," said Campbell slowly, "that the monstrance was the weapon in the bishop's murder. And, the killer still has it."

"Yes. Or has ditched it."

It was Campbell's turn to pause. "God have mercy," he finally said, quietly.

Adam gave him a moment, then asked, "How well did you know the bishop?"

"Quite well, I would say. He was a mentor to me, a kind man, a good leader. We spent quite a lot of time together."

"What do you know about his past?" asked Adam.

"He was regarded very highly in the church, and rose in the clerical ranks rather quickly," said Campbell. "I have never heard anything about his past that would make me think anyone would want to kill him."

"No enemies, then, that you're aware of."

"No. I don't know of any. I think he had some concerns about a few members of the congregations here, but they were not personal. More about their . . . views on things."

"Views?" asked Adam. "What views?"

"Well, you sometimes have people who are not, perhaps, as forgiving or understanding as one might like. People who are . . ." he stopped.

"Racist? Homophobic? Unhinged?" asked James, with some vehemence.

Campbell nodded, reluctantly.

"Do you know the names of any of these people that the bishop was concerned about?"

"No. There was never a threat or anything like that . . . and to the bishop, of course, the privacy of the confessional was sacred. As it is to me."

Damn, thought Adam. He was hoping they'd stumbled onto something.

"Who has access to the monstrance?" he asked.

"Well, Ed, of course. I do. The secretary does. The deacons. There are a number of people."

"Would it be difficult to pick the lock on the cupboard?" asked Adam, silently kicking himself for not looking at it more closely.

Campbell sighed. "Probably not."

"Would there be people around all the time, or are there times when the altar area would be private?"

"Churches are not the busy places they once were. It probably wouldn't be too hard to pick the lock in privacy."

"I'm sorry to ask you this, Father, but can anyone verify where you were Sunday night between four-thirty and seven?"

"I was home most of that time, and Anna was there for a while. She is, essentially, my right hand — cooking, answering the phone and so on — and fending off visitors when she feels it necessary," said Campbell, with a small smile.

"We'll have a quick chat with her. Do you have a photo, by the way, of the monstrance?"

Campbell reflected. "I don't know, to be honest," he said. "I'll look around. Maybe one of the deacons has taken one. It's not common to take photos while the sacrament is being given, but it's possible."

"Thank you, Father. Please let me know if you find one. Here's my card with my email address, in case you have a digital copy of a photo. We really appreciate you coming in. Will you be in town for the next few days? We may have more questions."

"Yes, I'll be here," said Campbell. "I have a congregation to look after. They just lost their bishop."

"Oh, one more thing, Father. Was it you who cancelled the Pride Chorus concert?"

"No. It's odd. I knew nothing about it."

Sixteen

I t was very odd that the priest knew nothing about the decision to cancel the concert, thought Adam.

"What did you think of the father?" Adam asked James, after the priest was shown out.

"He seemed genuinely shocked about the monstrance being missing," said James, grimacing after a sip of his acidic and cooling coffee. "God, can't we do something about this java? It's awful."

"Probably not. And yeah, he did. And he looked like hell — probably sleep-deprived and pretty upset. His hands were ice cold. Not that that knocks him out of the running for murderer."

"I've seen him preach a couple of times, and he's pretty good. He seems like, you know, a man of God in the pulpit."

"So, like, you actually go to church?"

"Sometimes. Shifts get in the way."

"Sure, blame it on me." Adam smiled. "Did you believe him when he said he didn't know about the concert cancellation?"

"I guess so. I mean, he responded immediately, didn't mess around; and it does seem odd that he wasn't informed."

"Yeah, that's what I thought too." Adam paused, looking into his cup of coffee. It really was disgusting. "And we can't exactly ask the bishop. By the way, how's Bruce doing?"

"He's okay, I guess, thanks for asking." James looked away for a moment. "He didn't do it, Sarge."

Adam just nodded. What could he say? He couldn't agree, since Bruce had no alibi — James was working and actually at the murder scene that night, while Bruce said he was at home. Adam doubted Bruce was a killer, but he couldn't officially rule him out.

Steve Delaney, Mark Williams and John Powers were standing in the emergency room triage area, screwing up their courage. They were very fond of Grace, and none of them looked forward to seeing her, beaten and bruised, in a hospital bed.

"Why is this so hard?" John finally asked the other two, deciding he had to break the mood.

"Hmmm," said Steve, clearing his throat. "Well, it's nasty to see someone you care about hurt, especially if it's bloody. And it sure does point to the fact that journalists aren't always safe."

"Yeah. I take your point. So let's go."

They found Grace sleeping in her emergency room bed, and Grace's sister sitting in a chair, staring at her. When the trio of visitors quietly drew aside the drape, Hope raised a finger to her lips; but Grace opened her eyes.

"Hi John! Hi Steve! Hi Mark!," she said enthusiastically, and then immediately started to cry.

"Oh Gracie," said John, going over to her and trying to hug her around the bandages, tubes and messy bedding.

A clumsy and confusing embrace followed, but it seemed the best thing; the funny side of the scene made Grace laugh instead of cry.

"Thanks for coming," she said, looking at Steve and Mark, and clutching John's hand.

"Grace. Of course we would come. How do you feel? You look a little pale," said Mark.

"Not too bad," lied Grace. "And I usually look pale. How are things going down at the shop?"

"Well, we miss you," said Steve. "And frankly, we don't know what to do about you, either."

"Hey, you're not going to fire me because I didn't call in?" Grace said, trying a joke.

The editors all laughed politely. "You know what he means," said John.

Yes. She did. Her attack was violent and had already made the news as a brief, although she had not been identified in the police press release. They would have to decide whether to reveal that she, Grace, was attacked. It was definitely newsworthy, particularly in light of the bishop's murder, her profile in the community, the fact that she had found the bishop dead — not to mention it was also a public service, to warn people that a crazed, homophobic jerk was out there.

"Have you met my sister?" asked Grace, changing the subject to give her a little time to think. Thinking was tough slogging with a head injury.

"Hope, this is Steve Delaney, my editor; Mark Williams, my managing editor; and John Powers, the news editor. Hope Rampling."

As the pleasantries and handshakes were made, Grace mulled the pros and cons of being identified as the victim of the attack outside Divas. Would people think she was LGBTQ? If so, did it matter? Would it be helpful to identify as hetero, to show that anyone in support of the LGBTQ community was at risk — and how homophobia could affect anyone? Or would that just seem like protesting too much, that she wasn't gay? What a weird situation.

Grace was under no illusion that this was probably not over. That guy had been specifically after her, and he still might be. Maybe it would be better if he thought she was either dead or nearly so. On the other hand, maybe he would try to attack her again, and the police could arrest him? What were the chances of that?

She needed to talk to Adam Davis before she made a decision about going public. Besides, he would probably be apoplectic and yell if she made what he saw as the wrong decision in his case. The thought made her smile.

"What's funny?" asked John.

"Nothing. Really, absolutely nothing is funny. I think I need to talk to the sergeant before we decide. We want to make sure we don't mess up his investigation; the most important thing is that this guy, or these guys, get caught, right? And I can't think my way through this. My brain's too foggy and my head hurts too much."

"You're right," said Steve. "We have an obligation to the truth and to the community, but when the truth should be told and what's best for the community are up for discussion. When do you expect to see the sergeant again?"

"I don't know. He came and photographed my head — when was that, Hope?"

120

"This morning. Can it really have been just this morning? Wow. Time goes pretty slowly in this place."

"I could ask him to come tomorrow?" suggested Grace. "I have his card somewhere . . . I actually have no idea where my stuff is. Do I have stuff? I don't even know if it's here or in that alley. Can someone call the cop shop, and ask him to come down to the hospital?"

"I'll do that as soon as I get back to the newsroom," offered John.

"Thanks, John. And thanks for coming," said Grace, her voice threatening tears again.

"Grace, for God's sake, of course we'd come," said Steve. "Take care, and after you've talked to the sergeant, we'll decide what to do. Does that sound okay? And take your time. This is your life, and you have to decide how much of it you want everyone to know about."

Adam was re-reading the bishop's file, and questions were popping out at him. We need to know more about his past, thought Adam. Then he turned over the report, and saw the news clipping of the story written by Grace that ran the day after the bishop's death. Grace, and Lacey McPhail.

Adam picked up the phone.

"John Powers," the night editor answered.

"John, it's Adam Davis. How are you?"

"Fine, apart from missing my best reporter. Right now, I'm wondering if you're psychic. I was going to call you, as soon as I got a minute. We were wondering if you could do us a favour."

"Sure, if I can. What's up?"

"We have to make a decision about whether we are going to release the fact that it was Grace who was attacked at Divas the other night. Obviously, we have printed the basic news coming out of your release; it's still news when someone gets beaten up outside a gay bar. But it was Grace.

"First of all, she's our reporter; second of all, she is not part of the LGBTQ community; and third, she found the bishop, so she is a witness in that case, and we don't know if they're connected. I don't know if you know yet.

"Anyway, we're struggling to put all those pieces together, and it's really important to Grace that we don't mess things up for you. She was wondering if you could pop by the hospital, maybe tomorrow, and let her know what your preferences are? I mean, as far as I'm concerned, most of this is up to her — her life, her attack — but she wants to do the right thing."

Adam was trying to concentrate on what John was saying, but his brain was off in all directions. First of all, Grace was definitely heterosexual. He knew that in his soul, but it carried some strange weight to hear it out loud. Second of all, she wanted to see him. And third, would it indeed be useful or detrimental for the public to know it was she who was attacked?

"I'd be happy to go see Grace, of course," said Adam. Happy didn't exactly cover it.

"But you called me," said John. "What's up?"

"There's something I better tell you. It will come into your decision. And I have to ask you to keep this to yourself."

"Okay," agreed John.

"Grace was not attacked randomly, John." Adam gave the news editor a moment to digest that. After hearing John's big intake of breath, he continued.

"I think there has been some assumption that it was a crime of opportunity — someone who likes to attack gay people, or perhaps women. No. Whoever attacked her knew she was there, knew who she was; it was personal."

"Oh, my God. How do you know this?"

"Because of the specific things he said to her. It had to do with her being at Divas."

"That definitely sounds personal. Of course, it occurred right after her story on the Pride Chorus ran. And the bishop story."

"That brings me to another problem. I was re-reading the story she wrote the day after the murder, and I just noticed there was a shared byline. With Lacey McPhail."

"Shit," said John. "Does that mean someone's out to get Lacey, too?

"I hope not, and I don't think so; but there is a possibility Ms. McPhail could be in danger, if the motivation for Grace's attack is that this asshole thinks running a story on a choir is dangerously pro-gay. God, what is the matter with people? But it is a possibility. Where is she now?"

"Here. I can see her. Thank goodness. She sits directly across the newsroom from me."

"I have to talk to her. Can I come right over? I also have to ask you a few questions about what Grace usually writes about. James Weatherall — that's the constable you met at the church the night the bishop was killed — has already started going through her stories at the library. Maybe you have a better library?"

"Probably do. Come on over. I'll make sure Lacey stays put. Thank you, Sergeant."

"Thanks, John. I'm on my way."

It was getting late in the day. The sun was starting to set. The chill remained in the air in this dirty, messy late March and Adam turned up the collar on his leather jacket against the wind. In minutes, he presented himself to the receptionist at the StarPhoenix, who was just packing away her lunch kit and gathering her scarf, gloves and hat.

Pretty, blonde Alison looked up from her end-of-day tasks and actually gasped.

"May I help you?" she said, practically beaming at Adam.

"Sergeant Adam Davis of the Saskatoon Police," he said. "I'm here to see John Powers, the news editor."

"I will let Mr. Powers know you are here, Sergeant," said Alison, staring.

She dialled up, and seconds later, John was opening the locked security door at the top of the winding staircase. "Come on up, Sergeant," he said.

Adam thanked the receptionist, turned, and took the curved stairs two at a time, unaware that Alison was powerfully appreciating the spectacular view from the back side.

Seventeen

L acey, John, Steve, Mark and Adam were gathered in Steve's office, drinking coffee slightly less awful than the caffeine at the police station. Coffee at the SP wasn't too bad in the mornings, but the afternoon dregs were bitter. Lacey added more milk, took a sip, made a face. Being a health nut, at least on the dietary side, she was trying to give up both coffee and milk. Maybe this would give her impetus.

The room was quiet. All four men were stirring coffee or looking at their feet.

"So what's up?" asked Lacey brightly. Something was definitely up, and it looked like she was going to have to open the conversation.

John began to say something, but Adam stopped him.

"John, thanks, but I think I better start. Ms. McPhail, I have to apologize to you. I realized today, when I re-read the story you wrote with Ms. Rampling after the bishop's death, that you shared the byline. It didn't occur to me, after she was attacked, until I re-read it today." He tilted his head at her, closed his eyes for a minute, and then said with feeling, "and I am really sorry."

Lacey just stared at him. "I don't understand. Why are you sorry, Sergeant?"

"You, as well as Grace, may be in danger. We don't know that you're in danger for sure, but it's a possibility."

It took some time, but Adam carefully explained the whole thing: that it looked like Grace may have been attacked because of the newspaper story. The attacker had viciously called her an awful name and it was pretty clear that he knew who Grace was, and where she was that night. That meant she was probably followed to the nightclub.

"We don't know yet whether he is focused on Grace, or on both of you."

Lacey was quiet. It was a lot to think about. The four men were quiet again, too, giving her some time to digest this.

Finally, John broke the silence. "Lacey. You okay?"

"Of course," said Lacey, looking up. "Sergeant, I appreciate and accept your apology, but I don't see how that would have occurred to you, since the story ran several days before Grace's attack. Please, don't feel bad about that. So now what?"

Reporters. God love them, they just get right down to business, thought Adam.

"Thank you, Ms. McPhail. Yes, so now what? John, Steve, Mark, have you thought about what you would like to say, or not say, about Grace? I know we still have to talk to her, but I wonder if you have some direction on that."

"I'm leaning toward not revealing that she was the victim of that attack, at least for now," said John.

"I'd like her to have some privacy around this, number one, and number two, if her name appears in the paper, we would have to say what her medical status is. That worries me, in terms of the attacker; he'd know more or less where she was, and she could be vulnerable."

"We have a twenty-four-hour guard on Grace," said Adam.

"You do?" asked Steve. "I didn't see him when we visited Grace today."

"Her. Plainclothes. Trying to blend into the hospital environment."

"I guess that's working then," said John, who didn't notice a guard either. "Even so, I'd rather not publicly declare that one of our reporters is lying helpless in a hospital. Steve? Mark? What do you think?"

"I agree," said Steve. "I think the public service aspect to this — telling people to be careful out there, especially in the LGBTQ community — has been sufficiently addressed without identifying anyone. At least for now. Mark?"

Mark nodded, then asked, "What about Lacey?"

"We need to put a guard on Ms. McPhail as well. How we're going to do that I don't know; it might be tricky with her out and about so much. But we have to. I'm sorry Ms. McPhail, but there is just too high a risk that he's after you, too."

Lacey choked on her coffee. "You've got to be kidding. How am I going to work and — well, eat and shower and drive to work with a guard? All those life things?"

"We're just going to have to figure it out. I'll try to get women on your detail, at least at home, so you can feel reasonably comfortable at . . . more private times. Do you — forgive me — live alone?" he asked.

Lacey nodded.

"Okay. There'll be no uniforms; and maybe you have an extra camera hanging around? We can put it around the officer's neck and say she's Ms. McPhail's photographer or something?"

"Woohoo. I like that," said John. "Extra staffer for free."

Lacey laughed, and then sighed. "When does this Siamese twin get attached?"

"Now. When I leave here, there will be a police officer waiting." He had hollered at Charlotte to arrange such a thing as he was leaving for the StarPhoenix.

Lacey shook her head. "So much for freedom. But you're the boss. Can I get back to work now?"

"Actually, no. The other important thing we have to talk about is the kinds of stories Grace writes; if there has ever been a story she has been particularly attacked for — I don't necessarily mean physically — in the past; and if she has any kind of history writing stories about LGBTQ people, or anything remotely similar. This is important," added Adam.

"Reporters get attacked all the time. All the time," repeated Lacey for emphasis. "Let me think a bit about whether any of Grace's stories drew particularly vile attention. Sometimes only the reporter knows; she opens her mail, and takes her own phone calls. At least two of our reporters don't even open their hate mail. And we don't always talk about it. It's so common, it's kind of weird or uncool to talk about it, unless it's particularly bad."

"Well, if a story pops out at you, please let me know," said Adam. "Does your library, by any chance, sort by the reporters' names? Some of the archives at the library are basically about turning pages until your fingers bleed — or your eyes spin in the microfiche room."

"Yep, you can sort by just about anything. Easy," said Mark. "Hey, while not posing as a photographer, maybe your officer could hang out on our digital library. We have an admittedly ancient, but vacant computer."

Adam broke into a grin. "Brilliant. Thanks, Mark." He had another thought. "Do we have to tell the other reporters about this?"

All four newspeople just laughed.

"We can try that," said John, "but reporters notice everything. Then they figure out what it means. For now, we can try to pretend that your officer is our new intern. That would only work, you know, if it's always the same person."

"Right. Well, let's see if we can work that out, for now, at least. If they figure it out, you'll have to tell them, but can we please keep it as quiet as possible?"

"You don't have to worry about that," said John, gravely. "Their first instincts will be to protect Grace and Lacey."

They walked out of Steve's office into the bright, open newsroom, and as Adam had predicted, there was a young female stranger sitting near the editorial reception desk. At a quiet word from Adam, they all quickly retreated back into the office, realizing more or less in unison that Adam's presence plus new person equalled two hundred questions from the staff.

Steve punched the quick-dial button to reach the receptionist.

"Hi, Jackie. Can you please show our visitor into my office?"

"Right away, boss."

The officer walked in to "Hi, Joan," from Adam, who introduced her all the way around and then asked, "are you any good with a camera?"

Eighteen

G race was no longer in emergency. The hospital had found her a room, and after an insistent call from Adam Davis, they had found her a private room.

There was no way Adam was going to discuss his case, from here on in, in front of other patients or visitors — or medical staff, for that matter.

Although Grace was feeling better, Dr. Bergan was still carefully monitoring her concussion and wanted her to remain very quiet for a few days — as much as possible, she thought wryly, for Grace was regaining some energy.

The wound on her head was also nasty, bloody and weepy, and needed frequent redressing. At least a couple more days, thought the doctor.

Hope had set up her own little camp in a reclining chair, and also decorated the entire room within an hour. There were flowers. Magazines were arranged on the window sill. Pottery mugs replaced plastic hospital cups. She brought a tiny coffee maker, a basket of fruit, and a pretty blanket for the bed.

She stood there for a moment, surveying the room with satisfaction.

Morning light was streaming in when Adam walked through the door.

"Wow," he said. "Looks almost like home. Good morning, Grace, Ms. Rampling."

"Call me Hope, please," said Hope. "Too confusing otherwise. How are you, Sergeant?"

"Just fine, thanks. How are you two?" asked Adam.

"I'm fine. Grace is fine-ish," said Hope, answering for both.

"Hi, Sergeant," Grace said. "Thanks for coming."

"My pleasure," said Adam. "John said you wanted to talk about some things, and they're probably the same things I need to ask you about. What's on your mind?"

"John and Steve were here yesterday, and we were talking about whether I should put my name out there as the person who was attacked. I didn't know . . . I don't feel like I'm thinking clearly . . . and I didn't want to mess up your investigation. But the most important thing is to make sure he doesn't attack anyone else."

Adam realized he had been staring right into her eyes while she had been speaking, lost for the second time in the direct, deep chocolate gaze of someone he was rapidly falling for. His witness, and now a victim, for God's sake. Be careful, he told himself.

"Right now, and I did talk to your editors yesterday, I think it's best to leave your name out of it. John made some good points about that — he said if they identified you, they'd have to release your medical status, and that might make you more vulnerable to this attacker. I tend to agree.

131

"What do you think? It's mostly your decision, Grace."

"Does that help or hinder you, either way?

"It may help a little . . . keep him wondering, which is usually good."

"Okay. I'll think about it a bit more, but I'll stay out of the pages of my paper — entirely, for now," said Grace, sounding a little bitter and a little sad.

"I have to ask you something else," said Adam. "I talked to Lacey McPhail about this yesterday. She said reporters are always getting hate mail and nasty phone calls, which wasn't news to me; but she also said that sometimes you don't even open threatening letters, or talk about them, they're so common. Do you find that's true?"

"Absolutely. There are just so many — everything from 'your story sucked' to 'I'll sue you' to 'I'll get you if you write one more word about me.' And you'd be amazed where the threats come from, sometimes. Like nice, normal, businesspeople. But there are also the crazies — I mean, literally; they are suffering from mental health problems. They think they're being followed by the FBI — in Canada, no less — or that the Workers' Compensation Board has a conspiracy going against them. Or that the police have a grudge against them. I bet that one surprises you."

Adam laughed. He heard that one all the time.

"Has there been one crazy or even not-so-crazy that stands out? A threat that sounded more real than the others? Anything?"

"I'd have to think. There have been many. But I'm getting the feeling you think this isn't just about that one story the day after the bishop was killed."

"It might be, no question. Some nuts go along doing petty stuff, maybe a bar fight, maybe robbing a store, until something seems to send them over the edge. And it's often something that seems like nothing — like a story about a choir getting booted from a church, say. A bishop dying. Who knows what makes them pull the trigger?"

Grace's eyes widened. "Oh, my God. Lacey had her byline on that story too," she cried, her voice rising as she struggled to sit up.

Hope and Adam both leaned in quickly to calm her down. "Grace, shhh, honey, shhh," said Hope, gently forcing her to lie down. At the same time, Adam was saying, soothingly, "Grace, we've thought of that. She's fine, please don't worry . . ."

Hope smoothed her hair and her blanket, and Adam touched her partly-bare shoulder reassuringly. He caught his breath at her soft skin.

"It's okay, Grace, honestly. She has a cop with her at all times. Just like you."

"Me?"

"Yeah. Right outside the door. Want to see?"

"No — I'll take your word for it. Thank you," she said, quietly. "Thank you for looking after us. Lacey and me."

Adam's face showed concern, mixed with a confusion of pleasure over Grace's thanks. She reached up suddenly, and touched Adam's cheek. "Shhh," she said, brow furrowing, and sounding just like Hope. "It's okay. What's the matter?"

"I'm sorry I upset you. You're supposed to stay quiet. Maybe I better go . . ."

"No — Adam — Sergeant — don't go. I just thought of Lacey and got upset. It's okay now," said

Grace, withdrawing her hand and slumping back onto the bed. "You were all over it."

"I wasn't at first," he said bitterly. "I caught it today, when I was going over the bishop's file."

"You've given her her own police officer," said Grace, more firmly. "And you actually thought of it. No one else would have or could have done that. Thank you."

Adam took another deep breath and sat down again. "Thank you Grace, but I should have remembered her byline."

"No. No, Sergeant. Easily done. No one notices bylines. And no one remembers them from five days earlier."

Adam was not so sure about that. Reporters always said no one noticed their names in the paper, but Adam was convinced that was not true.

"Well, let's agree for now that some people notice bylines. Certainly the people covered in your stories notice, and anyone who cares about the issue. Can you think of anyone who has been particularly difficult in your reporting past?"

Grace honestly couldn't. All the nasty calls, all the letters, seemed about the same to her. Most people angry about coverage — about things like tax evasion or court proceedings — threatened to sue her. But of course, it was public knowledge, and suing was pointless. They were upset that their names were in the paper, attached to something unflattering, and that was the only threat they could think of.

She shook her head.

"Do you often report on issues that arise in the LGBTQ community, or other human rights issues?"

Again, she shook her head. Those things came up for her from time to time, but less regularly than crime or business stories.

She had been solely a court reporter for four years, and still covered crime. She told Adam.

"Court? Queen's Bench? Provincial?"

"Both. Mostly QB, but if the provincial reporter was away, I'd do double duty."

"Any super-bad guys you covered, that you can recall?" Adam's voice changed, and Grace noticed.

"Plenty. Dozens, at least. When my brain kicks back in, I'll try to recall the super-super-bad ones. What are you thinking?"

"What if the choir-slash-bishop story was just the last straw? Maybe you've pissed off one of the bad guys in the past. I mean, you hear about this kind of thing happening in the bigger cities — journalists getting attacked for just covering stories. I assume it could happen here, too."

Grace felt sick. Sure it could, she thought. She had never thought about it, particularly, but it could. Saskatoon wasn't a metropolis, but that didn't change the violence and mental instability of the criminal element. It was just a smaller element.

"It could," admitted Grace. "But I really can't think of anyone who would come after me. That would be great, though," she added. "It would maybe mean Lacey wasn't in danger."

"Maybe. But even if this is a nasty blast from your past, the attacker might include Lacey in his anger. So I think we should stick to the police guards, and move a little faster on reading your old stories."

He thought for a minute. "Your job is getting more dangerous, isn't it?"

"Seems to be. In the past, once in a while, someone would show up calling you lovely names and threatening to beat you up. But I don't think I ever expected this."

Adam nodded. A new understanding, which had first dawned on him after his nightmare about Grace being shot, bloomed as she spoke. It wasn't just police officers who took a lot of shit, who risked their lives, who felt alone and frightened, and were often traumatized by the society they tried to serve. He just hadn't looked at it that way, hadn't been able to stretch his understanding after his own near-death experience.

He wasn't all that special, after all; not the only hero. He couldn't protect the world, or even himself. Nor Grace, although he was giving it his best shot. He was going to have to try to accept that.

He stood, and risked touching Grace on the arm. "Thank you, Grace. I'd better get back — lots of work to do. Keep me in the loop. Maybe you'll think of something that will help. I'll be back when I know more."

"Thanks, Sergeant. Apparently Hope found my stuff. It did make it into the ambulance with me, so I actually have your card and my cellphone. And thanks again for looking after Lacey."

Adam walked down the hospital hallway, pulling his phone out of his pocket.

"James," he said when the constable answered. "I've just left Grace. I don't know if I'm barking at the wrong car, here, but what if this guy who hit her is actually mad about something else? I mean, he's probably also pissed about that choir story, but maybe he had a weird thing about Grace before? She used to be the court reporter, and still covers crime much of the time," he added, realizing James needed some context.

"Yeah, that's a thought. It does seem strange that she got attacked out of the blue over one story, unless, of course, it's the same guy who killed the bishop. And that's dependent on whether the bishop or the Church cancelled the choir performance. Man, this is getting complicated."

"We need to get a fuller bio happening on the bishop, and if possible, find out if the bishop was gay, or even if people thought he was," Adam said.

"And it occurred to me this morning, too; if the bishop cancelled that concert, why didn't he tell the priest? It's his church, too. We need to talk to the secretary again. Maybe he can tell us who to call at the Catholic Church of Canada. We only have his word that the bishop told him to do it."

Adam hung up and called Joan Karpinski, who was at the StarPhoenix because Lacey McPhail was working the weekend.

"Joan, it's Adam. I need you to start looking for some of the criminals Grace has covered in the past. I think there might be a bad guy out there with a thing for her. Let's find him."

Nineteen

James walked over to the church office. It would have been ridiculous to take a police vehicle less than two blocks, which is how far away the office was if you took the alley behind the StarPhoenix parking lot.

It was still cold. It was going to be a late spring, which was good and bad: Good, because crime tended to be lower in winter, but bad, because James hated the cold. He was a shorts and T-shirt guy, whenever he could get out of his uniform.

But crime still bludgeoned its way through the winter, as the bishop's murder showed. That kind of crime did not take a weather holiday.

The secretary had not answered the phone, so here he was heading down Twenty-Third Street. He crossed at the alley, and turned the corner at the low brick building that housed the church office.

He tried the door, and it was open.

"Hello?" he called, not seeing anyone at the front or in the hallway. "Police. Is anyone here?"

No answer. James continued down the hallway, looking into each room — an office, a small boardroom, a little coffee area, another office.

Then someone came hurrying out of a doorway, and nearly ran right into him.

"Oh! Hello. Can I help you?" asked the woman.

"Yes. I'm Constable Weatherall, Saskatoon Police. I called out when I came in but no one answered. I'm looking for the church secretary. Who are you?"

"I'm the receptionist. Elinor Parsons."

"I've been trying to reach the secretary, Mr. Fairbrother," said James. "Is he in?"

"I don't believe so. Would you like me to leave him a message?"

"Yes. We need to talk to him right away. Please ask him to call me. Here's my card," said James. "How are things going, Ms. Parsons? I bet it's been tough, with the bishop's death."

"Yes, it has. He was a very nice man. I'll get Mr. Fairbrother to call you."

James thanked the receptionist and left, but peered into the offices as he went. No one else was about, that he could see. James decided he was going to see if Mr. Fairbrother was home, even if he wasn't answering his phone.

"Constable?"

James turned around. Elinor Parsons was standing behind him in the hallway.

"I don't know if this is important, but I was just thinking . . . "

"Yes?" said James, encouragingly.

"Well, last Sunday, I was in the office. I had to do some extra preparations for the service, since the bishop was coming, and then stayed for a while because he wanted to give confession. There was a phone call that afternoon — well, several — but there was one man who was very, very angry. He demanded to speak to Father Campbell or to the bishop."

"Why was he angry?"

"He said the church had no business cancelling the concert — that Pride choir. And he wanted to give someone a piece of his mind. Immediately. I really didn't know what to say. I knew nothing about it — the cancellation, I mean — but I offered to take a message. He said never mind, and slammed down the phone."

"Did you notice the phone number?"

"Well, sort of. It said private caller."

"Ms. Parsons, that is very helpful. Thank you so much. We may have to check your telephone log, and see if we can dig up that number. If you think of anything else, you have my card."

"Hopey."

"Grace. What's up?" answered Hope, putting down her book. Grace was awake again, after a short nap.

Grace moved restlessly in the narrow hospital bed. "It's so frustrating to be here. I can't work on the bishop story — my story! Even more than usual, that's my story. Can't do anything. And I'm hungry."

"Dinner is coming," said Hope.

"You're not cheering me up," said Grace. "How is someone supposed to get better eating that dreck?"

"Want me to go out and get something? Smuggle it in?"

Grace's face brightened. "Would you?"

"I would. What do you want?"

"Chicken parm. Or souvlaki, maybe. Glass of Malbec?"

"Fat chance on the wine, sis. You're on too many pain meds."

"Boo. I'd take a sandwich and some soup from that café on Broadway and Main."

"Yeah! Yum. I want some too. Okay, I'll zip out and get some food," said Hope, standing. Grace stopped her.

"Hope."

"Yes, Grace."

"What do you think of the sergeant?"

Everyone could see the sparks flying between Grace and Adam, hot enough to short-circuit the hospital's electrical system, and Hope was no exception. She cocked her head at Grace and said, "You like him, don't you, honey." It wasn't a question.

"I don't know what to think. He's being so kind to me and to Lacey, even though he saw me at the cathedral when I was at my worst, all upset and throwing up because of the dead bishop."

"And he's gorgeous," Hope put in.

"But my point is, maybe I'm just infatuated because of the situation? It's so bizarre. Maybe my lizard brain thinks he's my knight in shining armour or something . . . but he's really some macho control freak. Some cops are, you know. How would I know, before it was too late to turn back? And what if he's married?"

"Maybe it's time to find out. He doesn't wear a ring, by the way. Yes, I looked. Maybe you're generalizing, just a bit. And maybe you need to just let yourself feel the way you feel, and wait to see what happens when you're thinking clearly, once you're off the meds.

"For what it's worth, I'm willing to bet he does like to be in control, and that's part of his job. He's a detective sergeant. It doesn't necessarily make him a

141

macho freak. And Grace, he's not Mick Shaw," added Hope, referring to Grace's former boyfriend. "And he's not Melissa. Can you give him a chance? For God's sake, Grace. Isn't it time to take a shot?"

The thought of Adam being in control, under certain circumstances, sent an erotic shock through Grace. Oh hell, she thought. I have it bad. Stop thinking about the policeman, she told herself. Stop. Stop it. Even if he likes me, I'm still a witness. A victim. And a suspect in the bishop's murder — although that premise was showing as many holes as a police practice target, since her attack. But still she wanted Hope to be right that he wasn't Melissa or Mick.

Grace's face went through several contortions before resolving into a sad frown, as she roamed through her feelings.

"Yep," said Hope, as if she had read Grace's mind — which, more or less, she had. "You have yourself a situation. But think about what I said. You won't always be a victim, or a suspect, or a witness."

"Get out of here," said Grace, throwing a pillow at her sister, then wincing with pain. Ow. That was stupid. Her shoulder really, really hurt. "And get out of my brain," she added. "Can I have some real food please?"

Hope laughed, set aside the soft missile, grabbed her coat and handbag, and started out the door.

"I'm going, I'm going." She kissed Grace gently, sympathetically, on the cheek before she left.

StarPhoenix intern Joan Karpinski, aka Lacey McPhail's police guard, sat right next to her temporary ward and read Grace Rampling stories.

Joan was getting to be pretty good with a camera. They — she and Lacey — had been out shooting accidents, and the occasional theatre event. One of her pictures had actually made the paper.

The rest of the time, Joan pretended to be writing and researching — the latter, of course, she actually was.

A few of Grace's court stories drew her attention, more than others; and she was able to focus on the men, leaving out the women, since Grace was positive her attacker was male. That, at least, helped a little.

There was the case of a child pornographer, whose time in court was extensive; it took a week for the trial to unwind. There was a case of rape, a murder, a manslaughter, and a domestic case where no one could be named. There were several assaults, too, and Joan paid closer attention to those. Was it reasonable to assume that someone charged with assault, in a trial covered by Grace, would be more likely to assault her? Somehow that felt right, so she took particularly detailed notes on those cases.

There was one case where a man had hit another man with a chair at a bar, several times. Looked like your average bar fight. He went to jail for ten months. The victim survived.

In another court appearance, some lovely human being was on trial for burning a co-worker with a blow torch. That one was a real winner.

Here was another one, where a man had beaten another man nearly to death, leaving him partly paralyzed. This one had occurred outside a bar after closing time. Joan leaned in.

The attacker had been charged with attempted murder, ending up with seven years in prison for attempted manslaughter. He argued that he had been provoked, and very drunk. He took no responsibility, but the judge found that there were some mitigating circumstances, and it was his second offence; the first was a residential break and enter. He also ruled that the attacker would be required to seek alcohol rehabilitation and take therapy for his violent urges.

The trial took place over the course of several months, as the attacker went from one lawyer to another. He was one of those idiots who assumed it was his lawyer, not his own actions, that caused his problems.

Joan wrote down the names of the porn guy and the three men charged with assault, then headed to the boardroom and shut the door. She dialed Charlotte Warkentin's number.

"Hi Char, it's Joan," she said when Charlotte answered. "How're you doing?"

"I'm good, Joan. How's your new job?" asked Charlotte.

"If I ever get sick of being a cop, I can be a newspaper photographer. They actually printed one of my pictures today, after just one day on the job. I must rock."

Charlotte laughed. "Well, cool. And I know you rock. What's up?"

"I have some names for you," said Joan. "These are four bad guys Grace Rampling covered in court, sort of between seven and three years ago. I like the three assault guys, and one porn guy, because of the length of the trial, but less so. He was into kids.

"Thought I'd pass these along. I'm not finished going through all her stories, but my eyes are starting to spin, and I thought it might be a start."

"That's great, Joan," said Charlotte. "Thanks. Let me have them."

Joan gave her the names, spelling them carefully, along with ages and any other descriptions available in the stories. Reporters were amazing at describing the bad guys, whenever possible — their colouring, what they were wearing if they weren't in prison orange, and sometimes, the photographers would win and actually get a picture of a bad guy's face. The accused usually tried to cover their faces with their hands or clothing as they were transported from prison van to courtroom, but once in a while . . . snap.

Charlotte would then be able to search the police database, to see what was up with these particular bad guys — if they were in jail, on parole, or whatever.

"Got it. Thanks, Joan. That's a great start. I'll tell Adam if you like, or do you want to call him?"

"Nope, Char, let him know. I don't want to be hanging out in the boardroom for too long."

"I guess not. Okay, I will let him know. Cheers and hang in there."

"Cheers."

Joan opened the door and tried to sneak out, but almost bumped into one of the journalists, a handsome and Bohemian young man who was looking something up in the atlases located just outside the boardroom door.

"Hi . . ." said Joan a little weakly. "Just making a personal call. Ha ha…"

The journalist just smiled.

Twenty

J ames took Adam's unmarked car. He had looked up Fairbrother's address — which was not publicly listed, but he found it via his driver's licence — but Adam thought it might not be prudent to take his cruiser. He didn't want James to attract any unnecessary attention.

"If I have to go out before you get back, I'll take your car."

"Deal," said James, throwing him the keys, and heading out the door. Then he went back.

"Adam, there's another thing. The receptionist at the church office told me someone called the office on Sunday and kind of ranted about the Pride Chorus concert being cancelled. Private number, though. Whoever it was, he was male and refused to leave a message."

"Really?" said Adam. "I'll get on to SaskTel and see if they can find the numbers coming into the office that day. Sunday, you said?" James nodded. "Thanks. You go. I'll deal with the phone thing."

End of March, and the streets were still icy. James had the heat cranked and his big police parka on — sneaking up in an unmarked car was one thing, but he'd have to identify himself if he found Fairbrother, so avoiding the parka was pointless.

Spring seemed very, very far away.

Fairbrother lived in Eastview, a sixties' suburb that had almost become a core area after the city started to really grow, especially to the east. It was not the prettiest part of the city, but wasn't bad either — family bungalows and duplexes were ubiquitous, ranged along street after nesting street. Actually, it was a difficult neighbourhood from a policing point of view. It was so hard to find one's way around, with every street starting with East — East View, East Hill, East Heights, East This, East That.

Sure enough, it took a while to find it. After several wrong turns, James finally pulled up across the street and two houses down from Fairbrother's bungalow. He got out of the car, looked both ways and up the street, then crossed to the other side, taking in the tenor of the block. Mid-range housing, mostly well-kept. He absorbed every detail of his surroundings, which was partly what made him a great cop: full attention, curiosity, awareness of the environment.

Fairbrother's place was, simply, ugly and basic. It had aging, peeling wood siding, painted half white and half blue many, many years ago by the look of it. The driveway was shovelled, but otherwise the yard — even under its snow blanket — seemed unkempt. Unloved.

James was on the cracked front step and peering through the long, skinny window alongside the door. He couldn't see a thing inside. Neither could he see through the filthy front windows, largely because the shades were drawn. He saw no light, heard no sound, and wondered if the man was home.

James rang the doorbell, heard it chime inside, and waited. And rang it again.

Then he knocked hard and called out Fairbrother's name. Nothing.

James stomped down the three front steps and headed around the back, opening the gate gingerly in case of a large dog, which was unlikely since he had heard no barking. The back yard was as nasty as the front, but produced neither homeowner nor clue to his whereabouts. Still, James walked around the house to the side yard, and then returned to the back door, where he knocked again.

Then James called Adam.

"Adam, there's no one here. Well, at least, no one's answering to my repeated knocking and doorbell ringing. What do you want me to do? I was thinking of leaving a note in the mailbox or potentially breaking down the door," said James, frustration in his voice.

"Maybe the first option is better," suggested Adam, chuckling. "Worth a shot."

"Okay. Will do."

James returned to the warmth of Adam's car to write the note with ink that actually flowed from the pen instead of scratching frozenly across the notepad. He returned to the house, popped the note in the mailbox, and turned to leave.

Just as he did so, he saw a shadow against the drawn shades. Just for a second. He turned back and hammered on the door again. "Mr. Fairbrother!" he shouted. "Police. Please open the door."

But no one came to the door. The shadow had disappeared.

James gave the door one more frustrated bang with his fist. "I will be back, you know," he said loudly to the door, and left.

———————————

"He was there, Adam. I'm sure of it," James said, wrapping up his description of what had happened.

He and Adam were in Adam's office, holding hot cups of coffee in their hands. Adam contemplated this information, and what to do next.

"At some point, this man is going to have to speak to us again, and it looks like we may have to force him. I'll see if I can get a warrant. I did tell him to notify us if he had to leave town. What do we know about this Fairbrother, anyway?" asked Adam.

"Not a heck of a lot. Brown hair, blue eyes, five foot nine, as you could see in the interview. That could be me, give an inch or two. Father Campbell — I called him again, by the way — said he has worked in the office for about five years; that fits with what Fairbrother said. Before that, he was somewhere in southern Saskatchewan. Born in Ontario. Has a weird education history — tried theology but didn't finish, then English lit, then computer science, of all things."

"Interesting. Plus that awful house. Do you think he might be a gaming addict or something? Some other computer-related addiction? Might explain the condition of his property."

"I guess it's possible. The thought did occur to me that he might be short on money, more than the addiction thing. But either way works."

"We need this guy to explain exactly how that concert got cancelled," said Adam. "We can't really move forward until we have that information nailed down. The concert cancellation may or may not be connected to the bishop's murder, but we need to know.

"I'll get some paperwork moving on a warrant, see if a judge salutes. I'll try to persuade the court that

149

this guy might be a suspect, even though we have no grounds. But it might work."

After James left his office, Adam's mind turned to Grace. I have to see her again, he thought. The idea was irresistible. And dangerous.

Grace lay in her hospital bed, staring miserably out her window, thinking about what Hope had said the day before.

Adam is not Melissa, or Mick. How did she know that? But Grace felt it, too. This man was different. Did that mean he could be trusted?

She wondered how he felt about her; Hope certainly thought he was interested, but he couldn't really say or do anything to confirm that. Fraternizing with witnesses and suspects and victims was not on, for an ethical cop. Grace wouldn't want Adam, or any other cop, to be anything other than ethical.

And suddenly, there he was. Grace sensed him a split second before he knocked on the door, and quietly announced himself.

"Grace, it's Adam Davis. Is it okay to come in?"

"Of course. Come in, Adam. Sergeant." She still wasn't sure what to call him.

He swung the door open and Grace caught her breath in a little gasp. In casual weekend clothing, he was even more attractive, and sexier, than on work days. She could see the muscles in his chest and arms through the long-sleeved T-shirt that skimmed his body.

"How are you feeling?" asked Adam, drawing up a chair.

"I'm okay, thanks. Bored. I hope I'm going to get out of here soon. How is the case going? Well, cases, I suppose."

"Okay. We're working on a warrant, to check out one of the suspects in the bishop's murder. And we've made some progress on the stories you've written; I'll bring those files by as soon as they're ready. I just wanted to see if you'd thought of anyone or anything else, after we talked."

It was a weak excuse to visit. But Adam needed a case-related reason to meet with a witness.

Grace shook her head.

"No. There are so many. I think I'd remember many of them if I re-read the stories, but taken whole, it's just a blur. I'm sorry, I wish I could be more help."

"You've been all kinds of help. All witnesses should be reporters," said Adam, smiling at her. "And as brave as you are, too. I appreciate it."

"Me? Brave?" said Grace. "I took one look at the poor dead bishop and threw up."

"Grace," said Adam, looking at her intently. "Most people would have thrown up, but then they would also have screamed and run out of the church, and made a mess of the crime scene while they were at it. They sure as hell wouldn't have been taking notes until the police arrived, and then coherently explained what happened. And now you've been bashed up, too, with no complaint every time we come and ask you questions."

"That's lovely of you to say. Thank you," said Grace, and meant it. It did make her feel a lot better, and not as useless, lying there in the hospital.

"No. It's just the truth. You're a great reporter, Grace; all the prosecutors and the officers say so. How did you decide to become a journalist?"

151

"It was a bit of a tough call, at first. My parents are lawyers. There's a very strange fiscally conservative-socially democratic vibe in our house," she said wryly. "Dad is always taking on pro bono cases, for people who need it, but charges other people extra-big bucks to support his freebie habit. Luckily he's good enough to get away with it.

"Mom worked for Legal Aid for years. I considered law, but I thought I could change the world with my pen, more widely than one case at a time as a lawyer. Idealistic, I know. But I always loved writing, and was really nosy, even as a little kid."

"What does Hope do?" Adam asked.

"She's a social worker. David's the one who is following the parents into law; he's articling right now. And Paul was . . ." Grace stopped. She hadn't intended to mention him. It was still so painful. But he was in her heart and mind.

"Paul?" prompted Adam.

"Paul was going to be an engineer but ended up wanting to be a minister," said Grace quickly, then diverted the conversation. "Why did you become a police officer?"

Adam looked surprised at the quick shift, considering Grace was talking about someone called Paul. What happened to him? Adam let it go, since Grace obviously didn't want to discuss him.

"I always admired the RCMP officers out where I grew up," he said, slowly. "They were pretty cool with us, the kids in the district. And they saved my mother's life, or at least saved her from serious injury. I thought that was the greatest thing someone could do."

"They saved your mother's life?" asked Grace. "What happened?"

He hesitated, and looked down.

"You don't have to tell me," said Grace softly, seeing the expression on his face darken. It was clearly a tough memory, as Paul was for her.

"No, it's okay." Adam took a breath. "Mom was in the kitchen one day; I was thirteen, and my sister Jen was ten. We were upstairs, just doing kid stuff. Dad was away; he was really into farm politics then — still is, really —and was at the rural municipalities association meeting in Regina.

"I heard a clattering noise downstairs, and then I heard Mom give this sort of strangled cry. I went into the upstairs hallway, and I heard a man's voice asking if she was alone, and she said yes. It wasn't true; we were home. Hell," said Adam, who looked like he was reliving the awful day. Grace's heart was pounding in sympathy; she wanted to throw her arms around him.

"There was a phone upstairs," Adam finally continued. "Dad always said, if something ever happens, call the RCMP first, unless it's a fire. Then get the hell out first. So I called them. I told Jen to get under the bed and be quiet. She was so scared. I guess I was, too.

"I crawled into Dad's closet and found his rifle; it was heavy for me at the time, but the only gun I could find upstairs. Farmers always have guns, and they're usually loaded, as I'm sure you know.

"I went downstairs and saw a man trying to — well, assaulting my mother. She was fighting him off. She was incredible; so brave, so determined. But he was stronger. I didn't know what to do, so I shot the rifle into the air. Made a hell of a hole in the kitchen ceiling.

"It shocked him. He wasn't expecting me, or the rifle, so he stopped going after my mom and turned around, just long enough for me to point the gun at him. I held it on him until the RCMP arrived; I couldn't shoot him, because the gun was too heavy for accuracy, and I could have hit my mother. He was half-hiding behind her. But the police arrived really quickly, considering we lived on a farm. They took the jerk away, and even comforted my mother. I wanted to be like those guys."

Grace was staring at Adam, tears in her eyes.

"You were the hero, Adam," she said. "They just had the power to arrest him."

"It was Mom, really, who was heroic," said Adam, looking a little sheepish after telling the long, emotional story — and embarrassed about being called a hero. "Afterward, she hugged me and then went up and got Jen, and hugged her too, and told us she was fine, it was going to be okay. She would get better locks and an alarm system — and actually use them.

"She told us not to worry. She was so brave. She didn't fall apart; nothing was different after that. I don't know if I've ever met anyone with more grace under fire."

Grace's eyes widened as she heard him use her name as a descriptor. Had he noticed what he had said?

He had.

"Except you, apparently, Grace under fire."

He said the two final words as if they were her surname, then looked down again. And Grace was not under, but on fire. Those six words exploded the restraint she was trying to apply to her feelings. She had no idea what to say in response to Adam's opinion of her, or the favourable comparison to a mother he viewed as heroic. Grace simply held out her hand to him; he took it in his, and looked up. They stared at each another, breath coming hard. Until a nurse walked in.

"I'd better get going," said Adam, roughly, suddenly, standing up and nearly knocking over the chair. "Goodbye, Grace. I hope you're able to go home soon."

"Me too," she said, quietly, pulling the shreds of her composure back together. She had almost lost it, almost reached for him — whether to comfort him or feel his body against hers, she wasn't entirely sure. Both, perhaps. "Goodbye, Adam."

As he stumbled out the door and down the hallway, it began to make sense why Grace was affecting him, mind and body.

He thought she was beautiful — her surprising colouring, her silky skin, her modulated voice, her lovely figure. Admitting fully to himself that she was physically moving him, it was something more.

She did remind him a bit of his mother. Grace didn't look anything like Elizabeth Davis, who was dark like Adam and quite petite — Adam got his height from his father — but Grace had Elizabeth's dignity, courage and warm reserve, although Grace was far more outgoing.

Adam loved his mother dearly and admired her enormously. Now he saw some of her qualities in Grace.

When he met her at the cathedral, the crazy night she stumbled on the bishop's body, she didn't cry or scream or try to throw her arms around him, or anyone else. Adam experienced that on the job constantly — women, mainly, flinging themselves at him in melodramatic terror or feigned appreciation — and he always found it disconcerting and inappropriate; even, sometimes, revolting.

155

He was absolutely open to comforting a victim, but the excuse to touch him intimately was just dishonest.

It happened to him for the first time after a friend died in a farming accident; they were only seventeen. Adam was devastated by Bobby's death. They had spent a lot of time together, working and playing, over the years.

The day after the funeral, Bobby's very pretty, very popular girlfriend found Adam alone in the barn, threw her arms around him and tried to kiss him. "I always wanted you, Adam," she breathed in his ear.

He disentangled himself, pushed her away and told her he wasn't ready for any kind of relationship, then walked as quickly as he could to the house. How could she do something like that, so soon after Bobby died? he wondered. Later, he justified her actions to himself: she was just lonely, grief-stricken and confused, and needed affection.

It was many years ago, but that sensation of Jilly entering his space without question — not caring how he felt about her, or about Bobby's death — followed him into adulthood. It disgusted him that she could shift from Bobby to him, in a matter of days after his fatal accident.

Jilly, of the pretty face, heavy makeup and the jangling earrings, made a lasting impression. He had, in desperation, opened up to that kind of attention during his months of heavy drinking; but remembering it now, it sickened him. He hated how he had responded in those dark days. It was as dishonest as the minor-crime victims throwing themselves into his arms.

But Grace, with her beautiful face and unruly curls, her soft heart and remarkable composure, made him want her, in ways he couldn't act upon. What the hell was he going to do?

Twenty-one

SaskTel, the province's main telecommunications company and a Crown corporation, came through. In Adam's experience, they were pretty great at responding to police requests.

In his email Monday morning, Adam found a list of about twenty calls that had come to the church office the weekend the bishop was killed. Well, that's not too bad, he thought. At least it wasn't hundreds, like it sometimes was. I'll get James on this later today.

Meanwhile, he was preparing to hit up the court for an arrest warrant. The Crown prosecutor had set up a date for ten o'clock before Judge Mary Sutherland, and Adam was trying to work out whether she'd bite. She was a good judge, very balanced, but you never knew if she was going to side with your warrant or with the suspect's rights. They only wanted to talk to Fairbrother; there was no evidence against him at all. Indeed, thought Adam, why the hell would Fairbrother want to hurt his bishop? It didn't make any sense.

But they needed answers, and for those, they needed him. Was he dodging them? It sure seemed that he was, based on James' experience at his house; but he

157

had come in for an interview, willingly. Maybe he was sick or something.

He picked up his black leather bag with all of his information in it, pulled on his warm police parka, checked his face in the little mirror to make sure he was cleanly shaven and tidy — he always had an extra razor in his desk — and went out to meet the Crown prosecutor, stopping at James's desk on the way.

"Hey, James. I'm just heading to court with Sanj. Can I dump these numbers on you? SaskTel coughed up the list this morning," said Adam, dropping off a printout.

"Sure. I'm almost excited. We could use a break here," said James. "Good luck with the judge."

"Thanks. I think we're going to need it."

James wrapped up the report he was working on — it was the arson case that came up the same day the bishop was killed — and sent a copy of it to Adam by email. Then he grabbed the printout of the numbers that had called the church office the previous Sunday.

Five seconds later, James froze. Ten numbers down the list, staring him in the face, was his own home number.

The landline number he shared with Bruce Stephens, the love of his life.

Sweat suddenly pouring down his face, his mind whirling out of control, James wheeled around in his chair and vomited into the wastebasket.

Charlotte heard the upheaval from the other side of the room.

"Oh, honey," she said, hurrying over. "What's up? Do you have the stomach flu? Maybe you should go home."

James lifted his head and gasped out a "sorry." Pale, sweating and shaking, he did look like a victim of the worst possible stomach virus.

"I'm okay . . . I think. Yeah, maybe I should take a couple of hours and see how I feel," he said, wiping his face. He took the glass of water Charlotte offered. "Thanks, Char."

He grabbed the wastebasket but Charlotte stopped him. "No, no. That's what we have cleaning staff for. They've tidied up worse, as you know. Get out of here."

"Thanks, Char. Can you tell Adam I've gone, and I'll call him in a couple of hours?"

"You bet. Get," she said, with a gentle shove.

James staggered out of the station, with the printout in his jacket's breast pocket, and took a big lungful of the cold, crisp air.

Bruce had called the church office. It appeared that he had been lying all along — or at least not telling the whole truth, which was just as bad. Bruce was, again, officially the prime suspect as of five minutes ago.

It was incredible, but there was their number, in black and white, on that fucking printout.

James walked down to the riverbank, freezing as he went, but not really caring. Finally, after he managed to control his shaking, he pulled his cellphone out. Bruce answered.

"Hello, beautiful," he said. "Don't often hear from you during a shift. I hope you're calling to invite me out for lunch."

"No. Don't think I could eat anything. I need to see you. Somewhere private. Can you dash home?"

"I guess I could, sure. At noon? What's up?" asked Bruce, hearing the strain in James's voice.

"I'd rather not say until I see you. Like I said, private."

"You have me worried."

"Yeah, well . . ." James trailed off.

"Okay. See you at home. At noon. Love you."

James hung up. He walked back to the car, drove to a convenience store, and slugged back half a litre of ginger ale.

Then he drove home and brushed his teeth, and waited for Bruce to come.

Bruce strode through the doorway, wearing a perfectly tailored dark blue suit, white shirt, and blue-and-purple tie, topped with a navy wool coat worn open and swinging behind him. James's heart lurched, as it often did when he saw Bruce. He was so gorgeous. So elegant. So sexy.

"James," said Bruce, fingering off his black leather gloves and pulling off his coat. "Come on. I can see something is wrong and I could hear it in your voice. Now tell me. I'm here."

He tried to embrace James, but James just shook his head, regretfully. He pointed to the printout on the table.

"Take a look at that," he told Bruce. "You will notice that our phone number is on this list. Our phone number. Oh, my God," he stopped, and cleared his throat.

"This is a list of all the numbers — twenty of them — that called the cathedral office on Sunday," James continued. "The day the bishop was killed. And the owner of one of the numbers ranted at the receptionist, and wouldn't give his name or his number. He was mad that the concert was cancelled. And that particular call may have come from our home."

Bruce stared at the printout.

"Damn."

"What do you mean, damn? Did you do this? Did you think I wouldn't find out?"

Bruce closed his eyes and took a deep breath. Then he looked straight into James's eyes. "It wasn't me."

"Really. I suppose it was Eiffel." Eiffel was their dog, acquired after a particularly romantic trip to Paris.

Bruce smiled sadly, knowing that James was not trying to be funny. The situation was really awful.

"Tell me the truth, Bruce."

Bruce sat down, hard. He had a tough decision to make, and he had to make it quickly. Protect a loved one and lie to another, or endanger that loved one and tell the truth? James was a police officer. Whatever Bruce said right now, it wasn't going to be off the record, even with his spouse.

Truth won. Bruce looked down, and said, "it was Dad."

"Frank?" asked James, gratuitously. "What the hell? What did he think he was doing?"

"Dad was here — you were at work, remember? You had the weekend shift . . . "

"Obviously, since I identified the bishop."

"I was in the kitchen making coffee, and had just told Dad about the concert. He lost it. He was terribly angry. I told him, I can take care of this, I'm an adult, and I can take care of myself. But he wouldn't listen. So I went into the kitchen and waited for him to calm down. I heard him talking, but couldn't really hear the words; when he started yelling, I went back into the living room, and he was slamming down the phone."

"Then what? Did you ask him what was going on?"

"Yes. He just said he had given the church a piece of his mind. I told him that was unnecessary, but then we dropped it."

"That's it?"

"That's it."

"Why didn't you tell me, Bruce? You know how it looks that our phone number is on that list? And now Frank was the angry caller. Shit."

"Look at it from my point of view, James. To me, it was just Dad doing his usual thing. I wish he hadn't, and it's embarrassing, but how would it ever occur to me that this would turn into a big thing?"

James mulled that over, and his stomach quietened.

"I'm going to have to tell Adam, Bruce. I'm sorry. But I'm going to have to. Besides, he already has the phone numbers. He just hasn't had time to look at them. I don't want him finding out on his own."

"I know, James. And I'm sorry too. I just didn't see the issue at the time. I suppose I should have."

"No. I see why you didn't. And that didn't occur to me. Try not to worry . . . we'll get through this."

James stood up and walked over to Bruce, who was looking at his hands unhappily. He pulled Bruce to his feet and wrapped his arms around him tightly. Bruce responded to the hug, and they stood like that, quietly, in their kitchen, absorbing comfort from each other.

After a while, the phone call and the father were forgotten. The heat started to rise, as it never failed to do when they embraced, and James said into Bruce's neck, "I do love you. So much. I can't stand the thought of something happening to you. Like, jail."

"I love you, beautiful," said Bruce, undoing James's shirt and running his hands over the hard, muscular abdomen that never ceased to amaze him, and fire his senses.

"And I'm not going to jail. I'm staying here with you. Although, maybe not right here. The bedroom would be better."

James, by now having trouble breathing, started down the hallway, Bruce in tow. He would worry about telling Adam later.

Adam and Sanjeev Kumar, the Crown prosecutor, got what they wanted.

Judge Mary Sutherland, after a significant amount of convincing, granted them the arrest warrant to gather up Ellice Fairbrother, under the presumption that he could be a suspect, despite the lack of evidence.

Sanj had successfully made the point that they didn't know if he was a suspect because they couldn't gather crucial points of evidence if they couldn't find him. His evidence was an important part of finding the bishop's murderer; his previous evidence did not line up with the priest's; and besides, the entire political and law enforcement upper echelon was up in arms about a murderer running around free.

He also made the point that there was a reporter lying in a hospital bed who could also be dead right now, and just by luck was not; and that the police really had to find out if whoever attacked her also killed the bishop. If so, the guy was dangerous to others. If not, and the bishop's killer had only been interested in murdering him, that would still help solve both cases.

Sutherland told them she was a tad uncomfortable with the whole thing, given the lack of evidence, but she agreed that they made good points. And they were good enough.

"Here," she said, signing the petition. "Go get him. But be careful. Any trampled rights are going to be a particular problem in this case, plus it's a very high profile murder. Whatever you do will go under the microscope, so take care."

Adam thanked Sanj a dozen times between the courthouse and the latter's office. Sanj started to laugh.

"Adam, for God's sake. It's my job and I'm happy to help and I trust you. So quit thanking me." Sanj paused, and regarded Adam for a minute, as they paused outside his office at the Justice Building.

"What's up, man? You have a bug up your ass about this case. I can tell."

"You can?"

"Yes. I can. What's going on?"

Adam sighed. People he didn't even see all that often were finding his behaviour intense. He hadn't really realized it until this minute, but there it was.

"I want to solve this case before anyone else gets hurt."

"Bullshit," said Sanj. "If that's all you want me to know, like I said, I trust you. But if there's something you want to get off your chest, I'm happy to chat. Especially if it helps with this case. You're not the only one getting pressure, you know."

"It's only been — well, just over a week, for Christ's sake. Really?"

"The bloody Bishop of Saskatoon has been murdered, Adam. It's a big deal, and people want this solved yesterday."

"I know, I know. I'm working on it. So thanks for the warrant, Sanj. I'll stay in touch."

"Okay, Adam. Please do."

Adam walked back to the station, stewing in his many juices, and unaware that things were going to get even more complicated, immediately.

"Adam," said Charlotte as he appeared, "James is sick. Caught him vomiting. Might be stomach flu. He said he'd call in a couple of hours with a barf update, and that was a couple of hours ago, so you should hear from him soon. If he can talk."

"Thanks, Char."

"Did you get that warrant?"

"We did. I'm pretty stoked. This should move things along."

Back in his office, Adam started writing a memo to get everyone on shift — to the extent possible — into the squad room. It was time for an update, and to spread the word about the warrant. Then his phone rang.

"Adam, it's James."

"How the hell are you? Heard you were throwing up. Are you feeling any better? You don't sound too bad."

"I'm mostly feeling better. Just wanted to tell you I'll be back in the office in half an hour, so you didn't wonder. See you soon."

"Don't come in here, goddammit, if you're going to give me some life-sucking virus. That's all I need."

James burst out laughing. "Don't worry, Sarge. It's not a virus. Be in soon."

James hung up, rolled over, and kissed Bruce on the chest. "That was amazing. But I have to go in."

"You should have a shower first, beautiful. You reek like sex."

"Do I?" asked James, sniffing.

"Yes. Definitely. I probably do, too. Come on. Let's get wet."

James's body was humming from the thorough going-over Bruce had just given him. It was pretty clear that Bruce was trying to make amends over the non-mentioning of Frank's phone call, so James had his full attention. It was hard to concentrate, with endorphins surging through his brain cells.

"Hey, Adam," said James, knocking on the open door to Adam's office as he walked in. "Can I come in?"

"Looks like you already did," said Adam. "You're doing okay?"

"Physically, yes," said James. Adam didn't know the half of that. "But I have something to tell you.

"That angry call to the church office — the reason why we got the call printout — it came from our house." James held up a hand as he saw Adam's face darken and his mouth open to say something. Probably very loudly.

"Please, Adam. Let me finish. Apparently on that Sunday, Bruce's dad, Frank, was over — I was on shift, as you know — and Bruce told him about the concert being cancelled. They had some words, then Bruce went to make coffee; and Frank, in a fit, called the church office and in his words, he gave them a piece of his mind. It looks pretty awful, though, that my phone number, and Bruce's, is on that list."

"Holy shit, James. Well, we — let me rephrase that. I, not we, will have to get Mr. Stephens in here. And you will make yourself scarce. Dammit. We're going to have to take you off parts of this case, James. There's conflict here, at least until Frank is, hopefully, cleared. Worse yet, we can't really prove it was Frank who called," he added, feeling a bit sick and suddenly understanding why James had vomited and headed home.

"I know. Can I still try to find Fairbrother?"

Adam thought about that for a minute. "I don't know yet," he said. "I'll have to think about it. On the bright side, we got the warrant."

"You did!? That's great." Then James visibly deflated like a punctured tire. "Well, let me know what you decide."

"Did you give Bruce hell for not telling you?" asked Adam, then rethought that question. "Sorry; I shouldn't have asked that. Never mind."

"It's okay, Adam. I did. But I kind of see it from his point of view — it didn't really occur to him that it was a huge deal. He just felt embarrassed that his father would call the church, sort of on his behalf, as if he were a bullied ten-year-old and his dad was calling the school."

"Yeah, I guess I see that. I'll find Frank. Why don't you catch up with Charlotte, for now, and see where she's at with these perps Grace used to write about? Char's pretty busy. She might need some help. It'll keep your hand in without compromising the case. Just until I talk to Frank. Okay?"

"Okay," said James. "Thanks, Adam."

Hell, thought Adam. Bloody hell. Relationships made these cases twice as complicated, as the Frank Stephens fiasco showed. Even he had gone too far, at the hospital, spilling his guts to Grace. Getting too close. Somehow, she just drew him out. She was so sympathetic, so beautiful . . .

Well, that all of that had to stop. It was just too complicated.

Twenty-two

Adam remembered what Grace had said, the day they shared coffee and a walk to the police station. Frank had called her after the first story ran, and congratulated her, and suggested that she had had a long Sunday night. He was now very worried that Frank Stephens had much more to do with this case than they originally thought.

Adam called Stephens and asked him to please come down to the police station at his earliest convenience, unless he wanted a police cruiser to pick him up. Right now.

Adam was angry. This was such a stupid situation, with his best officer's father-in-law, basically, involved in a murder investigation. You've got to be kidding, he thought. He wanted to get this interview over with.

Frank showed up pretty quickly, disinterested — as Adam knew he would be — in having a police car turn up outside his home. Charlotte showed him into the interview room.

"Mr. Stephens. Thanks for coming down. Please, have a chair."

Frank sat.

Adam turned on the tape recorder and said the date, time, his name and Stephens' name into the device.

"I understand, Mr. Stephens, that you're the father of Bruce Stephens, a member of the Pride Chorus, and that the chorus had its concert cancelled at St. Eligius. Can you please tell me how you reacted to that, and what you did about it."

Frank cleared his throat. He already knew from Bruce about the phone number showing up on a list of calls to the church office, so there was little point in diverging from the truth.

"I called the church office. I was angry. It's hard having a gay kid, much of the time. He may be grown up, but he's still my kid. I gave them a piece of my mind."

Adam made an effort not to smile. He had heard that "piece of my mind" phrase three times now, in the last few hours.

"When you say 'them,' to whom did you speak?"

"I think it was the receptionist. She told me the priest and bishop were out, but that she would take a message."

"But you did not leave your name or phone number. Why is that?"

"I didn't want to tell her who I was. I just wanted to talk to someone in authority."

"If you don't leave your name, they can't call you back."

"I don't know. I decided not to."

Adam suspected he felt embarrassed after losing his temper on the phone. Unless, of course, he was the killer and didn't want to leave his name.

"And what did you say to the receptionist, Mr. Stephens?"

"I told her that the church was messed up and asked her how they dared cancel the choir's concert. She said she knew nothing about that. I — I guess I asked her if she was an idiot or something. Then she offered to take a message. That was about it."

"Did you threaten her in any way?"

"I told her I would come down there and have it out with the priest and bishop. Give them a piece of my mind."

Adam's eyes widened. Jesus.

"And did you?"

Frank paused, and looked around — a little wildly. Adam, alarmed, asked the question again.

"Mr. Stephens, did you go down to the office or the cathedral and confront the bishop?"

"Yes," he said, quietly.

"Could you please speak up for the tape, Mr. Stephens," said Adam, getting that sick feeling again.

"Yes. I did."

"And when was that?"

"Sunday afternoon."

"Did you find the bishop at the cathedral?" asked Adam, knowing the bishop had been there hearing confessions.

"Yes."

"Did you, indeed, give him a piece of your mind?"

"No."

"Did you change your mind about it? Why didn't you?"

"Because he was dead."

Adam was not expecting that. Shocked, he reared back, speechless for a moment. "Mr. Stephens. You better give me the entire story, chapter and verse. Let's have it."

—————————————————————

Adam called James, who was in the police library, and asked him to come to his office.

"Brace yourself," he told James. "Frank Stephens was at the cathedral on Sunday. Come down and I'll tell you about it."

"Oh, my God. He wasn't. Really? Is he a suspect?"

"Damn right he is. What a stupid thing to do. Either that, or murderous. Take your pick."

When James arrived, Adam told him what Stephens had said.

"So, claims Stephens, he gets to the cathedral ready to let it rip. It's dark in there, and he goes in calling for the bishop anyway — just steaming pissed, I gather. He's storming down the aisle shouting, 'Halkitt! Get out here!' And he stumbles on the body. Just like Grace did — maybe fifteen to thirty minutes before, if he had the timing right."

"And he didn't tell anyone," sighed James. "Why not?"

"He was afraid. He thought that if we found out about the phone call, and then about him being at the church, we'd think he was the killer.

"And he's right. And he could be. We can't discount the idea, James. Almost anyone is capable of a crime of passion."

"How did he get the monstrance, then? And where is it now, if he did it?"

"I haven't worked that out. Maybe the monstrance was still on the altar? Someone had forgotten to lock it up? As to where it might be now, it could be in his house, or in a shallow grave in his yard, or in the South Saskatchewan River. Who knows."

James closed his eyes. Adam was betting that James didn't want to tell Bruce his father was a suspect.

The afternoon wore on. James was reading the bishop's biography, to the extent it had been put together thus far. There were no red flags, no investigations by the church or the state, no newspaper stories apart from announcements regarding his various appointments and his rise within the church.

His colleagues were out looking for Ellice Fairbrother. Adam was doing sergeant things. Saskatoon didn't stop churning just because the department of detectives was obsessed with a murder case.

James looked up and saw Charlotte flying by. Mother Superior of the Saskatoon Police Service. She was really moving.

He leaped from his chair and followed her, right into Adam's office.

"….think I found something, Sarge," was what James caught of the end of her sentence.

"Yay," said Adam, unenthusiastically. He was feeling down about the case, which a week and a half on felt glacial, progress-wise. "I'll take any news right now."

"Can I listen in?" asked James, strolling into the room and sitting down before hearing the answer.

"Sure," said Adam, resignedly. He didn't have the heart to boot James out of his office. "Charlotte. What have you got?"

"Well, I've been phoning around Westmoreland, that southern Saskatchewan town, like you suggested,

Adam. It turns out that the bishop, who was a priest and teacher at the time, was accused of inappropriately corresponding with a ten-year-old boy."

"What? Holy shit — that didn't come out in our research," said Adam.

"No, because it never led to charges. According to my source, the parents of the boy accused Halkitt — the boy himself did not believe it was the bishop — and the RCMP looked into it. I'm still fuzzy on the details, but I have the parents' number. Just haven't reached them yet."

"Who's your source?"

"Previous RCMP officer, who handled Westmoreland cases at the time. Retired now. He doesn't have his notes any more, but said he thought he recalled that they switched their investigation from Halkitt to someone else, but never found him. Or her. The letter the boy received was signed with Halkitt's initial, but it was typed, so there was doubt about its origin. You know how priests have been accused, rightly and wrongly, of child abuse."

"How old would that boy be now?"

"Maybe twenty-five? I don't know if he is at home with his parents any more — kind of doubt it — but hopefully I'll find all of this out soon. Thought I'd dash in and tell you what I knew right away. And there's more."

"More! Charlotte, you are amazing. Bring it on. Tell me."

"That church secretary we're having trouble finding for a second interview. Fairbrother. He was a deacon in Westmoreland while Halkitt was serving there."

There's an old saying about a penny dropping. An entire coin bank unloaded its contents into Adam's brain.

The expression on his face, closely related to joy, was enough praise for Charlotte, whose own face widened into a huge smile.

"You're welcome, Sarge," said Charlotte.

Adam stood up, walked over to Charlotte and hugged her.

Twenty-three

J ames. We have to find out if Howard Halkitt was gay."

"Yes, Adam," responded James, looking up at his sergeant leaning over the carrel's wall. I'm on it."

"And we have to find out what was in that letter."

"Yep. Got it."

"I think we may have to hit the road to Westmoreland. Make sure the parents of that kid are home, though, before we go. I'll call Father Campbell, and see what he knows."

Adam was fairly sure he now knew the motive for the murder. He was quite certain it had something to do with the bishop's sexual identity, active or celibate, perceived or real.

That, however, meant he did not know who had attacked Grace. He was now quite sure it was not the bishop's killer, although the motivation for her attack was not precisely clear in his mind. It absolutely had to do with her story the day after the murder.

Joan Karpinski, who was keeping an eye on Lacey McPhail, had provided Charlotte with some names. It was time to show them to Grace.

Speaking of Grace, was she still in the hospital? He would have to find out. Easy enough, since there was still a twenty-four-hour watch on her. What would it be like to see her after that intense conversation, the last time he visited her?

Plus, Adam realized he was a little embarrassed. He was worried that Grace might think he was an idiot, after downloading the story of the attack on his mother on her — maybe she thought he was seeking sympathy? — and not seeing his role in it. But he hadn't. It was Grace who made it clear to the thirteen-year-old boy inside him.

He steeled himself. Hard as it was, he absolutely had to keep his distance. He had to remain professional.

Grace, in fact, was going home.

Dr. Bergen was sending her off with a smaller bandage on her head, and detailed instructions on how to care for her bruised clavicle. She was also going to see a nurse every day from Home Care.

Hope had already signed up to come at dinner time — it was high time she got back to work — and of course the policewoman would be standing guard. Grace still hadn't met her guard, and figured now might be good.

"Do you feel ready to go home, Grace?" asked the doctor. "I mean, this has been nasty, but I can't keep you much longer, since you're doing so well. Still, it doesn't have to be today, either."

"I think I'm ready. I would really love to go home, and I don't feel all that awful.

"Besides, I am not sure I can handle the food here one more day. No, make that one more meal."

177

The doctor made distracted sympathetic noises as she continued with a final checkup. "Mmm. Ugh. Yes. Well. Disgusting. Yes."

Laughter burbled in Grace's chest. Her doctor was so funny and human. She really liked her.

After getting her dressed, the nurses helped Grace into a wheelchair, and took her downstairs, where Hope and David were waiting with David's car in the loading zone.

"I'm going home!" she exulted to her siblings.

"We know!" said Hope in exactly the same tone, teasingly. "Come and get in the car," she added, taking one of Grace's arms as David took the other.

"And we're glad, honey," said Hope. "We're so glad you're okay."

It was Tuesday. Grace had been in the hospital for six days — long enough to know that it was a good thing she hadn't become a medical professional. Even if she could stand the blood and vomit and screaming patients, she couldn't stand the food, especially the smell of it. She couldn't wait to get home, and then, hopefully soon, back to work.

They rolled up in front of her tiny bungalow, followed closely by the policewoman in an unmarked car, and in plain clothes. Where were they going to put her? Grace hoped they had figured that out.

Hope and David walked Grace in, helped her to get settled in front of the TV in her living room, and then investigated the refrigerator. David had gone through the box a couple of days before, worrying about soft fruit and rotting meat, but it needed another going over. They made a list: bread, milk, eggs, fruit, vegetables, cheese and a few other staples, and showed it to Grace.

"Whaddya think?" asked Hope. "Will this get you through?"

"You bet. Thank you, you guys, so much. Hey, when are Mom and Dad getting home?"

"Next week. Just as well. You know how they would've freaked out at the hospital. They'll probably call tonight."

"Yeah, the first time they called, I wasn't really making sense. I'll calm them down when they call."

"Okay, we're off. Will return with groceries and if you're lucky, a possible bottle of wine. If you promise to have just one glass," said David.

"Cross my heart," said Grace, doing the motion. "See you soon. Thanks again."

Grace turned on the TV, but felt too restless to watch it. It hurt her shoulder to do too much, but she decided a cup of tea might be good. Better than water, which was the only other thing to drink in the entire house. First, she stopped in the bathroom . . . where she caught a glimpse of her face.

It was paler and thinner than it had been just a week ago; her revulsion over hospital food hadn't helped. Her eyes looked enormous and haunted; her hair seemed redder than usual in contrast with her pale face, and the bruises on her cheek and upper chest were ghastly against her white skin.

God, thought Grace, woozily staring at her reflection in the mirror. I look awful. At least I can eat again, after Hope and David get back with food.

Heading for the kitchen, she wondered where the policewoman was, and peered out the window — where she saw her on the sidewalk, talking to Adam Davis.

Grace's stomach turned over. Or was that her heart? Her natural vanity returned in a flash, and she wasn't sure she wanted Adam to see her looking like this — pale, sick, dressed in not-very-clean sweats. In the hospital was one thing — couldn't be avoided, of course — but now? Yet there he was, nodding at the policewoman, striding up the path to the house. Like it or not, here he comes, thought Grace.

He knocked on the door. Grace hesitated. Maybe she should pretend she was asleep? Or too sick to stand up? There was some truth to that . . .

She opened the door, and her legs nearly didn't hold her up. Looking at Adam standing in her own doorway, she wasn't sure she was going to make it through another investigative, or even personal, chat. That last conversation in the hospital had changed things. Profoundly, if she was honest.

"Hello, Sergeant," said Grace, aware of the policewoman and therefore using his title. She was weaving just a bit. "Would you like to come in?"

"May I? How are you feeling? Do you think you have the energy to look at some names?" he asked, stepping in.

"Um. Sure," Grace answered, after a moment. "Would you like some tea? It's all I have in the house, or I'd offer you something more exciting. Water's on."

"Thanks. That would be nice," he said — distractedly, Grace thought, not knowing he couldn't help gazing into her fathomless eyes, and at her pale, blue and purple face.

She led the way into the kitchen, where the water was just starting to boil, and went about making a pot of black tea.

"So," she said, filling the silence. "Names, you say. Sugar? Honey?"

Adam laughed, breaking the strange tension between them. It sounded like she was asking about people named for sweeteners.

"No, more like Duane and Terry," he said. Grace caught the small joke, and laughed too.

"Who are Duane and Terry?" she asked, setting and slightly spilling mugs of tea on the table, along with both sugar and honey, plus teaspoons.

"They are two of the four bad guys you reported on, that Joan — our police officer in the StarPhoenix newsroom — sorted out of your stories. She thinks there's a chance one of them is your bad guy, for various reasons — timing of release, homophobic attacks, that kind of thing."

Grace blanched, looked down, and felt the hot prick of tears behind her eyes.

"Oh, man. Grace. Are you ready for this?" asked Adam with heavy concern in his voice, leaning forward. "God, I'm sorry. I didn't think."

"I just haven't had much sleep, or any decent food, in about a week — and way too many drugs — so I'm feeling a little weird. Light-headed. Let me take a look," she finished, straightening her shoulders and holding out her hand for the four reports Adam had brought with him.

As she scanned them, he explained further about how Joan had picked these particular people out of her court stories. He was particularly interested in the three men with assault convictions. This Duane Sykes person had beaten someone up outside a bar; the victim lived, but was paralyzed, and Sykes got seven years, serving the whole sentence . . .

Grace looked up to ask a question, but forgot it instantly as her eyes landed on his face, then fell on his mouth. Gazing at his full, remarkably curved lips and the even, white teeth behind them, she stopped hearing the words he was saying; she only heard the thrum of his rich, deep voice. She was falling into him, completely absorbed in his beautiful mouth, remembering the moving things he had said to her in the hospital.

What would his lips feel like? she wondered. Slowly, she leaned forward, reached out with her right hand and gently touched them with her fingertips.

Adam stopped talking. He caught his breath at her touch, and froze.

She leaned forward further, sliding to the very edge of her chair, and ever so lightly, very slowly, just barely touched his lips with hers. Twice. Three times. Then she actually kissed him, gently pressing her lips against his.

Adam's resistance completely gave way.

With a sound he'd never heard himself make, Adam fell to his knees on the hard kitchen floor, pulling Grace off the edge of her chair at the same time. Holding her face between his hands, his long fingers tangled in her curls, he kissed her deeply, wildly, lost in the soft sensations created by her lips and tongue.

Grace burrowed into him, craving the feel of his hard-muscled body. In that moment, Grace was too far gone to remember that Adam was legally off limits, at least until this case was solved. The pain, the hospital stay, the medications and now this ridiculously beautiful man — she felt completely out of control. So here she was, either dreaming or madly kissing Adam Davis on her kitchen floor.

Until, finally, chest heaving, Adam pulled away to look into her eyes.

"Oh, my God, Grace," he breathed, then kissed her again.

Then it hit her.

"Oh, no. What have I done?" said Grace, ending the kiss, rearing back and looking into his eyes. "I'm sorry . . . I didn't mean to complicate your case. Oh, no . . . I just . . . "

". . . let all the animals out of the zoo," he said in a deep growl, pulling her against his chest. His chin was on the top of her head, his hands were running down her back to comfort her. Instead of being comforting, his touch was inflaming.

"I'm sorry, Adam," said Grace, now visibly upset. "And that police officer is right outside — and Hope and David are coming back."

Grace pulled back far enough so she could look into his face, his clear, dark blue eyes. "What is the matter with me?"

"Me, I hope."

"Do it again."

"If I do, I will never leave. I have to solve this case, Grace; for you, and for me, as much as for any other reason. Honestly, Grace, if anyone finds out about . . . this . . . it could seriously be a problem."

He rose slowly to his feet, gently pulling Grace up after him, mindful of her injuries. He lightly touched the bruise on her cheek, and the one on her clavicle.

"And you have to finish healing, and figure out if any of those names on the table mean anything to you," Adam finished.

Grace closed her eyes, briefly, tasting him. Damning him for his ethics, the same ethics she prized in him a day ago.

"I will. Go, before I can't stand it . . . "

He backed away. "I'm going. Please, go through the reports. Talk to your guard when you've finished."

He swallowed hard. "Goodbye, Grace."

Grace nodded goodbye. She was speechless with arousal, exhaustion and wonderment, fearing a flood of tears if she tried to talk. And, she was baffled at her own behaviour, her loss of control. She turned away.

Adam reeled out the door, only to see the policewoman waiting in her unmarked car. He nodded to her, got into his vehicle, and drove away, a little too quickly.

He stopped after a few blocks, got out of the car and doubled over, breathing hard, his entire body stinging. So much for keeping his distance. Grace had his blood raging, and he was going to have to figure out how to live with it.

He also had to figure out how to catch the bishop's killer. That was the main thing, the thing keeping him from Grace — a victim in one of his cases. His witness, and his suspect, in the bishop's murder. Even though that was ridiculous, the rules of engagement said otherwise.

The door was unlocked. Not good. Hope drew her head back, then looked at David, who grimaced and shoved the door open.

"Grace!" he called. No answer.

"Grace!" Hope called. "Where are you?"

No answer. "Let me go look for her," said Hope to David. "She may be in the bathroom or something."

"Luckily there's a cop outside," said David, heading for the kitchen with the groceries.

Hope found Grace, after checking the bathroom, on her knees on the floor of her bedroom, sobbing as if her heart was breaking.

"Oh no, honey, what's wrong? Grace, talk to me," said Hope when Grace didn't answer, rushing to her sister. "You're freaking me out. Are you hurt?"

Hope dropped to her knees, put her arms around Grace and rocked her for a few minutes, waiting for the weeping to subside. "Honey, the door was unlocked, and now you're crying. Tell me what's going on. Are you okay?" asked Hope, anxiously doing a quick scan of what she could see of Grace's body.

"I kissed him," said Grace, through sobs.

"What? You kissed who?" said Hope, immediately knowing who as the question left her lips. "You mean Adam, don't you?"

Grace nodded.

"Honey, why are you crying so hard? Tell me what happened," she said.

"We were sitting in the kitchen having tea, and after a few minutes I leaned over and touched his mouth. Then I kissed him. And then he kissed me."

Hope's eyes widened and flashed. "Why did you do that?"

"I couldn't help it," said Grace. "What the hell is the matter with me?"

"I would have done the same thing," said Hope, soothingly, rubbing Grace's shoulders. Grace reared back, staring at Hope, and found a glimmer of her normal personality.

"You would not."

"No, I wouldn't. I'm just trying to calm you down."

Grace stared at her sister for another moment, then burst into laughter. So did Hope. They laughed so hard they had to lie down on the area rug, until the spasm passed. Gasping for air, Grace put a hand to her shoulder, which was aching from the hilarity.

Finally, Hope said, "So, why did you do that?"

"I don't know. It just happened. Painkillers and feeling really vulnerable, I guess."

"And because Adam, I assume."

"Yes. He's . . . beautiful. But I need to respect the law, and his place in it. I also have to get off these godawful pain meds and back to normal."

"Grace, don't kick yourself so hard. Except, you didn't lock the door behind him, apparently; you have to pay attention, sis. But what's so bad about kissing someone, really?"

"You know what's so bad. He can't be fraternizing with a victim. Or a witness. Or a suspect. I feel terrible."

Hope sighed. "Well, it could've been worse."

"How?" Grace demanded.

"You could have slept with him. Take it easy, honey. You had enough control not to let it go too far. Just for God's sake don't tell anyone else."

"He had enough control," said Grace, bitterly. "Not me. And you don't have to worry about me telling anyone else, or doing that again. I'm pulling it together. Starting right now."

Twenty-four

After taking many deep breaths and walking around the block a few times, Adam got back into his car and distractedly drove around for a while, thinking. He had to focus, get down to doing something, to keep his mind off the encounter with Grace.

As much as possible. Every time she returned to his thoughts, which was constantly, he felt shaken with passion.

That thing she did, touching his lips gently with her fingers, as if asking a question, then kissing him so lightly . . . he had never been so aroused.

It told him, too, that there was an imaginative erotic passion just under this woman's surface, and he wanted it. As much as he admired her composure, he wanted to explode it under his touch. His own imagination couldn't stop returning to a vision of covering Grace with his body, making her writhe, call his name.

He drove back to the station and tried to focus on what was coming up next. He and James were planning their trip to Westmoreland. The parents of the ten-year-old who had received the letter were returning home in a couple of days.

They still hadn't found Fairbrother. If this continued for more than another few hours, he would absolutely get a search warrant for his house, thought Adam viciously. Officers had stopped by again to see if he was home. Again, no one was there. James had called Father Campbell, who said Fairbrother had called in sick a couple of days ago. He hadn't seen him since.

Adam knew he was going to have to visit Sanjeev Kumar, talk about another warrant, and tell him about what had happened with Grace. If it came to light, at least he would have told Sanj. He trusted Sanj. He was an ethical, passionate prosecutor and a good friend. Maybe he'd even have some advice.

Not long after Adam left Grace's bungalow, and while David was unloading groceries in the kitchen, the policewoman out front grabbed her overnight bag and came to the door.

"Hello?" she said, knocking. "It's Constable Painchaud. Denise Painchaud. May I come in?"

David turned and welcomed her in while Hope and Grace emerged from the bedroom, Grace's face puffy from weeping – and laughing so hard.

"Hello, Grace. I'm Denise. I'm moving in, I'm afraid. How are you doing?"

"I'm not too bad, thanks, Denise. This is my sister, Hope, and my brother, David, who are trying to keep me fed."

Nods and nice-to-meet-yous were made all around. The constable offered to make coffee or tea, and perhaps sandwiches?

"That's very nice of you, but David and I can manage," said Hope. "Why don't you settle in? Grace, are you up to showing her the second bedroom?"

"Shurr," said Grace, weaving down the hall. "Follow me."

"Oh, oh," said Hope to David. "She's slurring again. Let me just make sure everything's okay, and then I'll come help you. "

Grace was showing Denise the linen closet, waving toward the bathroom door, and looking like she was going to keel over. Hope caught her as she stumbled.

"You're going to bed, sister. Come on. Let's go."

Grace didn't object. She was exhausted from it all. Leaning on Hope, with the constable right behind, she realized she was completely blasted, and allowed Hope to help her slide under the covers.

"Get some rest, Grace. Please."

"Kay," said Grace. And promptly fell asleep.

Hope led the policewoman to the little second bedroom, and inexplicably began to cry again. The constable turned to Hope and gave her a quick hug.

"I'm sorry, Miss Rampling. I know this has been very hard. But don't worry. I'm here. Grace will be fine."

Hope gave her a shaky smile. "Thank you, constable. That really means a lot to us. I feel much better knowing you're here."

A few hours later, Grace was up and eating a ham and cheese on whole wheat bread, with crisp lettuce and fresh tomatoes, accompanied by homemade iced tea. It was so delicious she could hardly believe it.

Mmmm . . . real food, thought Grace. Concentrate on the food, she told herself. Not Adam.

Denise Painchaud was across the little table from her, also with an iced tea, and both of them were reading the reports Adam had dropped off. Charlotte had attached some of the newspaper clippings of the stories Grace had written.

"Do you recognize the guy you're reading about?" asked Denise after a while.

"Sort of. There were so many, sometimes it's hard to distinguish between them. This guy decided using a blow torch was a great way to get back at a co-worker." Grace shook her head. Even after years on the court beat, she could still be amazed at human behaviour. "Other than that, nothing really leaps out."

They traded files. Grace was now reading about Duane Sykes, the guy who had nearly beaten someone to death outside a downtown bar. There was a partial photo of him published with the story — he hadn't quite been able to cover his face before the photographer snapped a shot of him. Grace did remember him, at least vaguely.

Then a flash of memory slapped Grace into high awareness.

"This one. Duane Sykes. I think he called me from prison."

"Did he? Do you remember what he said?"

"It was quite a while ago, but I think it was the usual thing. It's not all that rare for us to get calls from prisoners. It was about how he didn't deserve to be in jail, and the whole thing was a miscarriage of justice, and the guy he beat up totally deserved it, that kind of thing.

"He wanted me to write another story about him; he said he understood why I had written what I did based on court proceedings, but he wanted to give me the real poop."

"Can I see that file again?" she asked. Grace handed it over.

"Released February Twenty-third," it said on the bottom of the file. Denise showed no reaction.

"Okay, Grace, that's interesting. I'm just going to call the sergeant."

I wish she hadn't said that sergeant word, thought Grace, her mind spinning back to earlier that afternoon.

Denise went into the living room and called Adam, who answered immediately.

"Denise. What's up?" he asked, his big baritone humming through the phone, laced with a thread of anxiety. "Everything okay?"

"Grace is fine, if that's what you're asking. I'm calling because I think we've made some progress with the reports on the cons she covered on the court beat."

"Really. Tell me."

"Duane Sykes," said Denise. "Guy went to prison for seven years for nearly beating someone to death outside a bar. He was released less than a month ago."

Charlotte had checked the names provided by Joan Karpinski against the police database, and had only provided to Adam those who were alive and no longer imprisoned. But the timing of his release . . .

"Grace says he called her from prison. Told her the victim deserved his beating, and wanted Grace to come interview him in jail and write another story, about what really happened, in his view."

"Does this happen to her often, this calling from prison thing?"

"Grace says yes, pretty often. Well, it's not rare, anyway."

So it wouldn't have necessarily occurred to or alarmed Grace previously, Adam thought, if this happened occasionally. It was starting to look like Karpinski was going to need a promotion. She had a good instinct for bad guys. Painchaud did, too.

"Good work, Painchaud. Stay close to Grace. I'll start looking for Sykes."

The head nurse was feeling disturbed, but he didn't exactly know why. A man had come by the desk asking for Grace Rampling early that afternoon. He claimed to be a cousin, so the nurse told him she had been discharged.

Now he was feeling uneasy about it. Should he have told this person anything? Somehow it seemed hard to believe that this twitchy, strange, reeking human being could be related to Grace and her siblings.

In retrospect, the nurse didn't much like the tattoo on his forearm. Not only did it look like a jailhouse effort, it didn't look too healthy, either.

So maybe I'll look like an idiot, thought Arthur Lampe. It beats something bad happening. He dialled the police station and identified himself.

"Hold on, Mr. Lampe. I'm going to put you through to the detective sergeant on the case," said the police officer on the desk.

"Sergeant Davis, a call has come in on the Rampling case. Can you take it?" asked the officer, calling Adam on his line.

"You bet. Who is it?"

The officer explained, then patched through the head nurse. "Hold on for Arthur Lampe, Sarge."

There was a click, and Adam said, "Sergeant Davis. How can I help you?"

"Oh, yes, Sergeant. It's Arthur Lampe, the head nurse on days at Royal University Hospital. We met briefly."

"Yes, I remember. What's happened, Mr. Lampe?"

"Well, early this afternoon, a man came looking for Grace Rampling," said Lampe. "I didn't think much about it at first; he said he was her cousin. I told him she had been discharged. Now I'm feeling that I may have done something wrong. If so, I'm sorry. I thought I'd better call."

Adam's mind raced. If this visitor was also her attacker, he now knew she was alive, and no longer in the hospital. At least Grace was at home, thought Adam, and not going out in the evenings or to work.

"Can you describe him for me, please?" asked Adam.

"Well, he had dark hair, reasonably tall — maybe just under six feet — and a blue tattoo on his left forearm," said Lampe. "He didn't give me a name. He left right after I told him she had been discharged."

Adam was taking quick notes as Lampe spoke. "Anything else?"

"Well, he had a very bad odour — sort of sweet and nauseating." Bad enough to mention it, thought Adam with interest. "I wonder if he has a chronic illness — or he may have just been drinking too much."

Stinky. Grace, through a blur of pain and medication, had said the man who attacked her was stinky. This is him, thought Adam.

"Mr. Lampe. This is a very important piece of evidence. When you say a chronic illness, what kind of illness would make a person smell awful?"

"Could be diabetes, maybe a liver condition."

"If you had to guess?"

"I'd say diabetes, uncontrolled or badly controlled. They call it the diabetic smell, in fact. It can be carried on the breath, but can also cause a pungent body odour. It's an effect of ketoacidosis — when acids build up in the blood because the blood sugar is too high."

"Thank you, Mr. Lampe," said Adam, with feeling. "Thank you for calling. It might have been better if you hadn't said anything about Grace, but your calling in and your description of this guy is beyond helpful. If you see him again, or if anything else occurs to you, please call me back. Here's my direct line," Adam added, reeling off his cell number.

Hanging up with Arthur Lampe, Adam immediately looked up the database copy of the report on Duane Sykes he had printed for Grace. He glared at his mug shot, found another photo featuring the tattoo on his arm, then called the prison.

Sykes was diabetic. Now Adam just had to find him.

He started with the Corrections Service of Canada, since there was no address in the police file forwarded by CSC. As he feared, CSC confirmed Sykes was living in Saskatoon, but indeed had no listed address. That was rare, but it happened occasionally when convicts were released after serving their entire sentences.

A friend had picked him up at the prison gates, and that was that. Either Sykes had no family in the city, or he had no family willing to take him home.

He started calling all the Sykes households in Saskatoon; there weren't many. No one answered at four of the seven numbers; voicemail kicked in at one; and two calls were answered by people who denied knowing or being related to a Duane Sykes.

Now what? He asked himself. Come on. Think. Where would you find this piece of shit?

Adam left the station, got in his car and started hitting the bars, the report beside him on the passenger seat. He wasn't sure exactly where he was going, but the man went to prison for nearly killing someone outside a bar. Maybe he was up to his old tricks.

Adam looked at the report, found the name of the bar Sykes had frequented before he went to prison, and headed for it.

He wasn't there. Adam kept driving.

Hours later, while Adam was still roaming the city, a 911 call came in.

"911. What is your emergency?"

"Assault at Logan's Bar and Grill. Third Avenue and Twentieth Street. Downtown."

"Do you need police or ambulance, sir?"

"Both."

"One moment," said the operator, quickly dispatching.

"What is the nature of the problem?"

"We have a guy in pretty bad shape here. He was beaten up. The dude who did it took off, don't know where he went."

"Okay, sir, help is on the way."

Adam heard the call for assistance on his scanner. Only blocks away, he turned on his siren and screamed around a corner, hurtling toward Logan's.

Pulling up, he saw four police officers getting out of two cruisers, and an ambulance arriving.

"Hey, Sarge, what are you doing here?" asked one of the officers.

"Heard the call. Sounded like it might be someone I'm looking for. Let's go."

The five officers made a big impression as they walked into the bar, paramedics close behind. A man was lying, bleeding copiously, on the floor; two other men were standing by the bar, with towels pressed to their noses. Everyone else stood around, more or less silently, watching the police as they came in.

"What happened here?" one of the officers asked the bartender, as the others, along with the paramedics, attended to the bleeding patron.

"Some guy was mouthing off. I asked him to leave, but he swung around and just clocked that guy," he said, pointing to the victim on the floor. "Hit him a few times. Then these two tried to pull him off, and he hit them, too. He was crazed, man. Kept screaming bad shit. I knew he was gonna be trouble from the get-go. I shoulda kicked him out sooner."

"Where did he go?"

"I don't know. After he hit these two guys," the bartender said, indicating the men with bloody noses, "they let go of him, and he beat feet outta here."

"What did he look like?"

"Dark, medium height to tall, bad skin. Wearing jeans and a hoodie. The usual."

"Did he smell bad?" Adam put in.

"What? Didn't notice. Everyone in here smells bad."

No kidding, thought Adam. The place itself reeked of old smoke, sweaty bodies, spilled booze and ancient wood. He thought he could see the grease from the bar food wafting through the air.

"Thanks. Got to get some air," he told the police officer asking the questions.

"Don't blame you. See you in a minute, Sarge."

Adam hit the sidewalk and gulped air. A couple of minutes later, the police officer joined him.

"So, do you think that might have been your dude?"

"Could be. If you catch him, call me right away."

"Will do, Sarge."

"How's the guy on the floor?"

"He'll be okay. Needs to go to the hospital, but he will be okay. I think he's lucky those other two guys were there and willing to help him out, though."

"Yeah. This guy sounds out of control. Let's put his description out there. Better find him before he hurts someone else."

At least Grace was safe, thought Adam. He was positive Duane Sykes was on a roll. He had to find him, before he hurt someone else.

Twenty-five

D enise Painchaud was relaxing, more or less, in Grace's spare bedroom, reading a book, with the door open. It was very quiet, very late and completely dark. There were few streetlights in the older parts of town, and in the summertime, many of them were obscured by the canopies created by huge trees in full leaf.

She got up every hour and did a quick perimeter check, looking for cars idling in the street, people lurking and for any disturbances. It didn't take long. Grace's nine hundred square foot home, on a thirty foot lot, didn't have a lot of perimeter.

But her ears were on full alert at all times, and her cellphone was on vibrate, just in case the sergeant needed to get in touch. Her gun was right beside her.

She put the book aside and looked out the window, her eyes automatically scanning the block.

A scuffle. A grunt. The sudden, soft noises were unexpected and made Denise jump and look around. She was sure Grace didn't have a pet . . .

Then Grace screamed. Denise, thinking her charge was having a nightmare, leaped across the hallway and knocked at Grace's bedroom door. No answer.

"Grace, can I come in?" she asked, loudly.

A strangled sound. And Denise knew.

She threw open the door to the dark bedroom, gun drawn, shouting "freeze, police!" and flung herself at the greasy, reeking man sitting on Grace's pelvis with a hand over her mouth, the other hand pinning her injured shoulder to the bed.

He immediately balled up the left hand and lashed out at Denise with his fist, catching her on the jaw and sending her staggering. Her gun flew out of her hand, backwards into the hallway, skittering along the hardwood floor.

Grace had a second's leverage and pushed Duane Sykes with all her strength. Enfuriated, he slapped Grace hard, just before Denise launched herself at him a second time. On impact, he and Denise landed tangled on the floor, punching and kicking, and Denise yelled, "Grace! Get out! Call 911."

Grace scrambled out of bed, pulling her torn nightclothes up over her shoulders, and stumbled into the living room. She had just snatched up the phone when she heard Sykes and Denise in the hallway, still fighting.

"She's mine!" Sykes was screaming, trying to hit Denise in the face as she fended off the blows. "Get out of my way, you bitch!"

He grabbed Denise and threw her down the hallway and onto the floor, stunning her, then came for Grace again. "You're mine. Tell her to fuck off."

"You're insane," Grace hissed at him. "I don't even know you."

He grabbed her by the hair, pulling her head back, and snarled into her face, his sickening breath making Grace's stomach flip.

"Don't you remember? You made me famous. I was your guy, all those days in court. I could tell. But I was pretty mad when you started making nice with all those faggots. Who are they to you? Hey?" he said pulling harder. "Lucky I just scared you last time. You and me, girl. We're gonna be together now."

Denise, coming out of her momentary daze, managed to get on her hands and knees and crawled over to Sykes as quietly as possible. On all fours behind him, she looked up at Grace and jerked her head. Grace, catching Denise's gesture out of the corner of her eye, mustered all the strength she had left and pushed Sykes again — backwards over Denise's crouched body.

He fell heavily, knocking his head on the leg of the kitchen table. Grace picked up the phone, shaking, and dialled 911.

"911. What is your emergency?"

Grace said it was a home invasion and gave her address, wondering if the dispatcher could understand her, her body and voice were shaking so hard.

"Do you require police and ambulance?"

"Police."

"One moment," said the dispatcher. "Okay, police are on the way. What is the nature of your emergency?"

"I've been attacked. The man is still here . . . he's knocked out, but he could get up at any time. And police constable Denise Painchaud is also here."

"Are you hurt?" asked the operator.

"We are both hurt."

"One moment," said the dispatcher, sending two ambulances. "Medical help is on the way. Do you need any further assistance? Does anyone need CPR?"

"No," said Grace, collapsing onto the floor, then reaching out a hand to Denise. "Are you okay?"

"I've been better," Denise said, struggling to sit up. "Do you think you could manage to get outside? Police will be here right away, but I don't want this asshole waking up with us here, inside."

Too late. Sykes was waking up as she spoke, snorting and swearing, and reaching for Grace — who slid backwards on her backside, eyes wide with disgust and fear, as Denise grabbed her weapon.

Gaining strength, Sykes lunged at Grace, as Denise trained her gun on him screaming "Freeze, asshole!" just as the police broke down the door, yelling as they came.

It was chaos. Grace was dimly aware that Denise kept her weapon pointed at the man who had his arms wrapped around her legs, as four officers poured in — grabbing Sykes, shouting orders, turning him over and pulling him to his feet. Denise rolled over and collapsed on her back as the police cuffed the cursing attacker.

And then Grace, still sitting on the floor, saw Adam — between the heads of the officers and the filthy, stinking man who had now attacked her twice.

"Adam," she said, getting to her feet. He dove around the officers and the struggling attacker and covered the distance between them in four strides, taking in the ripped nightgown, the new purpling bruise on her cheek, her snow white face.

As he came toward her, Grace almost imperceptibly shook her head, mouthing "no." Standing up straight and squaring her shoulders, tears pouring from her eyes, she said it out loud, just above a whisper. "No."

Adam stopped a foot away from her, so close he could have wrapped his arms around her. Past caring, he would have, but she took a step backward, shaking her head again.

"Grace." He held his arms rigidly at his sides, willing himself not to reach for her. "God, Grace . . . "

Then, "the ambulance is here."

Four paramedics waded through the madness, adding to the strange tumble of people shouting and swearing and milling about the kitchen. Two medics headed for Grace, and two for Denise.

Finally, Duane Sykes was dragged out the door by three police officers, leaving one behind to take statements from Denise and Grace. The paramedics looked at Grace's face and Denise's head, where a huge rising bump testified to her aggressive contact with the hallway floor.

Adam backed off and stood in the doorway with arms crossed, mouth set in a grim line. Be strong, he told himself. Like Grace. God, he wanted to touch her, hold her, comfort her . . . and himself.

"We should go to the hospital," suggested Jeff, the paramedic, to Grace. "Looks like a nasty bruise, maybe a cracked cheekbone underneath it." More quietly, Jeff asked her, "did anything else happen?"

Grace shook her head. She knew what he meant. Had she been raped, or otherwise sexually assaulted? Sykes had tried, immediately after he crept through the window and she felt his hand on her mouth; but she fought him, biting his hand hard and distracting him for just long enough so she could scream for Denise.

There was a bruise, she could tell, where he had grabbed her breast, another on her arm, and probably one on her inner leg. But they were minor.

She only cared that she would never have to feel, or remember, that crazed, disgusting man inside her.

"Are you sure?" Jeff asked, gently.

"He tried," said Grace, very quietly. "I bit him."

"Wow," said Jeff. "That was brave. Did you break the skin? Was there blood?" he asked.

Grace shook her head.

"Thank goodness, Grace. That should eliminate most concerns about HIV or Hepatitis C infection. Are there other injuries I should know about?"

"A little bruising . . ."

"Okay, let's take a look."

Grace's eyes flicked downwards, telling the paramedic that the bruise check would require some privacy. There were still six people in her living room.

"Would you feel more comfortable in another room?" he asked. "Jennifer will come with us," he added, referring to the female paramedic.

Grace nodded, and supported by the two medics, left the room.

Adam knew what that meant, and his mind travelled into the bedroom with Grace. What other awful things had happened to her? Oh God . . . he felt sick at what awaited her.

In her bedroom, Grace drew down her ripped nightgown and exposed the side of her breast, then showed the paramedics her arm and inner thigh.

"Grace, I'm so sorry, but we have to get photos of this. We'll have to go to the hospital."

"I'm not going back to the hospital," said Grace.

"These bruises are evidence. You have to be seen by a doctor."

"I was not raped. I told you, I fought him off. I'm not going to the hospital again."

"Again?"

"He attacked me a week ago, and gave me a concussion and a cracked clavicle. I just got home from the hospital. I'm not going back."

"Let me speak to the police," said Jeff. "Just a sec, okay?"

Jeff approached Adam, still standing rigidly in the kitchen, and told him he suspected sexual assault. Regardless, Grace's bruises and cuts should be photographed for trial. But she was refusing to go to the hospital. What did Adam think they should do?

Adam's head filled with blood, fury rising from the thought of Sykes sexually touching her — touching her at all. He couldn't think for a moment, the disgust and anger washing over him.

Clearing his throat, he asked Jeff, "did she say she was attacked sexually?"

"She didn't put it that way, but she was. She says she was not raped. She fought him off. Bit him, in fact."

"That's . . . wow. Good for her. Can I have a word with her? Maybe I can talk her into going to the hospital."

"Okay. First let me see if she's, you know, decent."

A couple of minutes later, Jeff called to Adam that he could come in.

He walked down the hall, mustering some strength, then knocked on the door and opened it to see Grace sitting bolt upright on the bed.

"Grace," said Adam, gently, crouching in front of her so they could be more or less face to face. "Tell me how you are."

"I'm fine. And I'm not going to the hospital."

"You know, if we're going to convict this pervert, we may need the evidence of your injuries. A doctor is going to want to check you over. We need to know if you're okay. Can I persuade you to go?"

At that entreaty from Adam, Grace fell apart. She dropped her face in her hands and wept, trying not to sob aloud. "I don't know if I can stand it," she said.

"I know, it's awful, and you're exhausted. I'm so sorry, Grace, so sorry, but it could be important."

She looked up and studied his face. Adam felt his resolve not to touch her melting under her steady gaze, even as tears dropped off her eyelashes and onto her cheeks. Grace knew she couldn't say no to him.

"Okay. I will go. Only if I don't have to stay after the exam and the photos."

Adam knew he couldn't promise that; the ER might keep her if something was wrong. It was killing him to persuade her to go in the first place.

"I'll walk out, Adam. I swear I will," said Grace.

"No one can prevent you from that. Thanks, Grace . . . it means a lot to me."

Adam was lying; he would rather she didn't have to go to the hospital again, but it was his job to ensure all possible evidence was gathered. He had to convince her. He had to convict this attacker. He deeply understood, as he never had before, why police ethics demanded distance between officer and victim.

"We have to nail this guy, so he never gets out of prison again," said Adam, unable to keep his voice from shaking with passion. "So he can never, ever do this again."

"I'm going to have to get dressed then . . ." started Grace, but the paramedic stopped her.

"I'm afraid we have to take you in just the way you are. I'm sorry.

205

"Can we find a bathrobe, maybe? And then put your coat over that? They will want to take pictures of the nightgown too," said Jeff, as gently as he could.

"Let's get this over with," said Grace, suddenly enraged by the situation and the night's events. She reached around Jeff for her robe. "Let's go."

Grace and Denise were side by side in emergency, just a drape between them. The doctor was examining Denise's head.

"Grace," said Denise. "Can you hear me?"

"Yes I can, Denise. How are you doing?"

"I think I'm okay. Mild concussion, probably. Grace, I just want to say I'm so sorry. I don't know how this went wrong. I should have shot him. Right away. But I was afraid I might hit you, with him flailing around."

"Denise, you saved my life — or at the very least, saved me from being raped. And got banged up for the pleasure. Denise. Don't beat yourself up. There's been enough of that, okay?"

Then the doctor came in, and Grace started to cry.

"Denise, can you come in here with me? I feel like a victim in one of those awful violent movies. I don't want to do this. Do you feel okay?"

Denise scrambled out of bed and around the curtain, glad she could do something for her charge.

"I'm here, Grace."

Grace grabbed her hand, and looked at the doctor. "Okay. Get on with it," she said, wishing Dr. Bergen was on duty tonight.

The examination was long, intimate, invasive and occasionally painful. Photos were taken at every angle, of every bruise and cut. Although Grace objected, they did a full rape kit. By the time it was over, Grace felt thoroughly invaded, and thought she was going to pass out.

"Can I go home now?"

"Do you really want to?" asked Denise. "There are probably cops crawling all over your house right now."

"Yes, I do. I don't want to stay here another minute."

"Okay, Grace. Okay. I'm coming with you. We can share your spare room until the police are gone."

The two women, Grace a mess and looking bizarre with her coat open over her robe and nightgown, and Denise in her dirty, ripped uniform, locked arms and walked out of the ER. Denise asked one of the police officers still standing in triage to take them back to Grace's, and although his eyebrows flew up, he agreed.

On the other side of the ER, Duane Sykes was handcuffed to his bed, police officers standing all around him. Doctors were checking him over to make sure his apparently minor injuries from the fight with Grace and Denise were, in fact, minor.

"He has a mild concussion," Dr. Brian Ashern told Adam. They knew each other well. "A few bruises. He will be fine, but to be on the safe side, we'd like to watch him for a few hours."

"Is that necessary?" asked Adam.

"Do you want him dying, or even getting sick, in cells before you can talk to him?" countered the doctor, who was seasoned in dealing with injured criminals. You really had to make sure they were well enough to leave, or bad things happened. And sometimes, they would pretend to be sick, or battered. "I mean, it's highly unlikely, but do you want to take the chance?"

"I see your point. No. Particularly not this one. Okay, Brian. Can you let me know when we can pick him up?"

"How about if I let Warkentin or Weatherall know? You look done in. Go home and get a few hours' sleep. He'll be here until mid-morning, at least. I want to watch him for a few hours."

"You can call me."

"I can call Weatherall. Get out of here and get a few hours, or you'll be no good talking to your bad guy. I mean it, Adam. You look like shit."

"Okay, okay. You don't have to rub it in. I'm going."

Adam caught a glimpse of himself reflected in the emergency room window as he left the ward. He did look like shit. He felt sick about Grace being attacked. He wanted to rip the attacker apart. He wanted these cases to go away, to be with Grace. But all he could do was keep working on them. He had no choice.

Twenty-six

Adam awakened to the ringing of his cellphone. It was ten-thirty in the morning. Despite the bloody mess of the night before, he did have one positive thought.

One down. One to go.

As far as he could figure it, this asshole Sykes had some bizarre thing for Grace. That made it much less likely he had killed the bishop — although, he supposed, he might have. As far as Grace's attack went, he had Sykes dead to rights. He would mop up this guy, and try not to kill him while he was at it.

Then he'd find the bishop's murderer, if he was right about it being a different guy.

"Davis," he answered briefly.

"Morning, Adam. We have Sykes in custody at the station," said James. "Want to come and play?"

"I'll be there in an hour. Make him sweat a bit . . . if he's the kind of guy who sweats at all. I'm wondering if he's completely nuts. What's your take?"

"I'm leaning that way, Sarge. Looking forward to finding out. See you soon."

"Cheers, James. Thanks for the wake-up call."

It was all very well for Adam to talk about letting Sykes sweat. He couldn't wait to start questioning him.

But food and a shower wouldn't be a bad idea first. He didn't want Sykes to see that this case was personal, for him — plus, he was starving.

He jumped out of bed, grabbed an apple and headed for the shower. He couldn't stop wondering how Grace was feeling, how she was doing, how soon he could see her again. And he'd have to get a blow by blow explanation from Painchaud — how that all went wrong.

Well, it also went partly right. Thank God she was there, or what would have happened to Grace? And it was also a good thing that Sykes was alive. He was going to get answers.

James and two other police officers were waiting in an interview room with Sykes when Adam arrived, already blowing steam. Between James's phone call and getting to the station, Adam's fury increased by the minute over the idiocy of how one lunatic could nearly wreck a beautiful life like Grace's.

James intercepted him at the door.

"Good morning Adam. Don't take this the wrong way, but you have to stay calm."

"Of course I'll stay calm," said Adam, big voice rising.

"You already don't look calm and you haven't even clapped eyes on him yet."

James just stood there in front of Adam, waiting for the capitulation that usually came.

"You can't go in there like this, Adam."

"I know. I know. Thanks, James," said Adam, breathing deeply and waiting for his heart rate to slow.

"I've got your back, Sarge," said James, opening the door.

Adam took one look at Sykes and wanted to lunge across the table, whether to strangle or punch him he wasn't sure. He swallowed hard.

"Mr. Sykes. Thank you for joining us."

Sykes just glared.

"Are you comfortable? Can we get you anything?"

"Coffee."

Perfect, thought Adam. Coffee may well have a positive effect on his bladder, from a police point of view.

"Constable, could you get Mr. Sykes a large coffee? What do you take in it?"

"Two milk, two sugar."

The constable left, and Adam sat down.

"So, Mr. Sykes. I believe we have plenty of evidence to convict you, at the very least, of home invasion and aggravated assault. There's no point to denying it. Maybe we could start with you telling us why you were at Ms. Rampling's home last night."

"Went for a little visit," Sykes grumbled.

"What do you mean by a little visit?"

"Wanted to see her again."

"Again?"

"Saw her a lot when she came to court. Covered my trial, didn't she, for the paper."

"So you saw her a lot then," Adam prompted.

"Saw her a lot," Sykes agreed, a sickening grin spreading on his face.

"I knew she liked me. Came every day. Looked right at me. Then every day she put my name in the paper. I thought she knew what I done was right."

"What did you do?"

"Punched a guy out. He came on to me at a bar. Not right for them faggots to be out with regular people, trying it on. He deserved what I gave him."

The constable returned with the coffee.

"You hurt him pretty badly, Mr. Sykes. He was in the hospital for weeks. He could have died. Do you think that was a good idea, punching him so hard that he almost died?"

Sykes shrugged. "Not my fault faggots are so delicate," he said, sneering. "She knew."

"She? You mean Ms. Rampling? Knew what?"

"It was important. She wrote all about it in that newspaper."

Adam was starting to get a bead on this freak.

"So why did you hit her with a — a what, a crowbar? Piece of pipe? — in that alley a week ago? Why, if you like her so much?"

Sykes' face suffused with blood.

"She wrote that story about the fag choir. Then she went to that fag bar. I was going to follow her home that day, but she went to the fucking fag bar instead. Why did she do that? She shouldn't have done that. Needed a lesson about what to write. Who to party with."

Well, he and James had been right about that, thought Adam. The story had, partly, brought on the attack in the alley.

"Did you want to kill her?"

"What do you mean? I was just mad. Glad I didn't kill her. She's so pretty. Always wanted to fuck her. Thought I'd go visit her and make up."

Adam swallowed hard, again. The thought of him anywhere near Grace . . .

"How did you know where she was, and where she lives?"

"I knew she was out of the hospital. Nurse told me. Then I just followed you, Sergeant. Easy as pie."

His words were like a physical fist in the stomach. Adam nearly doubled over. This lunatic had found him somehow, followed him to Grace's house — then returned later. Adam came out of his chair, muscles tensing, and looked like he was going for Sykes, but James stopped him — physically. "Adam. Don't."

Adam turned and stormed out of the room.

He had led this deranged freak right to Grace, if he was telling the truth. How could that have happened? How was that even possible?

"I seen you at the hospital, Sarge! I seen you there! Then I followed you!" Sykes screamed through the door.

Sweat rolling down his spine, Adam lurched toward the men's room and went straight for the sink, shoulders heaving, hunching over the basin. Sykes had been stalking Grace, probably since soon after he got out of prison; and he had also been following Adam.

Adam went through the chain of events in his mind, and found the tiny consolation that when he went to visit Grace, he didn't yet know that Sykes was her attacker. Still, how could he have been followed without noticing? The bastard apparently didn't know at the time that Grace had a guard. If he had seen her at Grace's house, maybe he thought she was just a visiting friend.

He ran cold water into the sink and plunged his face into it. Get back there, and get this guy's statement over with before you lose it altogether, Adam told himself. Drying his face, he looked in the mirror. Smarten up, he told himself, staring into his own crazed eyes.

He stalked back into the room, pulling the shreds of his dignity together.

"Sergeant Davis has re-entered the room," said James, giving Adam a warning look.

"So you followed me, did you," said Adam, as if nothing had happened, and no time had elapsed. "How did you manage that?"

"C'mon, Sarge. Easy as pie, like I said. Just waited across from the station until I saw you leave. Lucky for me you were going to her place. Worth a shot, since she was out of the hospital."

"Let me try this scenario on you," said Adam. "You follow me to Ms. Rampling's. Now you know where she lives." Grace's address was unlisted, Adam knew. Many reporters were unlisted; too dangerous.

"But I'm there. So you decide to get a load on, right? Haven't been out drinking or beating up gay people or breaking into houses for a few years, until lately, have you? You were missing that, if I'm right.

"You head downtown, go from bar to bar until you end up at Logan's, already drunk. You hang out for a while, making snarky comments to the guys at the bar, until someone says something that you think gives you the permission to punch him. He 'came on' to you.

"Then two guys pull you off him. You give them a couple of pops, then run out the door before the police show up. You get in the car, all revved up from punching and drinking, and after the bars close, drive over to Ms. Rampling's.

"You're pretty sneaky, aren't you? Pretty quiet. Pretty good at picking locks and opening windows. Lots of practice, am I right? Your first crime was a home invasion. I checked your file. How many others have you done, and not been caught for?

"So you slip in the window, awakening Ms. Rampling. It's three in the morning. Before she can scream or defend herself, you're on top of her with your hand on her mouth. You're ripping off her clothes. You're going to . . ." here Adam paused, unable to get the word out. He changed his language. "Attack her. Sexually. You're pretty rough; you leave bruises. But she bites you. You take your hand away from her mouth. She screams.

"Then an unexpected visitor comes into the room. You hit her, send her gun flying. You weren't expecting a cop in the next room, were you? Then you have a Donnybrook with a couple of injured women — and they win the fight." Adam let that sink in for a minute. "You're a real man, aren't you? So, have I got that about right?"

Sykes snarled. "Think you're pretty smart, doncha, Sarge? Hey, it was two against one, and one was a cop. Yeah, I'm a real man. Grace knows I am. She knows I wouldn't put up with homos."

"Except that guy you nearly killed seven years ago: he's not gay, you know."

"Looked gay. Acted gay."

"But he isn't. Neither was the guy you laid out at Logan's. So I guess you know shit. You also know shit about Grace Rampling. She barely knows who you are."

"Bullshit! We were gonna get it on. After the court case. I could tell. Just got a little delayed when I got locked up. That's all."

"No. She told me she barely remembered you, and then only after I showed her your file, and we found the stories she wrote about you."

Sykes' face was scarlet, his eyes were rolling. He was spitting bits of curse words and denying what Adam had said.

Things were finally going Adam's way. He couldn't resist a grin.

"Mr. Sykes. While we're at it, what do you know about Bishop Halkitt?"

"Nuthin," he said sullenly. "You're not pinning that on me."

"Really? Where were you last Sunday, say about five in the afternoon?"

"How'm I supposed to remember that?"

"It's a lousy couple of weeks ago, Sykes. Where were you?"

Sykes stared at Adam, then finally said, "chatting with the bishop."

That surprised Adam, but he didn't reveal it. "What were you chatting about?"

"Homos. In the confessional. I told him, I slapped out some homo in the bar. He gave me some Hail Marys and I left."

"You're Catholic?" he asked, answered by a nod from Sykes.

"You left the church," Adam continued, sarcastically. "Right. You didn't come out of the confessional, pick up some religious object, and smash his head in?"

"No way. Bishop was a good guy. Cancelled that stupid gay concert, didn't he? Wanted to thank him."

Damn. That was consistent with Sykes' world view. Adam's hope had been rising that Sykes was the murderer, but that was now fading. Still, Sykes had been in the church, and he could be lying.

"How did you know the concert had been cancelled?"

"Saw a note outside the office. It said it got toasted."

"Did you see anyone else around?"

"Nope. Quiet in there."

"Did you see a big gold cross anywhere?"

"Nope."

"You don't like gay people, Mr. Sykes. Why is that?"

"Learned it from my daddy. He hated homos."

Adam saw the foundations of Sykes' loathing in his squirming, messed-up brain. That, mixed with his low IQ, started to coalesce into a personality profile. It probably didn't help that he had badly-controlled diabetes, either, from a mood control standpoint.

"Hated homos, did he? Did he punch them out too?"

"Yeah. All the time. When he got mad."

"Did he get mad at you, too?"

Sykes gave an unpleasant laugh. "Sure. Just like any other daddy. Give me a whipping with his belt, told me not to be such a faggot. That kept me on the right track, I tell ya. 'Don't be a gay boy,' he said. 'Don't be a faggot. The Lord hates faggots, and so do I.' That's what he'd say."

Runs in the family, this hatred of people different from themselves, thought Adam. He threw a glance at James, to see if he was doing okay; but James was standing impassively, arms crossed, right behind him.

Sykes was beginning to shift uncomfortably. Adam saw his chance to question him again on the bishop's death; the coffee was kicking in.

"You claim you didn't kill the bishop," he continued, leaning back in his chair and crossing his arms to give the impression that he was settling in for a much longer chat.

"Look, I done the things you said," Sykes said. "I didn't do the bishop. I just did confession. He could of been a fag, for sure — lots of priests are — but he proved he warnt when he toasted that stupid concert. Right? Am I done? I gotta piss."

Adam regarded him for many seconds, not moving. Finally, Adam decided there was nowhere left to go with this interview. Sykes had coughed up — although he had little choice — and Adam doubted he was going to move on his assertion that he hadn't killed the bishop. He did have a confession on Grace's attack, an attack on a police officer, and as a bonus, the attack on the guy in the bar. He hoped it would lead to a guilty plea, and Grace wouldn't have to appear in court.

Still, Adam was not in a giving mood, especially with this person who had assaulted Grace and followed him. He got up, whispered "let him sweat a bit more" into James's ear, and left the room as Sykes yelled, "Where're you going? Let me out of here!"

Adam grinned.

The downside of interviewing Sykes was that Adam couldn't be at the St. Eligius office at the same time, as he had earlier intended. He wanted to find the secretary himself. Instead, he sent another police officer, who now returned to say there was no sign of him.

"Is this guy a figment of our imagination? Some kind of ghost?" asked Adam in exasperation, although he knew better. He had interviewed him once; or was that a dream? "Maybe he's wearing his invisible clothes. Jesus. Where is this guy?"

"I don't know, Sarge. He sure is hard to catch."

"Okay, Jonesy, thanks for going over to the church."

Bloody hell. It was tough to serve a warrant if you couldn't find the warrantee. Adam pledged to get a search warrant the next day, for the man's house. He'd had enough. A residential search could well provide the information they needed.

He had to talk to Sanj anyway. Adam fired him an email asking him for an appointment the next day. It was going to be hard, admitting what had happened with Grace.

Twenty-seven

An email from the chief of police was waiting for Adam in the morning. Dan McIvor wanted an update on the bishop's murder, and could Adam step into his office at nine?

Sanj had also replied to Adam's request for an appointment. Luckily that was at ten-thirty. It was going to be a busy day.

Adam presented himself to his chief promptly, and was invited to take a seat.

"How's it going, Adam?" asked McIvor.

Adam updated the chief on what he had discovered so far: that Duane Sykes and Frank Stephens had both been in the cathedral in the afternoon of the day of the bishop's death, and were suspects; that they could not unearth the church secretary for a second interview, but he was going to try to get a search warrant for his house that morning; that he was quite sure what the murder weapon was, but that it had not been found.

He and James were headed for Westmoreland, Adam continued. He explained that there had been a brouhaha over a letter ostensibly sent to a child by the bishop when he was a priest and teacher there. It took them a few days to learn about it, since it never resulted in charges.

They were going to interview the child's parents and nose around for other information.

Since the Sykes interview had just occurred the day before, Adam explained how they had been searching for him originally without success, but the violent homophobe with a thing for the StarPhoenix reporter, Grace Rampling, had ultimately shown himself and beaten up five people, including Grace and Constable Painchaud. He had admitted to it.

"Hard not to," said Adam. "We caught him at the scene. I don't think he's the brightest bulb, plus he has uncontrolled diabetes and is certainly mentally ill."

McIvor nodded.

"Well done, Adam, and good idea to get on the ground at Westmoreland. I don't have to tell you, though, that I'm getting a lot of pressure on this bishop case. What, if anything, can I tell the mayor? Not to mention the media? They call two or three times a day — per outlet. That's something like twenty-five calls a day. Can we shut them up for a day or two with a release?"

Adam reflected. What could they say without messing up the case?

"Maybe we could say in the release about Sykes' arrest that he is a witness in the bishop's case? Which is true," suggested Adam. "That we're making progress, that sort of thing?"

"I'll buzz that past the communications people. Thanks for that. Well, keep me posted. Thanks, Adam."

"My pleasure, sir."

His next stop was Sanjeev Kumar's office. Adam wasn't looking forward to this conversation.

Adam walked to the Crown prosecutor's office, hoping to keep his head clear in the fresh, late-March air. It was finally starting to feel, at least a little, like spring.

"Morning, Sanj," said Adam, knocking at his door and poking his head in simultaneously.

"Morning, Adam, come on in," said Sanj, standing. He was always so courteous, even with colleagues he knew well. Adam appreciated it.

They shook hands. Adam sat down, suddenly tongue-tied.

"What's on your mind, Adam?" asked Sanj, kindly, leaning forward. It was obvious from the expression on Adam's face — a mixture of conflict, exhaustion, and something else he couldn't quite put his finger on — that something unusual was up with the sergeant.

"Two things, actually," said Adam, finding his voice. "I'll start with the easier one. We still can't dig up that church secretary. I'd really like to get a warrant to search his house. Unfortunately, I don't have any real reason to do so — except that the guy is missing."

"Why do you want to search his house? Do you think he's hiding in there, or that you might find some evidence, or what?"

"Both, maybe. I don't know. Probably — mainly — that we might find a clue as to where he is. I mean, it's hard to see him as the killer, but there's something strange going on. I think he's in Saskatoon, somewhere. There's no evidence he has left town. So where the hell is he?"

"That is strange. Maybe I can make the argument that since the bishop has been murdered, something unpleasant could also have happened to the secretary and it's our duty to check. That would get us in the door, at least. I'll try for a full residence search, too. What's the second thing?"

Adam felt his extremities tingle, and his heart rate jump. Sanj, across the table, could see Adam's body tense.

"Come on, Adam. Something's up. Let me help."

"It's a bit of a confession, Sanj. I never thought I'd be in a position like this, so it's hard for me to tell you. But I have to. Did you get the paperwork on Duane Sykes, by the way? Did it come to you?"

"I got it, but just this morning, so I haven't read it yet."

"It turns out he's the guy who attacked Grace Rampling, the reporter from the paper. That's a bit beside the point, except that he followed me to Grace's house the afternoon before he attacked her the second time. She had just returned home from the hospital, and I was there dropping off some files for her to look at — trying to nail down her attacker. Makes me sick. I can't believe a freak like that was able to follow me."

"Okay . . . that sucks, Adam, but shit happens. You couldn't have expected that. What else? That's not all, is it?"

"No."

"What, then?"

"It's Grace." Adam swallowed hard. "As you know, she's the main witness so far in the bishop's case. She found him, and because of that, her testimony can help narrow down the time window, plus give us a clear picture of what was happening in the cathedral at the time. Which was more or less nothing, but still.

"She's also, theoretically, a suspect, but only in theory. And she's a victim of two attacks.

"Both of these cases are mine, and they intertwine."

"You're such a poet," said Sanj, who noticed the mine-twine rhyme and tried to lighten the atmosphere as Adam paused. Adam was so tense, and his voice betrayed it. "All good so far. Next?"

"When I was there the other day, something . . . happened. Between us. Between me and Grace."

Sanj's face changed. "What kind of thing happened?"

Adam gave himself hell. Stop stalling, get it out there, and get it over with.

"While we were talking, she leaned over and touched my mouth. I was really surprised; I didn't quite understand what was happening at first. Then she kissed me. And then I kissed her."

Sanj's eyes opened in surprise. "When you say kiss, was this a friendly gesture or — shall we say, a more passionate event?"

"The latter. Jesus," said Adam involuntarily, remembering the moment, feeling it in his body. "It was intense, Sanj. I lost control for a few minutes, there, with her. It didn't go any further. We pulled it together. But it happened, and there is no way I could honestly testify — in either case — that I was in any way objective about her. If anything came to light. I'm sorry, Sanj."

Sanj was quiet for a moment. "This wasn't in any way taking advantage, was it? You do have a real thing for Grace?"

"You could put it more eloquently, but apparently I do. I didn't plan this. When I first saw her in the cathedral, I had an instant reaction to her. It was dark in there, but we turned on a flashlight, and I asked her to

come out from behind the pew, where she was hiding —
she knew the killer could still be in the church.

"It was like . . . I don't know, Venus rising or
something in the beam of light. Her hair emerged, then
her face, then the rest of her. She got to me at first sight."

"How is it that you didn't run into her before?
How long have you been detective sergeant?"

"Couple of years. I know, I wondered that too.
Maybe I've seen her around, but maybe she was in the
court gallery when I was on the stand. She stopped full-
time court reportage about three, four years ago, and
when I was staff sergeant at the time, I wasn't in court as
often."

Sanj took a breath. "Well, it's not perfect, Adam,
as you know. Thanks for telling me before all of this
unwinds. I really do appreciate it. I hope like hell it never
comes up — with any luck, you should be fine on the
Sykes front. Looks like you have him dead to rights.
Hopefully that case will breeze through the system, or he
pleads guilty. It may become an issue in the bishop's case,
but let's hope not.

"As your friend, what are you going to do about
Grace? You have it bad, if I can read people at all. She is
very attractive, and a very good journalist, and in my
experience a very nice person to deal with. For a
reporter," he added, smiling.

"So I get it. Try to hang in there until after the
case is solved. Avoid seeing her as much as you can, okay?
It will complicate things, and people might notice your
attraction to her. Meanwhile, I don't think this
jeopardizes your work on finding the killer. I really don't.
It can't be Grace, and at this point, she's a minor witness
in that case. You just have to get past the Sykes trial.

"Just be careful, gather your evidence methodically, and don't jump to conclusions just to get it over with. You're a pro, Adam. I know it, and so does everyone else. Just keep acting like one."

Adam relaxed a bit.

"Thanks, Sanj. Thanks for the advice. I'll follow it to the letter. Christ, I feel like some lovesick seventeen-year-old; it's ridiculous."

"No, it's not," said Sanj, who was happily married. "It's great. Just, like I said, hang in there a little while longer. Then see what happens."

Adam and James left at an ungodly hour the next morning, and reached the tiny town of Westmoreland, three and a half hours southeast of Saskatoon, about nine-thirty.

Their first stop was for some desperately-needed coffee. Their next job was to interview the parents of the child who had, years ago, received a sexually suggestive letter, presumably and apparently from then-Father Howard Halkitt.

The parents, Joe and Brenda Hagel, hard-working people in their late fifties or early sixties, answered the officers' knock together.

"Come in," said Joe, opening the door wide.

"Would you like some coffee?" asked Brenda.

First impressions being what they are, Adam and James had a good feeling about the Hagels because of their warmth and hospitality. Privately, Adam thought these people would never have made up a story about a letter.

"Thank you," said Adam, who still felt the need for caffeine. "That would be great."

They settled into the living room, as Brenda stacked cups, coffee pot, cream, sugar and homemade cookies onto a tray.

"Now. How can we help?" she asked, pouring steaming cups for each of them.

"As we explained on the phone, we're investigating the murder of Bishop Howard Halkitt, and we understand he was the priest here many years ago," said Adam. "When we learned about the letter your son received, we began to wonder about the motive behind his killing. It may not be connected, but we have to investigate. What can you remember about the letter? Did you keep a copy?"

"We didn't," said Joe. "It wasn't a happy event, as you can imagine. We turned the original over to the RCMP and let it be at that. We didn't want it in the house."

"What did the letter say, as far as you can recall?" asked Adam.

"It asked our son if he would meet Father Halkitt at the school after six p.m.," answered Joe. "It was unusual, because Father Halkitt had never requested such a thing before, and had never requested anything, ever, by letter. He always just spoke to the boys, and if they needed permission for anything like a field trip or something, the paperwork would just be an official form from the school. And the paperwork came from the school secretary, not the father."

Adam felt there was more to it. He hated to upset the parents, so many years later, but just a request to meet at the school didn't seem all that threatening.

"What else did the letter say?" he asked.

"It wasn't really explicit," said the mother. "But it said the meeting would be private, and that our son was his favourite boy, and if he could do a favour for the father, there would be a nice present in it for him. That sort of thing. We felt it was vague and inappropriate, and we were very upset."

"Did your son see the letter?"

"He saw it first. He brought it to us, wondering what it was all about; and, we had a family birthday party to attend that same night, so he wondered what he should do. He was only ten, a good boy, and quite innocent. I don't think he understood the undertone in the letter, at the time."

"How was it signed?"

"It wasn't really signed. The name was just typed, with an "H" scrawled underneath."

James made a note. They would have to ask the retired RCMP officer who had been on the case about that H.

"What happened, to your recollection? We understand that the RCMP didn't press any charges."

"Our son told the police that nothing like that had ever happened before; that the father had never approached him for any favour, or for any other reason other than schoolwork; and if I remember correctly, they determined that the typewriter used to write the letter was not the one at the church or the school, and the father didn't have one at home. Apart from the letter itself, nothing pointed to the father. I must say, we found it bizarre. We had a very good impression of Father Halkitt, otherwise."

228

"Did you know Ellice Fairbrother, as well?" asked James. "I understand he was a deacon here at about the same time."

"We knew him a bit, more or less to say hello to. We saw him at church, of course," said Brenda.

"So you didn't really have a strong impression of him, then?"

"Not really. He seemed to keep to himself, more than the other deacons over the years."

That didn't surprise James, who was still seething over not being able to find the man.

"Did anyone else in town know him better? Anyone we can talk to?"

Joe and Brenda looked at each other.

"I'm not sure," said Joe. "You could try the church and school secretary, of the time. She's retired now."

"Where is your son now?" asked Adam.

"He's working down Estevan way."

"Did he have any after effects?"

"Not really. Nothing happened after the letter arrived, and he's a strong kid. I wonder if he's forgotten all about it."

"Could we have his phone number, please, Mrs. Hagel? We may need to talk to him just the same. And the name of the former secretary?"

Brenda obliged, scribbling names, phone numbers and addresses on a piece of paper ripped from a pad by the phone.

"Thank you so much, both of you. We'll be in touch if we need anything else," said Adam, rising from the couch in tandem with James.

"I'll see you out," said Joe.

At the door, Joe said, "you know, I never believed that letter was from Father Halkitt. It just didn't sound like him. He didn't speak that way, his notes in the church newsletter used different language, and there was never another hint of impropriety. It was just hard to believe. But we had to take it to the police. His name was on the letter."

"Absolutely," said Adam. "You did the right thing. I hope this hasn't been too unpleasant."

"No, no. We're fine. Water under the bridge — our son was fine and safe, so we've been able to let it go, for the most part. But I've always wondered who wrote that letter."

James pulled out his cellphone and called the retired secretary, who, thankfully, was at home and willing to see them.

Miss Margaret Dolan was white-haired and slightly stooped with age, but her bright eyes and crackling personality had clearly not been diminished by time.

"Come in, come in, officers," said Miss Dolan. "Have a seat. What can I do for you? You've come a long way, eh? From Saskatoon?"

"Yes, ma'am, from Saskatoon," said Adam. "It is a pretty long trip. Thanks for seeing us at such short notice."

"No problem, young man. As you can see, I'm not as busy as I used to be. Bored out of my mind some days. Comes with retirement. How can I help?"

"We are investigating the murder of the Bishop of Saskatoon, your Father Halkitt. I'm sure you've heard by now?" asked Adam.

Miss Dolan nodded, sadly. "I was very sorry to hear it. Howard was a good priest and a good boss."

It was starting to amaze Adam that anyone would want to kill the man. Everyone seemed to admire and even like him. It was strange; public figures who were killed usually had a skeleton in the closet, or were roundly disliked. Not so with Halkitt, at least thus far.

"Well, I suppose you've answered my first question, Miss Dolan — your opinion of Father Halkitt. What was he like?"

"Devout. Kind. An aesthete. Good speaker. I never had a complaint, while he was the priest and headmaster here."

"Did you know Ellice Fairbrother?" asked James.

"Humph. Fairbrother. What a creep," said Miss Dolan. Adam had to smother a smile; the word 'creep' sounded funny coming from this elegant, sharp older woman.

"He was deacon here for a few years. Couldn't stand him. He was always looking over my shoulder. I hated that. He was always kind of snuffling around, making odd comments."

"Can you give us an example?"

"I don't know if I can. He was just one of those unsettling people who can't quite say the right thing — or don't want to — and always kind of held himself apart."

Then her eyes widened.

"But, oh yes. There was one time, when Father Halkitt was planning a sermon about loving your neighbour — a pretty standard theme — and he wanted to talk about all the communities, the constituencies that

231

good Catholics should be tolerant of. He was a bit ahead of his time on women in the priesthood, and gay people in the congregation. As I said, a good man.

"I was typing out a final version for him, and that idiot Fairbrother came up behind me, reading over my shoulder as always. I can't recall exactly what he said, but something derogatory about gay people and how Father Halkitt should know better. I backed up my chair into him. Rolled over his toe. Ha! He went away then."

Adam's eyebrows went up, and this time he didn't smother his smile. What a firecracker.

"Did you hear about the letter received by Scott Hagel, back then? He was ten at the time. Do you remember anything about that?"

"I did hear about it. People didn't talk about it freely, but there was a lot of whispering. It was very hard on Father Halkitt.

"You know," added Miss Dolan, "that happened just a few weeks after the sermon. I remember thinking how odd that was, how unpleasant. Here the Father is suggesting we open our hearts to everyone, regardless of race or sexual orientation or whatever, and then this letter comes up, suggesting he is a pedophile."

She shook her head.

Bam. It all clicked together, like puzzle pieces, in Adam's head. Miss Dolan's brain was apparently right behind his.

"It was Fairbrother," she declared. "Wasn't it? It was Fairbrother who sent that letter. Trying to discredit the father. I can't imagine why I didn't see it then. That jerk," she added, sourly.

"Well, it's hard to say, but I can certainly see why you would come to that conclusion, Miss Dolan," said Adam, carefully.

"Oh come off it, Detective. You know very well that's what happened. I can see it in your face. But I know you have to be careful in what you say. And I also know it was that creep, Fairbrother."

"If you're right, Miss Dolan, why would he have done such a thing? Just to get back at him for the sermon?" asked James, for whom the scenario had also come together.

"Maybe. I don't know. As I said, he held himself apart, when he wasn't harassing me, or the father. I always had the feeling that he was obsequious around the father, but then he'd come out of his office and make snorting sounds or roll his eyes. Could have been something else going on.

"All I know is I hated him, and he wrote that letter."

Twenty-eight

God bless Miss Margaret Dolan, thought Adam.

She apparently nailed what had occurred with Scott Hagel and the letter, as well as what sort of a man Fairbrother was. Adam was already cranky that he was somehow giving the police the perpetual slip; but now had even more reason to find him. What a creep, as Miss Dolan had said.

Furthermore, Halkitt and Fairbrother had had quite a long, and not a very good, relationship — at least on Fairbrother's side — in Westmoreland. They knew each other well.

It was a good day in Westmoreland, Adam and James agreed. They climbed back into the cruiser and headed back to Saskatoon.

"Well, that was worth every minute on this long and bloody road. I'm so glad we found Miss Dolan. I could have hugged her," said Adam.

"I know. She figured it out in the same minute we did."

"We're seriously on the hunt for Fairbrother now. I have Sanj Kumar trying to get us another warrant, this time for his house.

"If all goes well, we should be able to execute it late this afternoon or tomorrow morning."

Adam's mind was churning. Clearly, the bishop and the church secretary had quite a history together; and if Miss Dolan was right about the letter, that changed everything.

Back in Saskatoon, Adam dug out what they had already learned about Fairbrother, and started re-reading the file closely, in light of this new information.

He was born in a small town in Ontario, attending high school there before going on to St. Peter's Seminary in London. He didn't do well. The seminarians put up with him for a year, and then booted him — although his marks were not too bad. Neither were they stellar, but were they bad enough for expulsion? Adam knew nothing about how seminaries made decisions around who was fit to serve, and who was not. He knew quite a bit, though, about how doctors and psychiatrists were chosen for university education, and police officers for duty; and he wondered if it was similar for priests.

Fairbrother went on to York University and attempted an English degree, but after two years of that, went into computer science, finally graduating with a bachelor's degree. Again, his marks were unspectacular, but not dreadful.

It was twenty-plus years ago that Fairbrother was at St. Peter's. Would anyone there remember him?

Adam picked up his phone and called Joan Karpinski, who had returned to her usual duties after Duane Sykes had been arrested. Adam was sure no one else was going to harass or attack Lacey McPhail.

"Joan, can you do me a favour? Can you get the registrar of St. Peter's Seminary in London — that's London, Ontario —on the horn? I'm looking for someone who might remember the church secretary. Ellice Fairbrother. Start with the registrar, and see which faculty members have been around for a while. Fairbrother was only there for a year."

"You bet, Sarge. I'll get right on it."

"And Joan. You did a great job at the StarPhoenix. Thank you. Excellent, intuitive police work." Stop there, he told himself. Lately he had been thanking the hell out of everybody on this case, which proved to him how personal it had become. He hoped he wasn't proving it to everyone else.

"Thank you, Sarge. That means a lot to me."

"Well, I'm glad. I mean it, though. I'll be making a note on your file, and letting the chief know, as well. Call me when St. Peter's comes through. Thanks."

Adam returned to his thoughts about university acceptance to professional colleges. He had briefly had an acquaintance, during his university years, who had tried and tried to get into medicine.

Adam always thought the acquaintance was extraordinarily unsuited to caring for anyone; he was selfish, self-aggrandizing, and annoying. He treated the women in his life as disposable. Eventually, Adam made sure he wasn't around if the man showed up in social situations, and if he did, made an excuse to leave. He just didn't like being around him.

Ultimately, the College of Medicine stopped even reviewing his applications. The acquaintance made no secret of it; he was angry, and put the fault on the school.

They just didn't want him, and Adam could see why. He was impressed by the med school's awareness of which students would not make good doctors. The guy he vaguely knew was smart and had good marks, but obviously there was something else the school didn't like about him.

Adam wondered if it was something similar with Fairbrother, and if so, what was it the seminary priests sensed in him that didn't contribute to clerical behaviour?

Another thought occurred to him. Pulling up Howard Halkitt's curriculum vitae, which he had obtained from the Catholic Church of Canada, he re-read the bishop's date of birth, education and work history.

He had vaguely noticed it before, but now it leaped into focus. Halkitt was also at St. Peter's, and at the same time as Fairbrother. He graduated four years later, before taking his doctorate, with the highest commendations.

There it was, in black and white.

Success and jealousy. Reputation and obscurity. Love and hate.

Fury.

"Hi Adam," said Sanjeev Kumar, when Adam picked up the phone late in the afternoon. "How are you holding up?"

"I'm fine, Sanj. Major progress on the case today. How are you, and how is my warrant?"

"We're both good. Judge Sutherland coughed up, again. She's starting to get a bit alarmed about this case, and in my view rightly so. Her gut, she said, was attached to the fingers that signed that paper. I'm starting to really like Judge Sutherland. Anyway, I just emailed you a copy."

"So, can we give the house a going over? Like, rip the place apart? Or just peer inside for the man himself?"

"All of it. Shed, garage, car, house — whatever is on site."

Adam exhaled.

"Man, that is great news. Sanj, this guy had a long relationship with the bishop. They were temporarily at seminary together, but Fairbrother bombed out and Halkitt went all the way. There's way more to their connection than just bishop and church secretary. But we can't discount the admittedly very remote possibility that whoever killed the bishop is also after the secretary. We have to find him."

"Well, off you go then. Have fun ripping the place apart. Can you take Weatherall? I gather he's been panting to get in there."

"I don't know. Have to think about it. I'm not sure if it's wise to sic him on Fairbrother when Frank Stephens is still officially a suspect. Doing research work is fine, but tearing apart a suspect's house might be going too far."

"Good luck with that decision. And for God's sake, call me as soon as you can and give me whatever you find. We have to move on this as fast as possible. Cheers, Adam."

"Thanks for the warrant, Sanj. Cheers."

I've got you now, Mr. Secretary, said Adam to himself. Tomorrow, they would execute the warrant. It was going to be great. He hoped.

The last few days had been the most bizarre of Grace's life. It was strange enough to be bashed on the head in a dark alley, but somehow, that didn't seem completely ridiculous. Women were always being warned not to wander about in the dark alone. Somehow, as

awful as that — and the following six days in the hospital
— had been, it didn't blow her mind.

But Tuesday had. In the two years she had spent
with Mick, eventually following him all the way to
Australia, not for one moment did she feel the way she
did with Adam. Not intellectually, not collegially, and
certainly not erotically. And she hadn't even made love
with Adam.

Michael Shaw was gorgeous, tanned, easy-going
and hard-working, especially physically. He played hard,
liked to have fun in bed, and was a riot to go out with. At
first, Grace had a wild time with Mick, who for some
reason had stopped and stayed in Saskatoon in the
middle of his world travels. They met in the bar he
worked at — frequented by the StarPhoenix reporters —
and were immediately an item.

The sex was constant at first; direct,
unimaginative, but still intense. It was fun, actually, but
even early on Grace often felt it was too much fun, or
maybe just fun. Mick would crow with delight afterwards,
tumble her around in the bed, and ask her, "wasn't that
great?" Not "was that great?" Hours later, he'd be back,
asking, "want to fuck again?" Just once, she wanted him
to ask her to make love. Slowly. Erotically.

When he decided to return to Australia, he
persuaded Grace to come with him; but after two
months, she knew it was definitely over. It had been a
romp, not a relationship. It had been fun, but her brain
was rotting. She felt under-stimulated, both mentally and
physically. Grace came home, glad she had had the sense
to take a leave of absence instead of quitting her job. I
guess I knew all along, she said to herself.

She realized, not much later, that she had chosen
Mick partly because he just didn't take life, or anything,

seriously. He was a complete distraction. So, she didn't take him seriously, either. It was a good way not to get hurt. But it did hurt, a lot, when she realized that he didn't really love her — at least, not what she understood as love. And, she supposed, she didn't really love him, either. Not deeply. It wasn't enough.

Grace backed off. Off men, off love. She felt limp with disappointment, disgusted with her own decision-making. Not only was it hard to trust men, she couldn't trust herself.

Even if she hadn't felt so dispirited, she just didn't meet anyone who stirred her. Grace, despite her tendency to worry about trustworthiness, did love men, and sex; but after Mick, the potency of it all had fallen away. She wanted a real relationship with someone she could enjoy, respect, connect with and trust — or nothing. So, she immersed herself in work, and friends.

But now she had completely fallen into Adam. I've only known him two weeks, thought Grace. But I knew that day at the station. Instantly.

In retrospect, Grace felt powerful embarrassment and guilt over what had happened in her kitchen. She had kissed Adam in a crazy, stoned haze of wanting him and being unable to control her emotions — or her body. It helped her understand, just a little, why drug addicts behaved as they do. Those mental filters just weren't there. But part of her couldn't help being thrilled. His kiss was sensual, expert, delicious, passionate. What else could he do? It didn't bear thinking about. Not now.

All of that was followed by the freak who climbed in the window, tried to rape her and was apparently, in his twisted mind, infatuated with her or something. Grace had an uneasy feeling that there were unopened missives from Duane Sykes underneath a deep stack of reporter's notebooks in her filing cabinet. She indeed was one of those journalists who sometimes couldn't open her mail, especially if the scrawl on the envelope looked — well, disturbing.

She also felt uneasy in general, after the home invasion. What would have happened if Denise Painchaud hadn't been there?

After leaving the hospital, a police officer had driven Grace and Denise home. Denise had been right; Grace's house had still been stuffed full of cops. The two women had made tea, gathered cookies and then hidden in the second bedroom. Grace's own room was being swarmed.

"You're shaking, Grace. Here, put this blanket over your shoulders," insisted Denise.

"I'm not cold."

"You're in shock, for heaven's sake. Do the blanket. Please, Grace," said Denise, draping Grace warmly, then sitting beside her. "Want to talk about it?"

Grace started to cry quietly. "I don't know. I'm not sure what to say, except thank you for being here. I never thought this person was really after me. Never. And now it turns out he's been after me for seven years — or would have been, if he'd been out of jail.

"And I'm afraid that I'll be afraid to be alone. I know he's in custody, and it's pretty obvious he was — as they say — working alone. But I'm scared I'll wake up off and on all night, wondering if someone is climbing in the window."

"I know," said Denise. "That's the worst part of something like this, assuming you come out of it physically more or less okay. It destroys your confidence, comfort, sense of safety. I'm so sorry, Grace. I can't believe I missed him while he was still out in the yard. You really should have people staying with you for the first while."

"Well, you're here now. How are you doing? That wasn't exactly fun for you either. How's your head? Oh, man," added Grace, peering more closely at Denise's temple. "That's a nasty bump."

"It hurts a bit, but I'm okay. We should try to sleep, despite all the noise out there. Unless you want to hit a hotel room or something? It'll be tough to sleep here. That being said, it's pretty safe with all those police officers."

It was a bit noisy, but surprisingly, not too bad. The crime scene investigation unit was reasonably quiet, gathering up samples and taking fingerprints and so on.

"I'm going to try to sleep, I think. We can both just stretch out here — that's why I have double beds. In case I need to sleep with a police guard," Grace said, trying out some humour.

Denise laughed. "Okay. Let's try it."

Both of them were out in minutes.

The next day, for Grace, was even stranger in some respects. She spent much of the day dozing, on and off, and trying to take only Tylenol for pain. She hated that stoned feeling, and wished she had kissed Adam stone sober, but there it was.

Night approached again, and Grace was ready to pop out of her skin. Noises made her jump. She ached pretty much everywhere. She hated the thought of that Sykes person touching her. She wanted Adam to touch her. The wanting was painful; she closed her eyes and clutched her shoulders, trying to banish the thought of him.

It didn't work. She wondered how Adam was, where he was, and what he was doing.

Had she looked out the window, she would have known. After putting together and briefing a team for the warrant execution planned for the next morning, Adam drove by Grace's home, and sat outside in the dark for a few minutes, checking to see if the lights were on, if anything looked strange . . . he didn't actually know what he was doing there.

He wanted to know she was safe.

No. At least be honest with yourself, he told himself. I want to see her. I can't wait to see her.

Then he did, through the window. Grace was in her living room, wandering aimlessly, her arms wrapped around herself. She looked sad, and suddenly threw her head back, obviously feeling some strong emotion.

Adam wanted to know what it was. But he could do nothing. He felt, suddenly, like a voyeur; he put the car in gear, and drove off. If he waited another minute, he was sure he wouldn't be able to stop himself from knocking on the door.

Twenty-nine

G race was enveloped in Adam's strong arms. Their legs were tangled together, lips and tongues kissing passionately as they had been two days ago. She could feel his powerful chest against her breasts, heart beating strongly, so alive, so male. She moved her hips against him as he rose to meet her, entwining his fingers with hers, taking control. Grace was overcome with erotic pleasure and relief.

Then she opened her eyes; she had closed them, allowing herself to feel the sensations created by Adam's big body undistracted by sight. And over his shoulder she saw the reeking man, leering at her and wielding some awful piece of long metal, serrated with jagged and already-bloody edges, ready to slice Adam to pieces.

Grace screamed Adam's name, awakening in the utter darkness of three in the morning. It wasn't her first erotic or terrifying dream starring Adam or her attacker, but it was by far the most intense, the most realistic, and the first one featuring both of them.

Only after a few seconds did she realize she had been asleep. Grace tried to unravel the loving from the terror, her body twisting in misery and arousal. She was soaking in cold sweat and hot wetness between her legs.

Hope was at the door. "Grace! Grace! What's wrong?" she shouted, entering at full speed without waiting for invitation.

Again, Hope crawled into bed with Grace, half-covering her body and soothing her with the little sounds she knew would calm her sister.

"What's up, honey? Did you have another nightmare? Shh, Grace . . . oh no, honey," Hope trailed off, as Grace began to heave with sobs.

Grace couldn't speak. She let Hope hug her, and wept into her nightgown.

Finally, Grace was able to shudder through a brief description of her dream, leaving out the more intimate, erotic parts. She just couldn't explain them, not even to Hope.

"Oh, Grace, that's awful. I'm not going to say it's just a dream. Those terrible, realistic dreams are so awful. It's going to take some time to get over what you've been through," Hope said.

"I know it's incredibly distressing. I don't think all the pain meds you've been on are helping, either. They tend to mess up your sleeping patterns, making everything worse."

"I know, I know. But I have to get Adam out of my head, somehow. I mean, even if this case wraps up sometime in the next million years," said Grace, making Hope smile in the darkness at her exaggeration, "does he feel the same way? I'm going to go nuts if this keeps happening."

"So this isn't your first Adam dream."

"No. Not my second or third, either."

_____

It was seven in the morning when Adam arrived at his desk. He couldn't sleep, so he thought he might as well get an early start. It was going to be another long day.

Adam had his own dream, quite different from the ones that had haunted him for the last several years. This time it was just about Grace, beautiful Grace, erotic Grace. She sat across his thighs, her soft skin rubbing against him, her hair flowing over her breasts. She was running her hands over his chest and stomach. Then she swept her hair to one side, lowered her face to kiss him, and took him inside her.

He had never had such an explicit, intense sexual dream, and Adam was the king of dreams. He awakened, every muscle taut with desire, an unwanted orgasm wracking his body. He didn't want that, not now. He wanted it to happen with her, not as the result of a dream. God, Grace, why did you kiss me? He could taste her, feel her body against his.

Adam blasted himself with icy water before stumbling into his running gear. Five kilometres later, he had a warm shower, breakfast and badly-needed coffee. He pulled himself together. He was getting tired of having to pull himself together.

Now he was looking over the warrant, preparing for a pre-execution meeting in the squad room, more than ready to dive into Fairbrother's house and life and hopefully end this thing.

A hard knock at his office door preceded the immediate arrival of a visibly-agitated Joan Karpinski, who didn't even say good morning.

"Sarge, you're not going to believe this. St. Peter's Seminary — there's been a death. They just called me. A priest — like a professor-priest person — on the verge of retirement. They found him in his office this morning, dead."

"What the hell?" said Adam. It was so bizarrely coincidental, he almost asked, "Are you sure?"

Instead, a split second of revelation later, he said, "Let me guess. The guy had his head bashed in."

Karpinski nodded vigorously. "Holy shit, Sarge. What's going on?"

"We have our killer. I'll call the chief. We need a Canada-wide warrant for the arrest of Ellice Fairbrother. It's him."

"What do you want me to do first?"

"Do another search for Fairbrother on Via Rail, Air Canada, WestJet, Greyhound — all the usual carriers — but this time, do it Canada-wide. Not just out of Saskatoon. Before you do that, get me the sergeant in charge of the investigation into this death. What was the priest's name?"

"Father Terence O'Shea. Age 64. Professor of ethics and law at the seminary."

"I get another guess. He's been at St. Peter's for at least twenty years."

"Thirty, actually."

"He knew something about Fairbrother. Damn. I wonder if we can find out what he knew from another priest? Or would he be dead then, too?

"Get me that sergeant in London, please, Joan. I know he'll be very happy to talk to me, since I'm going to solve his case for him. Then get on the ticketing — and get someone to help you. Ask Jonesy. We need to know where that asshole is, right now.

"You're amazing, Karpinski," he added, as she headed out the door, beaming.

In fifteen minutes, Adam's plan for the day had gone from one search warrant to a massive break in the case and twenty tasks ahead of him. He couldn't wait.

He immediately called Chief McIvor on his emergency cellphone.

"Chief. Another priest has been killed, this time in London, Ontario. It's the same killer. I need a Canada-wide warrant for his arrest. And I might need a helicopter, or the plane. I don't know where he is, but if he's not in London and he's not in Saskatoon — and I don't think he is — we may have to fly out to get him. It may be somewhere too far to get to fast by cruiser."

"Okay, Adam," said the chief. "I'll make it happen. Go do what you have to do. I'll ask questions later.

"Sergeant," he added. "I trust you. Whatever you need, I will get it for you. Even if it costs us a small fortune. Go get this guy."

"Thanks, Chief. That means a lot. And we will get him."

Adam had to decide, and fast: Was he going to Fairbrother's home with the warrant team? Was he going to stay and be at the ready, in case he had to climb into a cruiser or a plane? And first, he had to talk to the London Police Service.

He decided. Barely pausing as he walked by, he asked James to follow him into his office.

"James, Frank Stephens, as bad as his behaviour has been, is definitely not our killer. I mean, we both sort of knew that, but we can now say he's in the clear. We have another dead priest. In London. At St. Peter's Seminary."

James's face brightened as if he were the sun breaking out after a rainstorm.

"Holy shit, Sarge. That's crazy. How did that freak get out there?"

"I think we were a bit narrow in our search. I hate to admit it, but it didn't occur to me he would try to kill someone somewhere else. We only checked tickets out of Saskatoon. I have Joan checking Canada-wide right now — at least, as soon as she gets the London sergeant on the phone for me. The chief is dealing with a Canada-wide arrest warrant and checking on whether we can get the plane or a chopper, or both, if we need it."

"What about the search?"

"You have to lead it. You're officially fully back on this case, now that your — ah, father-in-law? — is off the hook. I have to stay here. But stay in touch. Videotape everything. And I know I don't have to say this, but do it all by the book. Be careful. We have to nail this guy. Get the team into their gear, then into the squad room; I'll be there in a couple of minutes."

"Okay, Sarge," James said.

The phone rang. "Detective Sergeant Jeannette Villeneuve for you, Sarge. London Police."

Adam nodded as James dashed out, and greeted the sergeant, who obviously was not a he but a she.

"Sergeant Villeneuve. Thank you for calling back so quickly. I have some information for you, and I'm hoping you might have some for me."

"Sergeant Davis, my pleasure," said a lovely, Québécoise voice. "Your constable tells me you're going to solve my case for me."

"I sure hope so."

Adam explained, as briefly as possible considering the time constraints, about the bishop being killed, about being unable to find Fairbrother, and then about the

bishop's long history with his church secretary —
including their cross-over time at the seminary.

"We had just hooked up with St. Peter's
yesterday, to see if anyone there remembered our
suspect, and the registrar assured us he would start
asking among the priests and professors. I have a very bad
feeling that the priest we wanted to speak with is your
victim."

"I'm following your logic, Sergeant," said
Villeneuve. "We will start searching for your Fairbrother
immediately."

"I'll email his file as we speak," said Adam,
swivelling his chair in front of his computer. "Your email,
Sergeant?"

She rattled it off. "What can I help with right
now?"

"First of all, how long has he been dead?"

"Quite some time, sergeant. Possibly all night. We
are consulting with the forensic doctor right now."

"I gather he was hit on the head. Do you have a
murder weapon?"

"No, but one of the professors tells me that one
of Father O'Shea's statues of Mary is missing from his
shelf. He says it may have been heavy enough to do this
kind of damage."

Adam felt a frisson of certainty travel up his spine.

"Our bishop," he told Sergeant Villeneuve, "was
murdered with a monstrance. It's missing, as well."

Villeneuve, being Catholic, didn't ask what a
monstrance was. *Mon Dieu.* A perfect fit, I would say,
Sergeant Davis."

"My thoughts exactly. Any witnesses?" he asked,
with little hope.

"Of course not," she said, sighing. "We are seeking fingerprints but there will be so many — students, other professors, Earth's population — I think that will be of little help. We will go to the airport, bus depot and train station immediately. I will stay in touch."

"Thank you, Sergeant. So nice to meet you on the phone."

"And you. Goodbye, Sergeant Davis," she said, hanging up.

Adam was instantly out of his chair and striding down the hall to find James, who was discovered putting on his Kevlar vest and holster in the claustrophobic SWAT room. The police service really, really needed more space for this, Adam thought fleetingly as he always did when entering the small space.

"James. This priest in London was probably killed with a statue of the Virgin Mary, according to the sergeant in charge, and several if not many hours ago. This is the same guy. I know it. Keep a particular eye out for religious statuary when you get to his house."

"You got it, Adam."

Adam gave the officers a short speech and directions and headed back to his desk. On the way, he encountered the chief, who had come into the office. He stopped Adam to say the Canada-wide warrant had been issued, and the police service plane was now being landed for his use if he needed it. McIvor also had a chopper standing by, just in case.

"Thanks, Chief, you're the best," said Adam.

Adrenaline was flooding Adam's system as it always did when he was very close to wrapping a case. It was the most exciting and rewarding part of the job for him.

Once Charlotte had teased him by saying, "the game's afoot," as they surged out of the station with the tactical team. She knew when he had solved a case, and could see him vibrating, his face alive with certainty.

This case was particularly intense for Adam, from so many standpoints: high-profile, complicated, violent, and because of Grace. He kept his focus, hearing Sanj's words in his ears. You're a pro, Adam. You can do this.

Just as he returned to his office, Joan Karpinski came flying over from her desk, papers in hand.

"Sarge. Fairbrother bought a train ticket. VIA Rail from London through Manitoba heading for Melville. I think he must have fake ID, but the stationmaster responded to his photo. It's him." Upon request, Father Paul Campbell had managed to unearth a slightly fuzzy photo of Fairbrother, taken at a church event, and turned it over to the police.

"Where is the train right now?"

"Somewhere outside Winnipeg, on the Saskatchewan side. Let me see how many hours that is from Melville," said Joan, hauling out her phone and doing a quick Internet search. "Usually about nine hours, if the train is near Portage by now. Nine hours! Can that be right? But I don't know yet exactly where the train is."

Nine hours. Melville.

If the priest had been killed the night before, Fairbrother could easily have had a big head start out of London.

Adam thought fast. Melville was a main Saskatchewan stop on the VIA passenger train line — as odd as that seemed to him, but whatever. Why was that ringing a bell?

"Joan. How far is Melville from Westmoreland?"

She returned her fingers to her phone, and brought up a Manitoba-Saskatchewan map. "Maybe an hour?" she said. "A little less? Why?"

"He's been hiding in Westmoreland. I'm sure of it. Maybe he owned a house when he lived there, and never did — or never could — sell it. It's tough to buy and sell property in little towns like that. Maybe he still owns it.

"So he beats feet out of Saskatoon, maybe borrows a car or something, or has a second car he didn't have licensed? Check to see if he's licensed a car in the last, say, week or so. If he had fake ID by then, that won't work, but check anyway. Then he hides in Westmoreland for a couple of days. We don't know when he left Saskatoon, but it was after James first went to his house. James was sure he was there.

"Then he figures out some fake ID, or steals some, maybe doctors it — they're not as careful with ID on the train, it's not like flying — and goes to Melville, catches the train to London. He can't fly to southeastern Saskatchewan anyway, short of chartering a plane.

"And it's too far to drive all the way to London and back in a couple of days, so he risks the train, at least part of the way. Plus, it's good to mix up transportation if you're on the run.

"His blood is up. He's escalating. After all these years, he finally decides to kill the bishop, even though he settled for trying to ruin his reputation before. Now, a couple of weeks later, he wants to kill the priest who ruined his chances of graduating at the seminary.

"There's someone in Westmoreland who's next. He has to drive back there from Melville. And we need to know where the train is; find that out first.

"I have to call the team searching at his house. Joan, can you please zip down to the chief's office and tell him we're going to need both of those aircraft. Then please get your gear on — you'll have to join the search."

Constable Joan Karpinski stood amazed before her boss. "Yes, Sarge," was all she got out, then hurried away.

Adam called James, now on site with the warrant. "Adam. What's up?"

"How far along are you?" asked Adam.

"Just starting. This place is a freaking pig sty, Adam. I'm not going to say I've never seen anything like it, but it's right down there with the worst. We do see a lot of statuary, by the way. Amid the filth."

"I'm sending Karpinski over there in about two minutes. You and Charlotte have to get back here right now."

"No way!" James objected. "Come on, Sarge. What the . . .

"Look, I know you've been waiting for this search, but I need you here, James," said Adam, cutting him off. "We're going back to Westmoreland. We have to leave in an hour."

Thirty

James and Charlotte were back in minutes, having turned on the sirens and lights to expedite their return to the station. They walked in each carrying a Mac desktop computer.

"Wow," Adam said. "Two computers? Any idea what's on there?"

"Nope. They appear to have been wiped. And there are two more at the house. The team will bring those back with the statuary — several Marys, several Christs, a whole bunch of news clippings — that's another story."

"No monstrance?"

"Not yet. Let us get these to the crackers and we'll be right back."

With any luck, Fairbrother, the computer science grad, was not quite smart enough to completely wipe his hard drives. If anyone in Saskatoon could find his traces, it was the police information technology department. James dumped the computers on the desk of one of the info tech guys, also known as crackers.

"Hey, Dave. Here are two of the four computers coming from that suspect's home — the guy we think killed the bishop.

"No idea what we're looking for but I'm hoping there's something here. He wiped them."

"Okay. Will let you know."

"We're heading back down south in the plane, but call Adam whenever you find what was on there. We'll call you right back if we can't answer."

James ran back downstairs, where Adam, Charlotte and another very large police officer, Lorne Fisher, awaited him. All four crammed into a cruiser, fully armed, and set the sirens screaming.

"We're taking both the plane and the chopper," Adam explained as they raced for the airport. "I don't know if we're over or under-manned — or under-womanned, sorry Char — but we can only get four of us into these aircraft, so let's go."

Then Adam explained what he had told Karpinski: that Fairbrother was on a train heading for Melville, and Melville was an hour or less from Westmoreland, so they didn't have time to drive down there. They needed to catch him, fast.

"He's escalating," Adam said, as he had to Joan. "He's ready to kill someone else. I think it's Margaret Dolan."

James froze, staring at Adam. That would be terrible: Miss Dolan was such a character — and she had really helped to break the case wide open.

"He might have tried to kill her sooner, but he decided to hit the priest in London first, come back to Westmoreland, and stay for a while," said Adam. "He could have a hideaway there. Maybe he's had it since he lived there, under a different name, or a relative's name. How and why he thinks he's going to get away with three murders, I don't get, but he could be crazy enough. Or angry enough."

"He sure could be crazy enough, judging by his house," agreed James. "And Adam, I think we were right about some kind of computer or Internet-related obsession or addiction. Who has four computers, unless you're a software developer or a website designer or something like that? He's a fucking church secretary, for God's sake. But his house says he's completely obsessed with something."

The cruiser arrived at the airport, in seven minutes flat. As he was getting out, Adam's phone rang and he put it to his ear.

"It's Joan, Sarge," said the constable on the line. "I can't find a new car licence, but maybe he took the bus down? Still checking with the depot. Just sent them his photo. Then could he have a car under someone else's name down in Westmoreland? What do you think?"

"It's possible. Thanks for checking," said Adam. He turned back to James, Lorne and Charlotte as they walked toward the hangar. "We have to assume he has a vehicle, and act accordingly," he said. "We can't assume he'll be held up by catching the bus from Melville."

"Detective Sergeant Davis, we're ready for you now," interjected one of the pilots, standing by the plane.

"Okay. Let's go."

Adam found himself wondering where the hell they were going to land in or near Westmoreland. A farmer's field? The highway? He assumed the pilots knew where they were going, and where they were landing. Nothing he could do about it, anyway.

He had called ahead to the nearby RCMP detachment and asked if they could provide assistance and vehicles.

The flight, although short at about forty-five minutes, seemed to take forever. He felt confident that Miss Dolan would be safe, assuming she didn't kick out the RCMP officer sent to her home. He could hear her in his mind, saying she would be just fine, young man. Off you go.

But he still felt an urgency to be there — to be sure she was safe, to finally catch this killer who had murdered two people and turned his life upside down.

Adam soon saw the little town below, nestled among the farm fields of southern Saskatchewan, sere and brown in the early spring. The plane landed first, gliding to a stop on a rudimentary runway usually used by crop dusters. The helicopter landed a few minutes later, setting down in a clearing nearby. The four police officers jumped out of both aircraft, and met two waiting RCMP officers — and their cruisers.

It was only ten minutes into town. The RCMP pulled up a few houses away from Miss Dolan's, parking in the overgrown ditches that passed for alleys in little Westmoreland.

All six officers walked up the alley, feeling fairly secure that they had plenty of time to reach Miss Dolan's, just in case Fairbrother hadn't been picked up in Melville. And she had a cop with her.

One of the RCMP officer's mobile devices crackled into life.

"Sarge," said a voice, "he didn't get off the train here."

"What? Are you sure?"

"Afraid so. He wasn't on this train, not by the time it got to Melville."

"Shit," Adam said, viciously. "What the hell happened to him?" Then his phone rang.

"Davis," he said, shortly.

"Hey Sarge, it's Dave from the IT lab. How's it going?"

Adam almost laughed. Dave obviously had no idea what was happening in Westmoreland. He was making conversation. It was so incongruous.

"Dave, what have you found? We're in the middle of looking for this perp."

"Sorry, Sarge. I'll cut to the point. You've got a pedophile. Boys, girls, anyone ten and under, I'd guess."

Christ. That hadn't clicked for Adam. There was no indication of it anywhere in the files — then Adam kicked himself. Of course — that letter, to the kid in Westmoreland fifteen years ago. He had tried to string up Halkitt for a problem he had himself, or to lure Scott Hagel, or both. Of course he was a pedophile.

If Adam was right, seminary professor and priest Terence O'Shea of St. Peter's had figured it out twenty years ago; or at the least, his gut had told him. Then, perhaps much later, so did Howard Halkitt. He was willing to bet that Fairbrother thought Miss Dolan, who treated him like the piece of shit he was, knew it too.

"Dave, thanks. Well done. I'll call you back." He turned to James. "Pedophile."

"Oh, man. Yuck."

"Let's move," added Adam, who had been walking more slowly while talking. "He didn't get off the train in Melville, so he could be anywhere.

"Driving would be way faster than the train. He may have driven from Portage."

Reaching Miss Dolan's house, the Saskatoon Police and RCMP officers fell silent, turned down their phones, drew their weapons and crept to the door. Adam waved James and Lorne to the front door, while he and Charlotte took the back. An RCMP officer was with each Saskatoon police team.

Adam glared through the back door window, and soon saw James, straight through the little house, doing exactly the same thing through the front door. Their eyes met; neither could see anything unusual inside, within their range of vision. They shook their heads at each other.

The house was quite dark, although there was a sliver of sunshine coming in from outside; but the fact that there were no lights on worried Adam. Older people usually needed indoor lighting to see their way around. Was she home? She was supposed to be; they had sent an RCMP officer over to be with her, and no one had told them otherwise.

He tried the door, which was locked. He motioned through the glass at James to try the front door; it was also locked. Adam shrugged at James, and signalled to indicate he wanted to break in. If anything was wrong, he didn't want to alert Fairbrother with a doorbell chime or a knock.

Adam nodded his head emphatically — once, twice, three times. Go. James and Adam put their shoulders to the doors and broke them down simultaneously.

Two steps in, Adam stopped, aghast. On the kitchen floor, at the top of the stairs leading to the basement, was an RCMP officer lying in a pool of blood.

James sped through the living room, seeing nothing and shaking his head at Adam. Lorne was right behind him; Charlotte was behind Adam.

It was time.

"Margaret Dolan! Ellice Fairbrother!" Adam roared. Loudly, even for him. "Police! Where are you?"

They could only be in the basement. The door was open; the officer was lying before it, and one of his colleagues went to him quickly. Adam rapidly pieced together what had likely happened; the RCMP officer had arrived after Fairbrother, not expecting him to be there for another couple of hours or more. Fairbrother had hit him as he came in the door. With the monstrance? Or the Virgin Mary?

Getting no answer, Adam headed for the basement, as deliberately and quickly as possible, James right behind him. Sidling down the narrow, steep and rickety stairs, guns held pointing up, Adam yelled, "Police! Show yourself, Fairbrother. This is over."

Adam was temporarily blinded in the dark basement. He had to stop for a minute to let his eyes adjust. Then he saw what appeared to be a door near the back — leading to an old coal cellar?

Bang. It exploded outward, kicked by Fairbrother, followed by the report of a gun. Shocked by the noise and the understanding that there was a firearm in play, Adam crouched and flattened his body against the wall.

Fairbrother shot again, and this time hit the wall next to Adam.

Adam was enraged, doubly so by suddenly feeling a trickle of blood, sticky and wet, sliding down his forehead and into his eye. He refused to give in to the rising memory of being critically shot years ago. Throwing himself onto the floor, he rolled into the corner shooting

261

back at Fairbrother, yelling at him to put down the weapon. He hoped like hell that Margaret Dolan was protected behind something in the coal cellar. And not dead already.

James followed Adam, executing the same rolling manoeuvre and training his gun at the shadowy figure at the back of the dark basement. Both were flat on the floor. There was no room in the tiny space for three more officers, so they lined the stairwell and attempted to direct their guns at the killer through the gaps between the open steps.

But Fairbrother did not drop his gun. He shot again, and James screamed. Adam heard Fairbrother laughing. Cackling, more like.

"Fucking gay cop," said Fairbrother, who began to advance from the coal cellar's doorway into the main basement area. Was he nuts? Suicidal? Adam could finally see his eyes, gleaming feverishly in a slender thread of dusty light.

"Fooled you, didn't I?" he asked James, as he pointed his gun down, right at him. "Couldn't find me, could you? Who's better than you now, eh?"

Adam aimed just as Fairbrother's finger twitched, and shot him in the arm. The killer's gun fell to the floor as he dropped to his knees, right in front of James's face, clutching his shredded biceps and screaming in pain.

Adam scrambled to his feet and lurched at Fairbrother, knocking him onto his stomach. Adam grabbed his cuffs, not caring whether he hurt Fairbrother more, and yanked his wrists behind him.

Adam rolled away to make room for Lorne and one of the RCMP officers to grab Fairbrother and drag him up the stairs, then rolled back to James, half-covering him with his big frame as he felt for his heartbeat.

"James, James, stay with me," said Adam, feeling his constable's body for the wound, fear making his voice thick. James was bleeding copiously from his leg, and was shivering and shaking from shock. He didn't respond to Adam, who yelled, "Charlotte, help me! God, James!"

But Charlotte had already assessed the scene. She had backed up sideways into the kitchen, grabbed every towel she could find, and now was thundering back down the stairs. They put pressure on James's wound with the stack of towels.

Adam had forgotten, briefly, about Margaret Dolan. He was also running out of cops. He called for the remaining RCMP officer to come and check on the elderly lady — if she was indeed in the coal cellar. He hadn't heard a word or a scream from her.

The officer took a big step over the trio of James, Adam and Charlotte, curled together in a circle of thin light, and hunching to miss the beams that threatened to crack his head open, looked into the cellar. He called back to Adam.

She was there. Unconscious.

Fucking head wounds, Adam thought. He was bleeding rather a lot from the bullet's ricochet that grazed his temple. He kept his left eye closed as he and Lorne, who had returned from wrestling the screaming Fairbrother outside, struggled to carry James out of the basement. Charlotte led the way, arms full of bloody towels, muttering "be careful" and "oh! Gently!"

James was unconscious from the shock, which was a blessing since the trip up the narrow stairs would have been excruciating.

They carried him onto the lawn. Adam sank to his knees and cradled James's head muttering, "James, stay with me," as Charlotte took a closer look at the gunshot wound.

Westmoreland was too tiny to have its own ambulance. In minutes, a doctor from a larger neighbouring town, driven in at two hundred kilometres an hour by yet another RCMP officer, leapt from the cruiser and hurried over to James. He gave Adam a questioning look. Was this the first patient requiring care?

"Doc. Please. He's been shot. He's lost a lot of blood, he's in shock . . . " Adam didn't know what else to tell him. "He's my partner."

The doctor was looking around and clearly wondering about triaging the chaotic scene, but seeing Adam's wild eyes decided to start with the police officer bleeding in front of him.

The RCMP officer they had found on the kitchen floor was dead. Fairbrother's arm was in bad shape, but he would live. Margaret Dolan had a nasty bump on her head, and was still unconscious. They must have arrived just as Fairbrother pushed her down the stairs, Adam thought; she may have fallen against the wall or the floor, and he hadn't had time to finish her off before the loud bang of the doors being smashed in.

Finally, Adam heard ambulance sirens. He stood up, leaving James in the doctor's hands, and looked down the street both ways, wondering where they were coming from. If this bastard had killed James . . . oh God, no.

What carnage. Two priests in two provinces, and an RCMP officer dead. James, critically injured. Miss Dolan, suffering a head wound. And, indirectly, the attacks on Grace.

The paramedics took over with James, as the doctor attended to Miss Dolan and then Ellice Fairbrother.

James was loaded into the ambulance. The paramedics told Adam he was going to Melville — coincidentally, to St. Peter's Hospital, named for the same saint as the London seminary. Adam nodded, and just stood there, not knowing what to do next.

But Charlotte and the doctor then descended on him, Charlotte clucking a bit and the doctor peering at his head wound.

"You'll be fine," he assured Adam, dabbing alcohol on the small but bleeding wound.

"I know. What about James?"

"I'm sorry, Sergeant," the doctor replied, quietly. "I don't know. The bullet appears to have hit an artery; he's lost a lot of blood. We're doing everything we can."

Adam had heard that before. He hung his head and began to cry.

Thirty-one

Charlotte, true to self, flung her arms around Adam and made motherly noises about waiting and seeing and that she was sure it was going to be okay. Did he want her to stay?

No, said Adam. Go back to Saskatoon. I'll stay. Go, Charlotte.

Charlotte, terrified for James and worried about Adam, and a sad but stoic Lorne Fisher climbed back into the little police plane, and headed back to Saskatoon. The helicopter would stay, in case Fairbrother could be moved back to the city that night.

Adam followed the two ambulances carrying James and Margaret Dolan to Melville, driven by the RCMP officer who brought the doctor.

By the time he reached Melville, James was already in surgery. Adam paced the hallway, wishing that prayer made sense to him.

It was only then that it occurred to him: he had to call Bruce Stephens. He couldn't bear the thought. Adam had given many people very bad news, but this time — he couldn't keep his own emotions in check as it was.

Adam called the police station and caught Joan, who was just ending her day.

"Joan, it's Adam," he said, in as even a voice as he could manage. "I need you to please find Bruce Stephens, whether at home or at the office. When you find him, please patch him through to my cellphone, or give him the number, whatever works better."

"Oh, Sarge, how is James? How are you?"

"I'm fine. I don't know about James yet. But I have to reach Bruce. Can you do that for me before you go?"

"Anything, Sarge. I'm on it. Take care, okay?"

A few minutes later, the phone rang, with an already-frantic Bruce at the other end.

"Adam, what's happened? The constable wouldn't tell me anything."

"Bruce. I'm so sorry. James and I are in Melville. James has been . . . " Adam's voice cracked; his throat began to close up.

"What has James been?" shouted Bruce. "What the hell are you doing in Melville?"

"He's been shot, Bruce. In the leg. He's in surgery right now; they say it's going to take a while. I'm so sorry, Bruce."

"Is he going to . . . ?" Bruce couldn't finish the sentence.

"I don't know. You may want to make plans to come down."

"Oh, dear God. Oh no. James. If you see him, tell him I love him. I love him."

"I do too, Bruce. All we can do is hope and wait. Let me know when you're on your way."

———————————————

Hours later, an exhausted-looking doctor emerged from the operating theatre, covered in blood and dripping with sweat. Adam's legs wouldn't support him. He sat down hard, staring at the surgeon, unable to read the news in his face.

"He made it," said the doctor, sinking onto the waiting room bench next to Adam. "He's a fighter. He's in pretty bad shape, Sergeant, but he made it."

Adam's shoulders came down. "Thank you, Doctor." He closed his eyes. "He's my best cop. My best friend."

"You're welcome. But he did a lot of it. He'll have to hang around here for a few days, just in case. Sepsis, internal bleeding, and other shit can happen. We'll move him by ambulance back to Saskatoon as soon as we can."

"Yeah." Adam was past speaking in sentences.

"We have a couple of open rooms upstairs, Sergeant. I know; it's not what you usually hear about our hospitals, but we actually do. You could try to grab some sleep — until we fill up again, anyway. What do you say?"

Adam had no intention of leaving the hospital until he had seen James, awake and alive. That being said, he was pretty sure he was going to fall asleep sitting up on that bench, as the adrenaline began to seep out of him. Even a hospital bed sounded like heaven. At the thought, he bounced back, just a little.

"I'll take you up on that, thanks, Doc. Anything to eat in this place?"

"Cafeteria. Come on. I could use a steak myself."

Adam raised his eyebrows.

"Just kidding," said the doctor. "But there might be sandwiches."

First, Adam called Bruce. By now it was nearly the middle of the night.

"He made it through surgery," Adam told Bruce. "He's not awake yet. They're still watching him, but he made it."

"Thank God," said Bruce, who shouldn't have been on his cellphone. He shouldn't have been in his car, either, considering his state of mind, but he was driving hell bent for Melville. Nearly there.

After sharing a meal of turkey sandwiches, slightly-wilted salad and milk with the doctor and agreeing they could really kill for a beer, Adam dropped in on the last victim. He had learned from the doctor that Margaret Dolan had a concussion, and was resting fairly comfortably. That kind of injury was not a good thing for anyone, and especially not someone of her age, but she was a very tough lady. He dropped in briefly, to check on her and thank her. Profusely.

"I told you he was a creep," said Miss Dolan, groggily. "A bigger creep than I realized."

"Did you know he was a pedophile?" asked Adam. "My guess is he thought you did."

"No. I didn't know. But I suspected. Sure as hell something seriously wrong with him."

He finally fell asleep on the offered hospital bed. It was actually remarkably comfortable and quiet.

Well, compared to everything else that had happened that day.

In the morning, Adam wondered for a moment where the hell he was. Then it all came back.

Sweaty, dirty and bloody, he strode to the nursing station and asked a young nurse which room James was in, then at her direction headed just two doors away.

He looked like hell, but there he was, sleeping. And breathing.

Adam went to the bed, as quietly as he could, but James awakened. "God, Adam, you look like bloody hell," he said thickly.

"Just what I was thinking about you, Constable. Is Bruce here yet?"

"I don't know. I think this is the first time I've been awake. Hard to tell when you're snapped on morphine. What happened?" asked James.

"After you got hit, I shot Fairbrother. I actually have no idea where he is — here, or in Saskatoon. The RCMP took him away. Then you ended up here. You scared the hell out of me, James. You were in surgery a long time."

"You waited," said James, now understanding what was going on.

"Of course," said Adam.

James extended his hand. Adam grasped it, and felt emotion overwhelm him; he dropped his eyes, blinking back tears.

"It's okay, Adam. I'm okay."

Adam looked up, suddenly past trying to hide or submerge his feelings. He'd done enough of that.

"Jesus, James. What the hell would I have done without you, partner? Shit," said Adam, forced to wipe his eyes.

James beheld his sergeant struggling with his emotions. "I would have missed you too, Sarge." And he smiled, weakly, tears pouring down his face.

Adam found Bruce, standing stiffly with his legs wide apart, in front of a window in the waiting room. He was staring out, motionless. He looked like he would shatter if someone touched him, but Adam did anyway.

"Bruce," he said, putting a hand on his shoulder. "What are you doing out here?"

"Adam," said Bruce, turning. "I needed to — I don't know. Cry or something. Not awaken James. I find I'm just staring into space."

"He's awake," said Adam. "He's awake now. Go see him. It's going to be okay."

"What happened, exactly?"

Adam explained, as briefly as possible.

"And you shot him?" asked Bruce, referring to Fairbrother.

"Yes, in the arm."

"Wow. Great shot," said Bruce.

"No. I was aiming for his chest. I meant to kill him. He almost killed my best cop."

"And my lover. My partner. Oh, God," said Bruce, as he envisioned the scene. His face was working as he tried to manage the emotions tearing him into pieces, and Adam — who felt much the same way — pulled Bruce toward him and hugged the man who was so physically similar to himself. Both tall, dark, strong. Both beautiful.

"I was mad at you," said Bruce, in the middle of the hug.

"I know. I'm sorry. We had to come here. We had to catch him. He has now killed three people, and nearly killed a fourth. It's our job, Bruce, fucking terrifying as it is sometimes.

"And James is one of the very, very best at that job."

"I know. I'm not saying blaming you was rational. It just was. I've forgiven you."

They broke the embrace, smiled shakily at each other in understanding, and Bruce headed down the hallway to see James.

Adam bought razors and a toothbrush at the drug store, found a motel room, had a shower, wolfed down a huge lunch — this time, he got a steak — and then started figuring out how to get back to Saskatoon.

"I'm sending the chopper for you," said the chief, when Adam called him for a quick debrief.

"Really?" asked Adam.

"Yes. Head over to the RCMP detachment; they'll take you to the chopper. Shouldn't be more than a couple of hours. You've been through enough, Adam. We'll come pick you up. Besides, we need you back here pronto."

He walked to the detachment, which wasn't far, and presented himself to the desk sergeant.

"Where is Fairbrother, at this point?" Adam asked him.

"He's in Saskatoon, in hospital under guard. We took him up last night by air ambulance, after some preliminary medical care on that arm."

"Great. I'll want to question him when I get back, as soon as possible, so that's great. Thank you."

Feeling like some strength was flowing back into his body, he was ready and anxious to get back to the city and get this interview over with. Finally, the helicopter arrived; an officer drove him out to the pad, such as it was; and he was on his way back.

Just wait until tomorrow, you asshole freak, thought Adam. This is it. This is where I wrap this up. You are done.

"Where the hell is the monstrance?" Adam asked Joan.

"We've got it in evidence, Sarge. Not a mark on it, though."

"Unfortunate, but we don't need blood and hair. We have plenty of evidence. Where was it?"

"He had it locked up in a cupboard in his bedroom, hidden behind a fake wall panel. He wasn't kidding around. Six locks on the thing. I guess he didn't think he could travel with it. It is pretty big. And heavy."

"That's my assumption. He would have known that some kind of religious statuary would be in O'Shea's office. Do we have the Virgin Mary statue?"

"Yeah, that was in the coal cellar. He probably meant to give Margaret Dolan a whack with it, but didn't, for some reason."

"I think he didn't have time when he heard us come in — smashing in the doors probably distracted him. She was banged up enough from being pushed down the stairs. My main question, though, is how he got to Westmoreland so far ahead of time?"

"Our best guess is that he got off the train in Portage, and had arranged for a vehicle to be there. Maybe he left it there on the way to London? Caught the train at Portage, and not at Melville?

"Anyway, then he drove like a madman to Westmoreland, I assume. The train is actually even slower than we thought, so he would easily beat the train."

"Thanks, Joan. See you later."

Adam took the stairs, walked through the second floor, took another flight of stairs, and strode through the rabbit warren that was the police station until he arrived at the IT department.

"Hey, Dave," said Adam. "How are you doing? Sorry I had to cut you off, there, when we were in the field."

"Oh, for Christ's sake, Adam, don't mention it. You had way lots on your hands. How's Weatherall?" added Dave, his voice betraying worry. Everyone really liked James.

"He's hanging in there. Surgery went well; I hear he's pretty good today. So. Better tell me about this pedophilia on Fairbrother's computers."

"Well," said Dave, rapidly pulling up the files he had retrieved, "I think it was mostly about his own . . . um, pleasure? Goddammit, can I even use that word without puking . . . anyway, pleasure instead of broadcast. He shared some files in a pretty closed, small community, but didn't really get it out there. There were plenty, though. I've definitely seen worse, but they're bad enough."

Adam steeled himself. This was the worst part of the job. Period. He'd rather be shot again than examine child porn. They needed a different term for it; child pornography didn't cover this kind of abuse.

"Both girls and boys, I understand," Adam said to Dave, leaning forward to see the images on the computer.

"Yeah, both. Classic pedophile."

Classic pedophiles, as Dave described them, referred to those who were strictly aroused by children, due to their vulnerability and immaturity. Gender didn't matter to many of these men.

"He has never been caught for this until now," said Adam. "As far as we know, anyway. Can it be the motive, for killing Halkitt? I kind of don't think so, at least not entirely. Halkitt may have found out recently and threatened to reveal it, but there's more to this. Still, this crap, and shooting James, is going to keep him in jail for a long time. It'll buy us a while to stick the murders to him, too. Thanks, Dave. I'm going to go throw up now."

Adam wondered again, for the thousandth time, if Howard Halkitt had been gay but celibate. Fairbrother had screamed "fucking fag cop" at James, which brought up two questions: where did his loathing of gay people come from, and how did it hook up with the case? Make that three questions: how did he know James was gay?

There was another thing that still frustrated Adam. Tracking Fairbrother had all started with a simple two-part question the police needed an answer to: Who cancelled the gay choir's concert, and why? He still didn't have the real answer to that. But he did have Fairbrother.

Ellice Fairbrother's eyes were sullen, his skin was sallow and he wore dirty, rumpled clothing — and that was after being cleaned up at the hospital, where they had fixed up his arm. Adam considered him through the one-way window, as he worked his interview approach through his mind. I bet he reeks, too, thought Adam; his clothes are so filthy. I'm sick of stinking perps.

Adam had prepared his psychological profile of Fairbrother, and was mentally reviewing it before he confronted the pedophile. Fairbrother had wanted to be a priest, in part because of his religious upbringing and possibly his inability to relate to people; Adam guessed that he felt a priest could hold himself apart, and simply give sermons and dole out Hail Marys. That was probably why Terence O'Shea had not allowed him past the first year of seminary, although he may also have known, somehow, about the pedophilia.

Fairbrother would have been furious. His squirming mind decided that gay men ruled his world — weren't all priests gay? — and had ruined his chances at access to children.

Whether an individual priest was gay or not didn't matter. They were all part of the cabal. It was all about power, and Fairbrother didn't have it. He wanted it.

Eventually, he went into computer science, which would have been rudimentary at the time he was studying, compared with today. But it gave him a different kind of access to children.

He seemed to prefer boys, judging by the disgusting pornography on his computers, but that didn't mean Fairbrother was gay. He couldn't have normal adult relationships, and was sexually moved by the immature. It made Adam shudder with revulsion.

Adam wondered how hard Fairbrother would fight the murder charges. They had him, obviously, for shooting James and hurting Miss Dolan. But that was a far cry from three prison sentences for murder. He was already crying self-defence in the case of the dead RCMP officer.

Adam took a couple of deep breaths. He didn't have James with him, and that made Adam really angry, since James was the one guy who could keep him from acting on his anger with a just a word or a signal. Or a tackle, if necessary. Charlotte and Adam had a different relationship, but she could also manage him. Adam gave her sharp directions before this interview.

"Get in my face if I'm getting out of line, but don't let Fairbrother see it," said Adam. "Kick me if necessary. This has to be clean. And remember, when I pick up that weapon, back away, Char."

"Got it. Adam, we'll be just fine. I know you miss James, but we'll be just fine. We have to be good for him, too, you know."

"Did Fairbrother lawyer up?"

"Yes. He'll be here in a minute. Got held up in court."

Adam was ready. He looked at Charlotte, nodded, picked up the monstrance sitting precariously on the ledge of the window, and strode out one door and in the other.

"Good morning Mr. Fairbrother," said Adam. "This is Constable Charlotte Warkentin. I am Detective Sergeant Adam Davis. This is my case."

Fairbrother sneered, and gave a slight nod.

"We have a lot of questions for you. And we have all day. So the sooner you answer our questions, the better and the more comfortable for you. Would you like some coffee?"

Another curt nod. Charlotte stuck her head out the door and ordered it. Black.

"Would you like to wait for your lawyer?" Adam didn't think he would. Fairbrother had a strange arrogance about him, which he had, at first meeting, cloaked with nervousness.

"No. Let's get this over with."

"Let's start with who cancelled the Pride Chorus concert, shall we? Whose decision was that?"

"The bishop's," tried Fairbrother, sticking to his original story.

"Not true, sir. Want to try again?"

277

"It wasn't?" said Fairbrother, feigning surprise. "The Catholic Church of Canada?"

"I don't think it was the Church, either, sir. I think it was you."

"Me?"

"You."

"Why would I do that?"

"You tell me, sir. Why would you do that?"

"I can't imagine."

"Really. Do you like music, sir?"

"Of course. Doesn't everyone?"

"Do you like choirs?"

"Sometimes."

"Then why would you cancel a musical performance by a choir at your church?"

"Because it was a gay choir, Sergeant."

"So you did cancel it."

"I didn't say that."

"Yes, you did. I asked why you would cancel the choir performance, and you said because it was a gay choir."

Fairbrother stared at Adam. "I meant it in the general sense."

"Did you, now. So let us assume you just told the truth, and you cancelled the choir's concert. Were you upset that it had been scheduled at all?"

Fairbrother didn't answer. He was already floundering.

"You were, then."

"I didn't say that."

"You didn't make any effort to deny it. Did the bishop allow the choir to book the church?"

"Yes, of course. He signs off on all entertainments at the cathedral."

"Signed off. He's dead, Fairbrother. You killed him."

Adam stood up, and picked up the monstrance by the cross at the top. His considerable strength allowed him to swing the heavy item as if it were a camping lantern.

"This lovely item killed him. It was found in your house. Can you explain that?"

"I just had it for safe-keeping."

"So you lied when you said nothing was missing from the church, didn't you? And, it was kept safe in a locked cupboard at the cathedral. Why did you have to keep it safe?"

A thought struck Fairbrother; Adam could see his face change. His expression was crafty. "Because someone had taken it, been able to take it — and hurt the bishop with it. I didn't want anyone else getting hurt. Or the monstrance getting wrecked."

Good lie, Adam had to admit. But not good enough.

"Were you in the church, then?" asked Adam, trying to seem honestly puzzled. "After the bishop was killed? And found the monstrance? Because if so, why didn't you call the police? And why didn't you tell us earlier?"

Fairbrother thought about that for a second or two.

"No, I wasn't there. I found it later."

"How much later?"

"A couple of days."

"We interviewed you after we discovered the monstrance was missing. We asked if you had noticed anything out of place at the church. If you had it, why didn't you tell us?"

"It wasn't out of place. I had it locked up."

"Indeed. But you didn't bother to mention that."

Adam was still walking around the little room, swinging the monstrance in his fingers. It was hard to be insouciant with the thing — it was getting heavy — but Adam refused to show it.

"Maybe you pick up the monstrance after the service. Ed would have done so the next morning, since there was no evening service. Just confession. You see that the bishop is in the confessional; you hide in the one across the church."

Adam's pendulum arc became longer as he roamed the interview room.

"A man leaves the confessional, and then exits the church. It's dark, because you've turned down the lights. All is quiet. You see your chance. They don't come very often. You've been waiting a while, haven't you? You creep down the aisle, monstrance in hand. It's heavy. You swing it, to gain momentum," said Adam, still demonstrating.

"Bishop Halkitt is standing near the altar, possibly praying. Fury overtakes you. How could he allow gay people to sing in your church?" Adam closed in on Fairbrother.

"Gays. Right? You're a real man, aren't you? You have power over those babies you like better.

"The church hates the homosexual, and so do you. Including Halkitt. How could a fag like Howard become a priest, and then a bishop, for God's sake, when you couldn't do it?

"You're livid. You've waited forever, in the shadow of your friend and classmate. He becomes a big deal in the church, had a big future ahead of him. You've been demoted from deacon to church secretary. And one day, you blow it. You bring up a photo of a little girl, or a boy, on your computer screen at work. You just couldn't wait until you got home. And now the bishop knows. You'll be demoted again. Or go to jail."

Adam pulled back, just a little. He wanted to scare the hell out of Fairbrother, but he had to make it legal; he couldn't intimidate the witness. This couldn't go wrong.

He walked around Fairbrother, so the murderer could see what he was doing. He stood far enough away so that no intent to hurt would be clear to a judge and jury, not to mention his lawyer. Well, he did want to hurt him, but this approach was more likely to get him a conviction.

"It was time for Halkitt to die. You give it one last swing." Adam swung the monstrance high into the air, catching it with his other hand. "You grab it at the top of the arc, and you have the momentum. It comes crashing down on Halkitt's head. Bang," he said loudly, as he caught the monstrance in full downward force.

Fairbrother reflexively ducked and blanched, recognizing the action he had used to kill the bishop. He began to sweat profusely, and started to whimper. Adam had him.

"That's what happened," said Adam in Fairbrother's ear.

"You can't prove it!" screamed Fairbrother, galvanized by Adam's accusation.

"Oh yes. I can."

The lawyer showed up, but the interview, for now, was over. Adam and the monstrance left the room, followed by Charlotte, as police officers came to take Fairbrother back to cells. "That was amazing," breathed Charlotte, face alight.

"He totally freaked at your re-enactment. We've got that bastard. Don't we?"

"I think so. As long as the video equipment worked."

Adam was sure that a videotape would be visceral evidence for a jury, and they would see what he saw: the murderer reacting himself to what he had done to the bishop.

It may not be the nail in the coffin, but it was definitely a jury pleaser.

Thirty-two

G race really had to do this thing. She had waited too long as it was, but she knew she was going to get emotional, and had to find a day when she felt centred.

First, she called the bank. Then she got dressed, climbed into her car, and stopped at Bill's House of Flowers on Broadway Avenue. She bought a single, perfect, long-stemmed red rose.

Arriving downtown and miraculously finding a parking spot, she walked a block and then into the bank's reception area. She asked for Bruce Stephens. She identified herself and presented her card, but asked the receptionist not to tell Bruce who his visitor was. It was a bit of a surprise.

The receptionist, surprised herself at a personal visit to Mr. Stephens from this pretty woman holding a flower, said, "one moment, please, Ms. Rampling. Would you like to take a seat? I'll see if I can pull it off."

She called his number, and said, simply, "someone to see you, Mr. Stephens. Would you like to come to reception, or shall I send your visitor in?"

Susan was always punctilious about getting people's names, and never letting them get past her without the third degree.

"I'll come down," said Bruce. "Who is it?" But Susan had hung up, and winked at Grace. Something interesting was happening, and Susan wasn't going to spoil it — for herself, as much as anyone.

Bruce soon emerged through the elevator door, and clapped eyes on Grace.

"Grace! How wonderful to see you," he said, heading for her with his arms outstretched, hug at the ready.

Grace walked toward Bruce, and with a tiny bow, presented him with the rose, a reminder of the first night they had met in person at Divas. It was the night she was attacked and he saved her life, when he wore the flower in his lapel and wrecked his blue silk jacket with her blood.

He took the rose, and looking into Grace's eyes, which were welling with tears, asked her with his own eyes: What's up?

"I've come to thank you for saving my life," said Grace. "I should have done it weeks ago, despite the injuries and James being shot, and everything. I'm so grateful, Bruce. You were so brave that night. Thank you," she ended, then perched on her toes and threw her arms around him.

He hugged her back, tightly. They stood in the reception area of the bank, ignoring the clients in the waiting room chairs, staring at them. Grace cried in his arms, and tears began to roll down Bruce's face, as he remembered how shattered she looked that awful night, lying in the alley. He was also remembering his terror when he learned James had been shot. It had been a dreadful time.

"Anything, ever, Bruce. Anything. Ever," said Grace, finally able to stop crying, then backing up out of the hug and looking him in the eyes again, for emphasis.

"Thank you, Grace," said Bruce, in a shaky voice. He cleared his throat. "Dinner?" he suggested.

They both laughed. And knew they would always be friends.

The trial of Duane John Sykes was slated for late June. It would not be entirely about just finding him guilty. He was guilty, all right — assaulting a police officer, assaulting a bar patron, assaulting Grace Rampling.

The trial, or possibly a hearing, would really be more about which charges would stick against the sick and violent man, and how long he should spend in prison. Even his defence attorney was all over expediting this case, trying mainly to get his client's charges reduced and time in prison shortened.

As far as Adam was concerned, one of the charges should be attempted murder for the attack against Grace in the alley near Divas. He could have bloody killed her, he argued to Sanj, passionately. The longer he goes away, the better — so he can't attack anyone else, and especially not Grace.

"We're going to have better luck making this fast if we just go with five counts of assault, and one of sexual assault. We'd do even better if we left off the sexual assault — wait, Adam," said Sanj, putting up a hand as he saw Adam getting ready to object.

"He didn't manage to rape her, even if he did sexually assault her. We go to court with five counts of assault and ask for twenty years. What do you think?"

"The one thing that's kept me going is thinking about charging that asshole with attempted murder, Sanj. I just have to argue for it."

Sanj breathed in, and out, and regarded the angry friend and police officer across from him.

In a perfect world, he would charge Sykes with attempted murder; but the defence attorney would insist on a trial in that case — and he may not win it, but he'd have a shot.

In the real world, Sanj knew he could make the assault charges stick, and the hearing would last a day or two at most. The defence lawyer, he knew after several conversations, wouldn't kick up a fuss.

He explained this to Adam, again. Adam argued, again.

"How about if I talk to the head of prosecutions, and try both scenarios on him?" suggested Sanj.

"Fine," Adam groused, then relented. "I know you are trying to do the right thing, Sanj. For everyone."

"Yeah, including you. Have you seen Grace recently?"

"No."

"Well, you're going to see her in court in a few days. Are you ready? This must be brutal for you, Adam. Remember, it's almost over."

Adam fought the thrill coursing through his body at the thought of seeing Grace again. She was back at work, and he drank in her stories like a man dying of thirst. It was rare for the weekend reporter to talk to the detective sergeant; usually it was the staff sergeant or a communications person, so it wasn't strange that he hadn't crossed paths with her, professionally. He wondered what would have happened.

"How's the case going against Fairbrother?" asked Adam.

"Very well, thanks to you. And Char and James. Speaking of James, how is he doing?"

"Also very well. He's on half days, on the desk, champing to get back to real work, but he has a way to go with physiotherapy and all that before he can hit the street. God," ended Adam, remembering the day in Westmoreland. It could still choke him up.

"That would have been an awful loss for you. But he's okay, right? All good."

"So," said Adam, clearing his throat, "Back to Fairbrother. You have the video, you have the evidence, the computers, Miss Dolan's statement, the priests at St. Peter's, the statue of the Virgin Mary, the monstrance. What more do you really need?" asked Adam, who needed for Grace not to be a crucial witness any more.

"Nothing," said Sanj. "Absolutely nothing."

The riverbank in June was a happy, chaotic mass of people walking, throwing discs, necking on blankets. All the trees were bright with leaves, ranging from lime to forest green; flowers were budding in scarlet and purple. It was beautiful.

Adam walked down the Meewasin Trail along the water to the courthouse, needing the time to be distracted by a bustling city and to suck in as much oxygen as he could.

He knew that Grace would take up all the oxygen allotted to him in the courtroom. He had to keep it together. If she still had feelings for him, he didn't want to be a blubbering fool.

Reaching the courthouse, he wondered when exactly he would see Grace — how she would look, what would happen. He had no idea.

He walked into the courtroom after passing through security, and took a seat.

"All rise," said the clerk, and the judge walked in, took her seat, and waved everyone down.

The Crown v Duane John Sykes was underway.

The judge addressed Sykes. "You are charged with four counts of assault, one charge of sexual assault, and one charge of attempted murder. How do you plead?"

Adam held his breath.

"Guilty on the first five charges. Not guilty of attempted murder."

Shit. But at least he was going away for sure.

Sanj stood up. He threw a glance back at Adam, with a little sympathetic moue, and called Grace to the stand.

She entered the courtroom, walked to the stand and turned to place her hand on the Bible. Adam gasped audibly.

He realized with a start that it was the first time he had ever seen her in street clothes, apart from her parka and the voluminous sweatshirt and torn nightgown she was wearing at home the day of her attack. If he hadn't already thought she was stunningly beautiful, he would have started thinking so now.

More slender than she had been three months ago, she was also taller than Adam had previously realized — perhaps partly because she was wearing heels, but partly because he had rarely seen her standing. She was wearing a trace of makeup — mascara, lipstick — and a stunning grey-blue wrap-around dress, cinched at the waist with a black leather belt, matching her shoes. Her figure was slim, but curved. Adam couldn't stare hard enough.

She sat down gracefully in the stand, and suddenly was looking straight at Adam. He looked back. She gave him the tiniest, slightly sad smile. He didn't know how to respond; he didn't know what the smile meant, so he nodded, shakily returned the smile, and just kept staring at her, his heart pounding. He wondered if this beautiful, composed, intelligent woman would ever be his. It had been three very long months of waiting.

He had completely given up fighting his feelings for her. It was futile and, he knew that fight had been mostly driven by knowing he had to stay away.

Sanj asked Grace to identify herself, and then began asking her questions about the two nights she was attacked. For the first time ever, Adam wanted to clamp his hand over Sanj's mouth. This must be so painful for Grace.

"Regarding the first attack, Ms. Rampling. Did you think your life was in danger?"

"Yes."

"Why did you think so?"

"He attacked me with a weapon, which seemed at the time like a crowbar or pipe or something. And while he came for me, he called me a fucking fag-loving bitch." Grace didn't apologize for her language. She knew it would have an electrifying effect.

The courtroom, indeed, buzzed.

"You took that to mean he was very angry with you?"

"Yes, I did. I think he proved it by hitting me with a heavy piece of metal."

"Let the record show that the defendant has admitted to attacking Ms. Rampling. Your witness."

"Ms. Rampling," said the defence attorney, standing. "The confessional interview held with Detective Sergeant Adam Davis indicates that Mr. Sykes was pleased that his attack did not result in your death. Is it possible that you are exaggerating any of the circumstances around the event in question?"

Colour rose in Grace's face, and her voice changed slightly; but she kept her composure.

"Perhaps he realized later that he was pleased, because then he could climb through my window and attack me again. And attempt to rape me. But at the time, my life was in danger. He hit me with an iron bar, sir."

Wow, thought Adam. He could have applauded. Reporters. Man, they make good witnesses, he thought for the hundredth time. Especially this one.

Sanj later called Constable Denise Painchaud to the stand, who corroborated all of Grace's evidence about the events of that night in her bungalow. Sykes was specifically charged with assaulting a police officer, and that particular conviction was going to be a no-brainer from a sentencing point of view.

"Why did you not shoot the defendant on sight?" he asked Painchaud, who winced at the question.

"It was dark, and I was afraid of shooting Ms. Rampling. There wasn't time to find the light switch. I drew my gun, but decided to throw myself at Mr. Sykes to get him off Ms. Rampling instead of firing. Unfortunately, he hit me very hard, and the gun flew out of my hand and into the hallway."

Sanj nodded, and let it go.

Ultimately, Sanj took the court through the various pieces of evidence. The photos of Grace's head wound after the first attack were shown; and then the photos of Grace and Denise after the second attack were presented to the jury. Adam never wanted to see those pictures again.

Grace remained in the courtroom after her testimony, still in the first row with Lacey beside her madly taking notes, for she would write the story about this trial. Grace didn't hear a word Sanj was saying. She only heard her heart beating. Would she see Adam again? She had managed to pull herself together, after getting off the medication and back to work, which was blessedly busy and distracting. But she thought of Adam every day — really, all day — missing him and always wondering.

He was so handsome. Black hair, blue eyes, navy uniform, perfect mouth. She was completely certain that no heterosexual woman could look at him, or hear him speak, without being moved.

All she could do was wait.

But near the end of the trial, Grace couldn't bear it any more. She crept to the end of her row, bowed briefly to the bench, and slipped away. She knew she couldn't just make small talk in public with Adam, not yet. Actually, not ever. It was all, or nothing.

Adam watched her go, his heart contracting, hoping she left only because she had to get back to work.

Thirty-three

The Saskatoon StarPhoenix, June 23, 200_
Page One

Sykes convicted on all charges
By Lacey McPhail
of The StarPhoenix

Duane John Sykes, charged with five assaults as well as attempted murder, was convicted on all counts in Court of Queen's Bench Thursday.

Sykes attacked Grace Rampling, a reporter at this newspaper, using a large iron bar to hit her on the head and clavicle. He subsequently attacked her in her home, as well as Saskatoon Police Constable Denise Painchaud, who was guarding Rampling after the first attack.

The two women fought Sykes and were able to subdue him until more police officers arrived. Both attacks took place in March.

Sykes also beat a man in Logan's Bar and Grill on the same night, and punched two other men in the face when they tried to drag him away from the first victim.

Sykes had been recently released from prison, where he had served a full seven-year sentence for assaulting another man outside a Saskatoon bar, leaving him partially paralyzed. His apparent motive was that the man was gay and had approached him for sex. However, the victim was not gay and testified that he had only asked Sykes for the time.

Justice Deborah Lafond said in her decision that Sykes's actions were reprehensible and that he was unremorseful. His sentencing is slated for two weeks from today.

Trial set for man accused in bishop's murder

Ellice Fairbrother, the secretary of St. Eligius Cathedral and the accused in the killing of Howard Halkitt, former Bishop of Saskatoon, will stand trial.

The trial could take place as soon as February, Crown prosecutor Sanjeev Kumar said.

Kumar said the Crown has more than enough evidence in the case, and he expects the trial to last for about two weeks. He praised the Saskatoon Police Service for a thorough investigation, which encompassed two provinces and a gunfight in the small town of Westmoreland, Sask.

Fairbrother is also accused in the deaths of a London priest, Father Terence O'Shea, and RCMP constable Albert Devereaux; as well as an assault on Margaret Dolan, a resident of Westmoreland.

———————————————————————

"At least that one's over," said Bruce. "Now we just have to wait for the other asshole to be put away."

James and Bruce lay facing each other, hands exploring familiar, yet endlessly fascinating, terrain.

"James. I know I've said it before, but I have to tell you again . . . how desperate I was. How frightened. How unbelievably happy I am you are here."

James kissed him, fully on the mouth. "Me too," he said fervently.

"I hate to ask you this, but have you figured out yet how that secretary person knew you were gay?"

It was, of course, taking a while to put together the case against Fairbrother, and this detail was not top priority. But they were making progress.

"Well, we haven't figured it out for sure, but it looks like he was at Divas a couple of times, maybe more. Daril recognized him."

"Daril knows all. What the hell was he doing there, if he's such a homophobe?"

"Adam thinks he might have been there to lord it over people, in his mind — you know, I'm better than this lot of freaks. He may have been looking for someone. And I guess he saw me. Maybe you, too."

"I bet he was thrilled when you showed up on his doorstep," said Bruce, with a sarcastic little laugh. "Another gay person with authority over him. He'd have loved that."

"Yeah," said James, ruefully. "I think that worked against me — when he targeted me in Margaret Dolan's basement — but it gave us that moment to catch him without killing him. Or him killing Miss Dolan. Otherwise he may have stayed back in the coal cellar doorway. Who knows."

"Was the bishop gay?" asked Bruce. "Did anyone ever confirm that, either way?"

"No, no one ever did. I had a quiet conversation with Father Campbell, and while he couldn't say for sure, he really didn't think so. That's one of the remaining mysteries. Adam theorizes that Fairbrother just decided Halkitt was gay, evidence or not. It gave him a good reason to hate him; then he didn't have to admit to himself that Halkitt was better than he was, in every way."

"And then some."

"And then some. Now be quiet," said James, arousal getting the better of him as Bruce ran his hands down his thighs. "I'm going to love you so hard, you won't be able to speak anyway."

Thirty-four

I t's over, Adam," said Sanj, outside court. "Go live your life."

"Sanj, how did you get Sykes into court that fast?"

"I'm magic. Go."

It was Saturday. Grace was not working. In fact, Steve and Mark had finally released her from the weekend beat.

"I guess it's time, Grace. Thank God you're back," said Mark. "But you're right. It's someone else's turn."

Thank God for that, thought Grace.

She got up at nine in the morning — not six — and turned up the music, cleaned the house, had a shower, bought some groceries, a bottle of wine. Heaven. All of it. A Saturday, all to herself.

She called Hope. "My first Saturday off!" Grace exulted. "To most people, buying groceries on a Saturday is a chore. To me, it's freedom."

"That's awesome! Want to come over for dinner tomorrow? Mom and Dad and David — all of us? We can celebrate that — person going to jail. Woohoo. Want to?"

"You bet. What can I bring? Grace's famous potatoes? Oh . . . doorbell. I'll call you back."

Grace went to the door, unlocked it and swung it open.

Adam.

Her heart in her throat, she backed up four or five paces. The sight of him on her doorstep stunned her, threw her thoughts into a whirl. Has he come for me?

"Grace," was all he said, her own name caressing her.

She took in his face, his darkening eyes, his wavy, thick black hair; he wore a casual shirt that skimmed his abdominal muscles, tight blue jeans, boots. She returned her gaze, as always, to his mouth. What was it about his mouth?

He looked thinner, his face more angular, the expression on it more intense than she recalled. They had both lost weight over the horrors of the two cases. And the waiting.

"Grace," said Adam again, more insistently, and in one long stride closed the gap between them. Nothing was getting between him and this woman now — unless it was the woman herself. He had waited a long time. He wanted nothing, and no one, else.

Kicking the door shut behind him, he took Grace's face into both hands, watching her eyes; then he kissed her lips, feather-lightly, just as she had kissed him months ago — asking the questions gently, not with his words, but with his mouth.

Passion hit Grace like a storm. She reached up, thrust her fingers into his hair, and kissed him back, asking his lips to open with her tongue. She wanted him so badly, wanted him to kiss her like he had the first time.

She heard a sigh mixing with a groan in his throat, and then he kissed her madly, lips and tongue and mind and heart.

They finally broke apart, breathing as if they had been running, and just held each other.

"Grace."

"Adam," Grace finally said. "Adam."

"Thank God. I was so. . . I didn't know if you would . . ."

"I know. Me too. Those weeks were so intense, so crazy, so awful in many ways. And then these months before the trial. I didn't know what to think."

"I thought of you every day, every night," said Adam softly, against her lips.

"I dreamed of you," said Grace. Looking at him, all the erotic dreams flooded back. Now he was here, in her arms. She ran her hands over his chest, dying to see his muscular abdomen, wondering how his skin would feel under her mouth and fingertips.

The same strange absorption that came over her when she first kissed Adam returned. Maybe the drug wasn't Percocet; maybe it was Adam Davis.

She slowly pushed up his shirt, marvelling at the muscles, becoming further aroused by his deepening breathing. With a sigh of amazement she kissed his bared chest and slipped her tongue down to his abdomen.

Adam, rising hard, lifted Grace into his arms and strode into the bedroom, mouth moving against her throat. Gently setting her down, he stripped off his shirt in one quick movement then stopped and pulled her tightly into him.

"Jesus, Grace, I want you. Is this what you want? Tell me, Grace."

"I've wanted you since the day I came to see you at the station," she said, looking him right in the eyes. He kissed her again, hard.

Until she backed away to touch him again, and noticed the round, blue scar marring his shoulder.

Grace knew nothing about the event in which Adam had been shot, but she knew what this was. With a soft, sympathetic moan, she kissed the spot gently, then travelled down his chest and stomach, undoing Adam's belt as her tongue moved down his body.

Adam's head snapped back, and he released the sound that Grace alone seemed to draw from him. His body tensed as she kissed him all the way down, finally reaching the most sensitive part with her tongue, delicately surrounding it.

It was too erotic. Adam shuddered; he had to stop her. He lifted her face, kissed her again, then slipped her blouse off, pushed her bra straps down her arms, and kissed her shoulders. He couldn't wait to see her breasts. Face buried in her neck, he expertly removed her bra, then backed up to gaze at her.

"God, Grace . . . you are . . . " He shook his head a little, looking for a word more meaningful and descriptive than just beautiful. Not finding it, and standing inches away, with both hands he gently touched her round, soft, hard-tipped breasts, then looked at her face to see her reaction. How sensitive was she to that touch?

Grace couldn't look back at him. The erotic current flowing from her nipples to the rest of her was electric, almost embarrassing in its intensity, making her involuntarily flex at the hips. He continued to stare, and caress, his fingers running softly over the erect ends.

"Adam. For God's sake," she whispered, her body throbbing.

Adam slipped his hands down her back and then across her stomach, pulling off her slim-fitting athletic slacks and kissing her thighs as he crouched to push them to the floor.

Sliding the rest of the way out of his jeans, he picked Grace up, finally naked, and laid her on the bed, her hair spreading over the pillow. Adam lowered himself on top of her, his hands and lips everywhere. But he had to pull back, to try to regain some power over his body; he was damned if he was going to end this early.

He travelled down her stomach with his lips, hands on her breasts, Grace's hips rising under him. He could hear her breathing turn to panting, and felt her hands tug on his shoulders.

Sliding back up her body, his face came to hers. She dipped her fingers into her own wetness and smoothed it over Adam's erection, making him gasp. Grace didn't want to wait a second longer, and it wasn't just about her intense physical response to him. She wanted to welcome him in, be with him emotionally, even intellectually — wanted to feel that connection with this man she could love and respect.

Looking into her eyes, he entered her slowly, and heard her intake of breath, watched her lips open. Once inside her, he didn't move; the sensation was too exquisite, he had wanted her for so long. Grace waited, running her hands over his back and buttocks, trying not to move her hips.

Finally, reflexively, she began to move, rocking him. His eyes closed then, and he lost himself in the loving, knowing his body wasn't going to hold on any longer.

"Adam, Adam, Adam," he heard Grace say, a rhythm low in her throat; and even as the orgasm overwhelmed him, his brain said: She's calling my name. Not God's. Mine.

Then she arched her back, and cried out. Adam held on to her, lifting her hips slightly with one arm under the small of her back, as she came to the end; and his own body and mind exploded with one thought, the word he was seeking. *Unbelievable.*

Tangled together in her bed, they made the endorphin-saturated sounds of after-love, until Adam started to touch her breasts again. He couldn't help it. There they were, right there on the front of Grace, and they amazed and aroused him.

They made love again, wildly, more sure of each other, touching and looking at and clutching each other.

Finally, Grace suggested some food might be a good idea.

"We might need a few calories," she suggested.

"More than a few," agreed Adam.

They threw on a few bits of clothing and headed into the kitchen, where they mutually cooked herb omelettes and made seven-grain toast, sipping on glasses of white wine.

"Did I mention that . . . that was wonderful," said Grace, a little shyly, in the blissed-out daze of being thoroughly, physically loved.

"The omelette?" teased Adam.

"Very funny, mister," she responded, poking him in the stomach and kissing him lightly.

He pulled her to him. "That was unbelievable," he whispered into her neck, holding her hard against him.

————————————

Grace awakened at three in the morning. It happened often, after her attacks, but she didn't think it would happen tonight, being exhausted and ridiculously happy from the loving — and feeling safe in Adam's strong arms.

Something had awakened her, though, and she realized with a little shock that Adam was trembling. Oh no, she thought. What's wrong? Is he dreaming? Is he sick?

The trembling became more pronounced, and then he cried out. Grace, who had been sleeping curled into the curve of his body, turned and put her arms around him.

"Adam," said Grace, quietly. "Wake up, Adam. Wake up."

He did, with a start, and knew immediately that he had been dreaming and crying out. Damn. He slipped out of Grace's arms, swung his feet to the floor, and reflexively started pulling on his clothes.

"I'm sorry, Grace." He was so obviously sad and embarrassed, Grace's heart was breaking for him. It made her want him more, this strong, beautiful man who was also, suddenly, so human and so vulnerable.

"Why are you sorry, Adam? What's wrong? Please, tell me."

"I didn't think it would happen tonight. I thought I would just fall asleep and stay asleep, tonight of all nights."

He was pulling on his shirt.

"Adam, what are you doing?" asked Grace, alarmed. "Are you leaving?"

He stood up. "Yes."

"Why? Oh, Adam, please. Tell me. Tell me what's wrong."

He was taken aback; he found he couldn't, or didn't know how to answer that 'why,' precisely, except that this was his fear: that he would have these terrible dreams, be out of control, alarm the woman in his life. They would remind him forever that life was hard, and lonely, and dangerous.

"I don't want to be like this, and I don't want you to see me like this," he finally said, simply.

Grace crawled to the side of the bed, knelt before him and started removing the shirt he had just put on. Even in his state, Adam noticed her breasts and flat stomach gleaming in a sliver of moonlight. He gave a small, involuntary shiver.

"Tell me what happened," she said quietly, pulling him down on the bed and putting her arms around him, thinking he had a chill.

"I was shot, twice, a number of years ago," Adam began, factually. It felt strange. It was the first time he had ever told a woman, he realized. It was the first time a woman had asked — at least, sympathetically.

"I know. I can see," said Grace, touching the scar on his otherwise perfect shoulder, and then the one on his leg. "You had a post-traumatic reaction?"

He nodded. "Bad dreams. Really bad. I had one about you, when you were in the hospital."

"Oh, no, Adam. I'm sorry. I have bad dreams too. I wake up doing God knows what — crying, screaming, flailing. But I wouldn't leave you, I don't think. Why do you feel you have to?"

"Always have," he said. "I never felt I could do justice to a relationship. I could be killed at any time. I am a mess at night. I have no right to put any of that onto anyone else. And . . . there was a time when I didn't . . . behave well."

Grace was thinking hard. What could she say to soothe him?

"Everyone has the right to love, and all of us have done things we regret," she said. "Are the dreams better, worse, or the same as they were?"

"They're . . . better. Still intense, but I don't get them as often."

"You know, intellectually, that anyone can die at any time. Adam? Look at me. I was almost killed, twice. The bishop died. James was shot. People walk in front of buses. Die of diseases. I know your job is more dangerous than most, of course; but Adam, that doesn't take away your right to a life. Or my right to choose to be here, with you."

"After I dreamed about you, I think that did start to dawn on me, for the first time in six years," said Adam, slowly, visibly relaxing a bit. "That I was being a control freak, and was making myself feel special — different, apart — as a shield. As protection. It was the only way I could beat that sense of being a victim.

"I thought for a long time that if I didn't inflict my choices on anyone else, I wasn't a walking danger zone. Everyone around me would be safe. It took me a long time to start figuring out that wasn't true. It was partly what happened to you, I think, that made me realize it. But I also wanted you, right from the beginning. That started to change my point of view."

Grace didn't know what to say. "Oh, Adam," was all she got out. She straddled him and kissed him deeply.

"Adam, you are no victim," she said, passionately. "You are brave and strong and empathetic. Your experiences, bad as some of them have been, make you who you are. You were so good with me, so good — I am so grateful for your care of me, and Lacey.

"Maybe it's not surprising that you'd dream tonight, in a different place, with a different person, after what's happened. I'd love it if you'd tell me everything. In the morning."

Grace gently pushed him onto his back and moved down the bed, tugging his jeans off. She crawled on top of him, starting at his feet and slowing kissing her way up his hard thigh muscles, stopping to kiss the scar of his healed wound. Her own heat rising again, she passed her tongue slowly up his growing erection, along his abdomen, and then took him in her hand, moving her lips up to his chest and finally, his mouth.

"Is this a Rampling woman thing? This — body crawl?" he gasped, barely getting the words out as Grace came to a sitting position over him, and slipped him inside her.

"Yes," she said. "It's a love thing. Will you stay with me?" she asked softly, a little wickedly, pulling herself up by tensing her thighs and sliding him out of her.

He didn't answer right away. Instead, he lifted and flipped her onto her back, so easily, and entered her quickly.

"I will stay with you," said Adam, quietly, moving inside her. "Love thing."

Notes and Acknowledgements

In 2004, Saskatoon's Anglican cathedral cancelled a performance by the local gay choir, the Bridge City Chorus, and a second visting choir.

The local newspaper, The StarPhoenix, covered this event, and I wrote a furious column excoriating the decision. The cathedral, unsurprisingly, changed its mind after considerable media attention. It is doubtful that a church would try to do such a thing today.

Saskatoon is, in many ways, a better place than it was then. The LGBTQ community has gained better acceptance. The police service, as I depict it in this story of murder and love, is now a respectable force, having gone through a dreadful earlier period of violence and disrespect of local, and mainly Indigenous, citizens. Yet the Pride community still faces barriers; not a month before I finished the first draft, a gay friend told me he had been denied employment because of his sexual orientation.

Adam's Witness is, therefore, a piece of fiction inspired, as they say, by true events; it takes place somewhere in the mid-2000s, allowing for the widespread use of cellphones, modern databases and email, while also allowing for the police station to exist in its former location.

The plot erupted in my unquiet mind one early morning when sleep was impossible, as it had been for many months. It saved, at the time, my sanity. I don't know who to thank for that.

Obviously, the StarPhoenix is an actual newspaper. The gay nightclub actually exists, as well. The town of Westmoreland is a complete fiction.

The cathedral is, too. Saskatonians may recognize its general location, but I have for personal convenience expanded the space along the riverbank and inserted a different cathedral with a fictional name. It is not intended to represent the actual Catholic, nor the Anglican, cathedral.

All of the characters are fictional, although some have bits and pieces of personality that are, shall we say, gently adopted from people I greatly admire or love very much. Or, in other cases, disrespect intensely.

Certain members of the StarPhoenix newsroom of yesteryear may recognize parts of themselves, a little, in these pages. Of them, I beg forgiveness. The convivial environment at The SP as depicted, based on my days there, is not exaggerated. It really was an incredible place, populated by amazing journalists and kind, patient editors. It may still be.

Adam Davis is a complete fiction although he has traits from many inspirational men, one of them a police officer who had similar traumatic experiences and reactions.

Grace Rampling is a strong, intelligent, passionate and vulnerable person so very much like many female journalists I have known.

Hope Rampling is the closest thing to a real-life character in this book. My own sister and my best friend's sisters are the inspirations for the tough, loving little person who gets Grace through the worst of it. I have also stolen my own brother's Christian name. There was no other.

Finally, to all of you who put up with hours of chatter about this novel; who supported my crazy whim to write it – after all, it is simply a murder story, and a romance; who listened to me over lunch and put up with my text messages saying, "almost done," thank you.

I must profoundly thank my beta readers: Kathy and Bruce, Jennifer, Jan, Caroline (gifted creator of the cover – thank you!), Kristin, James, Carol, Philly and Ken. Thank you to content editor Bev Katz Rosenbaum for her excellent advice; Art Slade, Saskatoon author and library writer-in-residence, for encouragement, support and brilliance; and the magnificent Lori Coolican, the best crime reporter ever and a genius copy editor, for putting in so much time and effort for a couple of lunches and a bottle of wine. If anyone is Graceful, it is you.

Finally, thank you to my wonderful, supportive friends and family, who didn't actually laugh out loud when I said I would write a novel. And to Ken, husband and love, for everything.

Made in United States
Orlando, FL
10 April 2023

31959237R00173